PRAISE FOR CHARLOTTE MACLEOD'S
BESTSELLING
EXIT THE MILKMAN
AND THE PROFESSOR PETER SHANDY
SERIES

* * *

"Another series charmer!"
—*Library Journal*

"Macleod's MILKMAN delivers. . . . Her writing is infectious . . . her characters engaging, and her dialogue crackles with humor. . . . Readers will want to come back again and again."
—*Maine Sunday Telegram*

"An enjoyable story."
—*Chattanooga Times*

"The screwball mystery is MacLeod's cup of tea."
—*Chicago Tribune*

more . . .

Also by Charlotte MacLeod

CHARLOTTE MACLEOD

Exit the Milkman

THE MYSTERIOUS PRESS

Published by Warner Books

A Time Warner Company

MYSTERIOUS PRESS EDITION

Copyright © 1996 by Charlotte MacLeod
All rights reserved.

Cover illustration by Mark Hess

The Mysterious Press name and logo are registered trademarks of Warner Books, Inc.

Visit our Web site at
http://pathfinder.com/twep

Mysterious Press Books are published by
Warner Books, Inc.
1271 Avenue of the Americas
New York, NY 10020

A Time Warner Company

Printed in the United States of America

Originally published in hardcover by The Mysterious Press.
First Printed in Paperback: August, 1997

10 9 8 7 6 5 4 3 2 1

For Sara Ann Freed
and the Wonder Workers

1

"HI, PETE. WALKING THE CAT?"

Professor Peter Shandy, internationally acclaimed monarch of the turnip fields, refrained with some difficulty from grinding his teeth. This was the five hundred and eighty-seventh time since the halcyon day when the Shandys had acquired a frolicsome tabby kitten that Professor James Feldster had asked Peter that same damn fool question. Peter knew, he'd kept count.

Time had passed; that beguiling scrap of feline femininity had become a gracious lady cat of exactly the right size to occupy a favorite chair or a friendly lap. She was charmingly turned out in elegant tabby stripes of gray, grayer, and grayest, accented by a jabot and gloves of purest white; she'd been named after another dainty little lady, long gone but never forgotten. A brief visit from the present Jane Austen was considered a mark of honor by those neighbors who lived around the Crescent, all except Mirelle Feldster, Jim's wife, who hated cats on principle and didn't much care for people either.

Jim himself had been one of Jane's earliest conquests. She had him well trained to pause at the street end of the Shandy's front walk long enough for her to climb his faded blue denim pant leg, poke her pink nose inside the baggy white jacket he always wore, and discover which of his regalia Jim would have festooned himself with for tonight's lodge meeting. Whatever it was, it would clank. Jim's regalia always clanked, even when Jane wasn't around to check him out.

Although Jim Feldster stood six feet five in his milking boots, he was not the sort of man who got noticed in a crowd. His only claims to recognition were two. First, he was Balaclava Agricultural College's never-surpassed expert on the fundamentals of dairy management, a course that he'd taught with unflagging zeal for the past thirty-seven years. Second, he knew more secret handshakes and esoteric passwords than any other dedicated lodge brother in Balaclava County. Maybe more than all the members of all the lodges in all the states put together. Maybe even in the entire galaxy, if those provocative theories which quantum physicists and authors of science fiction stories had been propounding for quite a while should happen to be true. As why should they not?

Peter found such erudite speculations mildly interesting to muse upon, particularly when he happened to be wandering alone at eventide through the college's extensive turnip fields, as he sometimes did for no special reason. It would never have occurred to Jim Feldster, he thought, that either quantum theory or turnips might be worth investigating. And why should they? Professor Feldster knew more than anybody else about dairy management. He'd taken the trouble to learn a vast deal about mystic rites and earned the right to clank all he wanted to at appropriate times and places. Those ought to be enough for any reasonable professor to think about.

Jim did stop long enough to watch Jane wash her paws, paying scrupulous attention to each pussy willow toe. Cleanliness being among the most fundamental of Fundamentals of Dairy Management, he honored her with a ritual pat between the ears, then clanked resolutely onward toward his secret rendezvous. Had Jane been a tomcat, Peter thought, Jim might by now have taught the intelligent creature a few secret pawshakes. Here in Balaclava County, however, fraternal organizations were still bucking the national trend toward androgyny, doing their utmost to keep their arcane doings fraternal in the strict sense of the word.

So far, the ladies of Balaclava County had shown no great inclination to storm the barricades. Helen Shandy's opinion was that they couldn't be bothered because they had better things to do. She was probably right; Helen was a librarian and librarians always knew. Anyway, whatever the reason, Brother James Feldster would have been the last of his fellows to proffer the handshake of personhood to any female intrepid enough to expect one.

It was not that professor Feldster had any antipathy to females in general. Some of his best students were of the womanly persuasion and he'd never met a cow he didn't like. His stubborn defense of the male lodge brother's last stronghold was based solely on a primal instinct toward self-preservation. Any man, even any woman, who'd ever spent five minutes in the company of Mirelle Feldster didn't need to be told why her husband joined so many lodges and never missed a meeting.

Normally Jim would have been on his way to Charlie Ross's garage. He and Peter both parked their cars at Charlie's. Parking was all but impossible around the Crescent where the Shandys, the Feldsters, and a few other faculty families lived in houses that were owned by the college and rented out to the elect. Tonight, however, was Mirelle Feldster's bridge night. This meant that she would be using the Feldster car herself. Jim must be expecting to be picked up along the way by some lodge brother.

Peter didn't really give a hoot what either of the Feldsters would be doing tonight, but anybody who lived around the Crescent couldn't help knowing every last thing that went on there, willed he or nilled he. Or she. And what the Crescent knew, every last soul in Balaclava Junction would get to know because Mirelle Feldster would make sure in one way or another that they did; but not before she'd got the information twisted up, down, and sideways, blown out of context, and repainted in the murkiest colors possible.

Peter and Helen Shandy were among Mirelle's special targets though they lived circumspectly enough, never fought, didn't even raise their voices over a difference of opinion, gave no wild parties, kept their lawn mowed, and refrained from cutting down the magnificent blue spruce trees that had sheltered the small red brick house long before its present tenants had been born. Mirelle had been loudly and chronically opposed to the Shandys' touching so much as a twig until at last it dawned upon her that neither of them would ever have dreamed of assaulting their cherished spruces. Thereupon she'd executed a smart right-about-face and started bemoaning the Shandys' perversity in leaving those great, messy, dangerous old trees just where they spoiled the Feldsters' view.

Had the trees been taken away, their ever critical neighbor's only view would have been of the Shandys' bedroom windows, across which Peter and Helen were always careful to draw their curtains at bedtime. Mirelle had a habit of ducking in under the spruces with her binoculars at the ready and a glib tale of bat-watching on her lips in case they happened to catch her snooping.

The woman's chief problem seemed to be that she could find so little about the Shandys to revile, though she was always ready to do what she could with what she might find. Lately she'd taken it as a personal affront that Helen Marsh Shandy was getting so much cheap notoriety out of a stupid book she'd written about the Buggins family who, Helen claimed, had founded not only the college but all Balaclava County. (As, in fact, they had; but that didn't cut any ice with Mirelle.) Not to mention the pack of lies she'd dreamed up about an old souse called Praxiteles Lumpkin and his so-called weather vanes. Worst of all was the brazen way Helen

Marsh had managed to snare herself a husband practically the same day she'd set foot on campus. And look what she'd got for her trouble. Everybody knew Peter Shandy was crazy as a coot, and always had been.

And thus it went. What Mirelle might come out with at any time of day or night depended on the often faulty connection between her fevered brain and her forked tongue. What generally resulted was either a tempest in a teapot or else just a fly in the flue. More often than not, neither Peter nor Helen was aware of their neighbor's one-sided vendetta. If they did happen to notice, they generally found the situation mildly amusing.

Jim wasn't a bad old scout, though. Peter and he sometimes shared a table in the faculty dining room. Helen and Peter wouldn't have minded having Jim over to the house for a cup of coffee now and then, but that would have meant having to ask Mirelle too; chance meetings on neutral ground were less of a risk. Tonight, Peter wished his neighbor a happy lodging and accepted Jane Austen's suggestion that he and she take a little stroll around the Crescent.

Strolling with Jane usually meant her human escort's waiting as patiently as could reasonably be expected while she manicured her claws on a convenient tree trunk or chased after a squirrel almost her own size, just to remind it which small, furry gray quadruped was running the show in this neighborhood. All things considered, Jane could be rated as no pushover but an amiable malkin, willing enough to accept any small courtesy such as a gentle pat or a compliment on her fine stand of whiskers, but ready to retire to her favorite perch in the crook of Peter's elbow if a neighbor tried to pick her up.

As they passed the Porble house, Phil Porble, the college librarian and Helen's nominal boss, remarked that Peter and Jane reminded him of Samuel Johnson and Old Hodge going out to buy oysters. Peter replied that oysters must have been a damned sight cheaper then than they were now.

Jane's thoughts, as cats' meditations generally do, remained her own.

There was more than a hint of fall in the air tonight. Here in Balaclava County, the leaves were already beginning to turn. Students were moving their effects into the dormitories; tomorrow morning they'd be lining up to register for classes. Peter and his colleagues would be making last-minute changes in their schedules and giving the new lot of teaching assistants a final pep talk on how to keep a roomful of first-year students awake long enough to capture their full and complete attention.

Jane was tiring of her stroll. By the time she and Peter reached the Enderbles, who lived directly across the Crescent from the Shandys, she was up his pant leg and into his arms, yawning in that artless way young lady cats do, without bothering to cover her rose petal mouth. Jane's yawn must have been catching; John Enderble, professor emeritus of local fauna, was following her example.

"Hadn't you better go in, John?" That was his ever solicitous wife, Mary, one of the few persons whom Jane would allow to pick her up. "You know you have to narrate that program the Ameses will be filming tomorrow about the cabbage butterfly."

"Assuming we can find a butterfly, dear. And a cabbage."

"Oh, John! You silly old goofus. Tell him to go to bed, Peter."

Peter obliged. "Go to bed, John. You're a television star now, you know. Think of your public."

Peter wasn't trying to be funny; Professor Emeritus John Enderble was cutting quite a figure these days. Already widely known as the author of *Our Friends the Snakes, How to Live With the Burrowing Mammals*, and several other books both delightful and informative, John was capturing a new audience via Station WEED. Balaclava Agricultural College now had its own public broadcasting facility, focused exclusively on subjects of an environmental nature and subsidized by Professor Winifred Binks-Debenham, sole heiress to her late grandfather's immense fortune and an even more reliable authority on the burrowing mammals than Professor Enderble, having been one herself for a period of several years.*

John was ready to exchange a few more pleasantries but Jane, on a telepathic hint from Mary, broke up the meeting by leaping out of Peter's arms and racing for home. She made a quick stop behind a clump of coral bells in a new shade that Peter was trying out, tended meticulously to the tidying-up process that she'd learned as a wee kitten in the Enderbles' sandbox, and emerged ready to quit for the night.

Not so Peter. He could not resist going into the cubbyhole that he called his office to make a few more additions and corrections to his notes, knowing perfectly well as he did so that he'd forget them once he got on his feet before his first class and just tell the students what they needed to know. And they'd listen, by gad. Professor Shandy's courses were stiff, his examinations were frequent, he marked harder than a slab of New England granite, yet his students never missed a class.

After a while, Helen came down from her own office. Getting into it was a tight squeeze; all the rooms in the old brick house were small. The Shandys themselves were no giants, however, and liked the place as it was. Helen suggested a pre-bedtime cup of camomile tea; Peter offered an alternate suggestion.

A few days ago, Winifred Binks-Debenham had given them a jar of something purely organic made of elderberries, potato peelings, and no doubt a few more exotic odds and ends. Old habits died hard. Winifred had not been able to make herself disassemble the primitive and most likely illegal still that she'd rigged up from a banged-up stew kettle and a rusty tin funnel found in a burned-out cellar hole dur-

*Vane Pursuit

ing her Hobbit days. Winifred's potations were never twice the same but always worth sampling. Tonight, Peter recognized a soupçon of elderberry, Helen detected a hint of chokecherry, they both got the essence of dandelion. It made a pleasant windup to a somewhat hectic day.

Having performed their usual bedtime rituals behind drawn curtains, though with scant concern as to whether Mirelle Feldster might or might not be on the prowl, Peter and Helen gave themselves over to sweet conjugal repose. Jane strolled back and forth over their recumbent bodies a few times, selected a cosy spot in the bend of Helen's knees, spent a frantic minute or so washing her own left hind leg, purred her two humans a brief lullaby, and relaxed herself into that happy hunting ground where good cats go mousing in their dreams.

Serenity reigned in the Shandys' bedroom until precisely 2:47 A.M. by the illuminated clock on the nightstand. That was when all hell broke loose. Peter shot up like a startled woodcock, struggling to get his arms into his bathrobe. Helen switched on her reading lamp and dropped a quiet word to the effect that he might find his task less perplexing if he were to turn the robe right end up. As this seemed a reasonable suggestion, Peter tried again and succeeded.

"All set. I'd better go see what the flaming perdition's going on down there. That's Mirelle Feldster's voice, isn't it? What's she screeching for?"

"Who knows? You go downstairs, Peter, I'll be right along."

Helen was not about to face her neighbor in nothing but a pink chiffon nightie. As the howling and thumping at their front door got louder and wilder, she ran a comb through her short blond curls, dabbed on a bit of lip gloss, and slipped into a fairly dashing negligee that Peter had bought her for reasons of his own. She might as well give Mirelle a chance to titillate her bridge buddies with a juicy nugget about the lewd lingerie of libertine librarians.

Oddly enough, Mirelle didn't even appear to notice Helen. She was totally caught up in her own tribulations, which Peter, by dint of some fancy yelling on his own part, managed to boil down to the simple statement that Jim hadn't come back from his lodge meeting. Mirelle thought he might have stopped in to visit the Shandys on his way home.

Of all the blithering idiocy! Normally Peter Shandy was not the sort of man to get into a shouting match with a neighbor in the dead of night. Tonight, all Mirelle's nasty digs, her bossiness, her pushiness, her damnable poking and prying and spreading false rumors got rolled up into one scabrous wad; he let her have it right between the eyes.

"Of course Jim isn't here! For God's sake, Mirelle, did you have to wake up the whole Crescent? What do you think the neighbors are saying right now?"

The question was redundant. Peter knew damned good and well what the neighbors must be saying and he didn't blame them one iota. Mirelle Feldster's dramatic outbursts were no novelty but this was the first time Peter could remember that she'd gone to such histrionic lengths. But then she might never before have had reason to; as far as he knew, Jim had never stayed out so late before. Sighing, Peter damped down his righteous indignation and assumed the role that had been forced upon him several years ago, as Balaclava's apology for Sherlock Holmes.

"What time did you get home yourself, Mirelle?"

She had herself a little more under control now; she answered like a sulky child. "About a quarter to eleven. The rest of us wanted to keep on playing, but naturally Coralee had to get home to her answering machine. You know Coralee."

Peter did know Coralee Melchett, and wished he didn't. Being the wife of the only doctor in town, who was also the college physician, mainly because his father and grandfather had held the position before him; and being also the daughter of the man who had established a small, but highly regarded, chain of ladies' clothing stores around the region, Coralee felt it her civic duty to dress up to her station and look down on her neighbors, except for a chosen few, of whom Mirelle Feldster was a leading light. Peter remained unawed.

"So you've been sitting up all this time, waiting for Jim?"

That struck her in a sore spot. "Why should I? Jim never waits up for me. Not that I'm one to be running the roads, as you well know, but I do have to get out sometimes, don't I?"

"That's beside the point. Look, Mirelle, why don't we try talking sense for a change? I saw Jim walk past our house about seven o'clock. He stopped a minute to pass the time of day and pat the cat, then he walked on. I assumed then that he was going down to Charlie Ross's to get his car but that can't have been the case. You'd already taken the car to your bridge club, hadn't you?"

"It's my car as much as his. I believe I'm entitled to get a little use out of it once in a blue moon."

Since it was well known around town that Mirelle spent a great deal more time in the car than she did in her house, Peter didn't bother to answer that one. "Then I'm to assume," he said, "that Jim must have been meaning to get a lift from one of his lodge brothers. Would you happen to know which lodge he was going to last night?"

"I can't keep track of the foolish things." Mirelle spent a moment in silent glowering, then said grudgingly that it might have been those idiots who called themselves the Scarlet Runners. "They usually meet at the firehouse in Lumpkinton, though I can't see why Jim has to go traipsing all the way over there. They could just as well meet here at the Balaclava Junction firehouse, such as it is."

"Except that there's barely enough room here to squeeze in the fire truck, much less hold a meeting. Furthermore, all the Scarlet Runners except Jim live in Lumpkinton and their firehouse has a very comfortable meeting room, plus a special stall to park the old hose cart which they take out on special occasions, as you very well know."

Peter was warming up to the job. "If you'd only stopped to think, Mirelle, it might have occurred to you that Elver Butz, who's one of Jim's lodge brothers, has been over here on campus with his helpers every day for the past couple of weeks, replacing the wiring in the farrowing barn. Since you were planning to take the car to your bridge game, Jim most likely hitched a ride with Elver, which would have got him to the meeting all right but left him without a ride home. So the logical assumption would be that Butz has offered Jim a bed for the night and is planning to bring him back in the truck with the crew when they come to work. Which makes perfect sense all around and I can't see what you've got yourself so damned het up about."

Mirelle was not placated. "That's right, put the blame on me. Why couldn't Jim have phoned and let me know he'd be late?"

"Perhaps he did and you weren't around to take his call."

"He could have called back later, couldn't he?"

Peter was about ready to let off steam again. "Look, Mirelle, you told me just now that you weren't in the habit of waiting up for Jim. So that must mean you went straight up to bed when you got in, slept for two or three hours, and woke because you'd drunk too much coffee at the bridge party. You got up to go to the bathroom, didn't hear Jim snoring"—it was well known around the Crescent that the Feldsters occupied separate bedrooms, for whatever reasons they chose to give—"and went into a tizzy when you looked into his room and found he wasn't there."

"I don't care," Mirelle pouted. "He could still have called."

"What would have been the sense? Jim knew you'd be out playing bridge all evening. He also knew it's a toll call from Lumpkinton to Balaclava Junction and didn't want to run up Butz's telephone bill. He wouldn't have tried to call you collect because he'd known damn well you'd refuse to accept his call out of spite."

"So what I'm supposed to do now is go back home and worry myself sick all night, is that it?"

"Actually, it's three o'clock in the morning, but I suppose you can get in a fair amount of agonizing between now and daylight if that's what tickles your fancy. Or you might make yourself a cup of camomile tea and go back to bed like a sensible person. If you can't sleep, read a book. I'd escort you back home but I don't suppose you'd particularly want the neighbors seeing us together with bare legs and bathrobes, so I'll just stay here on the stoop and wait to make sure the goblins don't grab you before you get safely inside."

"Thanks for nothing! I ought to have known I wouldn't get any help from you, Peter Shandy."

"And how right you'd have been. Good morning, Mirelle."

If she'd been anybody less exasperating than Mirelle Feldster, Peter would at least have taken the time to phone the state police and find out whether any accident had been reported on the Balaclava-to-Lumpkinton Road that evening. He might even have got his own car from Charlie's and driven slowly with his high beams on over the route Elver Butz would most likely have taken, for whatever good that might have done. If Jim Feldster had been in any sort of accident, surely somebody would at least have made an attempt to reach his wife.

Maybe this show that Mirelle had just put on stemmed from plain boredom. Maybe she'd been out on a tear with the mailman and was trying to cover up. Maybe she'd strangled Jim with his Scarlet Runner regalia or just shoved him down the cellar stairs because she couldn't stand any more of his clanking. More probably, Jim had seen his chance to stay clear of Mirelle for a few extra hours and grabbed it, as any sensible man naturally would.

The Feldsters' front door opened and closed. Mirelle had left the outside light on. The screech owl that had taken up residence in the tallest spruce tree said something rude about humans who didn't know enough to perch quietly in their own habitats during an owl's hunting hours. During the whole time Helen had spoken no word nor made any sign. Seeing that the show was over, she scooped up Jane Austen, settled the little cat comfortably on her shoulder, and led the way back to bed.

2

"WERE YOU DREAMING LAST NIGHT, OR WAS I?" HELEN
Shandy picked up the coffeepot and gave it a gentle slosh. "I
think there's just about enough in here for one more cup.
Want it?"

"Let's each have half." Peter held out his cup. "To answer
your question, I'm reasonably sure that I was awake. If I'd
been in the mood to dream, I'd have picked somebody more
interesting than Mirelle Feldster to dream about. That
woman's a bigger nuisance than an epidemic of fire blight.
I'd say she was batty but I don't want to traduce the bat,
which is a useful critter in its own quiet way."

"And also cute," Helen added. "I do like those little round
ears and pointy wings, and the way they flap around going
eek!eek!eek! And what would Halloween be without them?"

"Good question," said Peter. "What's on your agenda
today?"

"Never you mind my agenda. What do you think we
should do about Jim Feldster?"

"Greet him politely when he comes home from the wars,
I suppose."

Helen sniffed. "Home to the wars will be more like it. All
I can say is, I'm glad I'll be able to barricade myself in the
Buggins Room all morning rather than dodge the flying ep-

ithets. Would you like to rescue me sometime around noon and carry me off to the faculty dining room?"

"Sure, cutie, my pleasure. I'll come to thee at noontide though heck should bar the way. It isn't every denizen in the groves of academe who gets to hang out with a gorgeous blonde who goes eek!eek!eek! Good gad, look at the time! I'd best be off to the greenhouses before the bush beans get rough with the thunbergia. Au revoir, then, but not good-bye."

What with one thing and another, Peter had no time to ponder the strange disappearance of Jim Feldster until he kept his luncheon date with Helen. She, of course, was primed with the goods. Librarians always got to know what was going on, even when they'd been penned in all morning by six generations of the Buggins family. The gist of her morning's research was that Professor Feldster still hadn't shown his face anywhere around the cow barns and chaos was rife in the animal husbandry department. The latest earth-shattering rumor was that the great Professor Daniel Stott, sultan of swine and bashaw of bulls, had actually consented to oversee Jim's classes himself, should a catastrophe have occurred and a reliable substitute not be found available.

Professor Stott had even taken it upon himself to telephone Mrs. Feldster. All he'd got for his solicitude had been a long diatribe during which she'd switched like a runaway jumping bean from unbridled fury to incipient widowhood and back again at top speed. Quickness not being Professor Stott's forte, he'd completely lost the thread of her plaint and excused himself on the reasonable grounds that the college cows must not be kept waiting.

Helen thought it would be an exaggeration to claim that Professor Feldster would be sadly missed by all and sundry should the worst have happened. She was not quite sure that none of his colleagues wished him ill. The mere fact that Feldster the ever predictable had suddenly turned up missing for no apparent reason was already making him a subject for wild speculation around the luncheon tables in the faculty dining room; not all the comments were lapped in the milk of human kindness. Neither Peter nor Helen cared much for wisecracks about the clanking cowherd; they ate their meal without taking any part in the unbridled conjectures.

While the dining room was technically restricted to members of the faculty, its hospitality could stretch to cover just about anybody who happened to be on campus for respectable college-related purposes. Among those present today Peter noticed Elver Butz.

Elver was a self-effacing man, quiet almost to the point of never saying anything at all unless it was pried out of him. It wasn't so much that Elver didn't care to socialize; it was simply that he never had much to talk about except the finer points of electrical wiring, and not everybody was so totally hipped as he on the nuances of circuit breakers and rheostats. Even his helpers got fed up. He didn't have any of them with him at the table today; they must either have brought their lunches or gone down to the hot dog stand.

This was not surprising. Helen murmured to Peter that none of Elver's helpers stayed with him long because they couldn't stand the silence. Peter raised an eyebrow and beckoned for the check. Helen noted that Elver had got to the stage of picking his teeth and debating inwardly whether to finish his last refill of coffee. The two left the dining room and loitered under a convenient maple tree, showing each other which of its leaves were turning the reddest, until Elver ambled out, still chewing abstractedly on his toothpick.

Elver was a big man, fair-skinned and blue-eyed; his hair must have been blond before it turned gray. He'd done some electrical work for the Shandys a while back, and showed no particular aversion to being greeted by a couple who paid on time and weren't pushy about getting him to talk. He even seemed mildly pleased that they'd noticed he was there. Peter extended a reasonably appropriate greeting, regretted that he had no secret handshake to offer, and got down to business.

"You know, Elver, that was a funny thing about you and Jim Feldster last night. Funny in the unfunny sense of the word, that is. As it happened, I was outside with our cat—you remember Jane—when Jim came along in his Scarlet Runner regalia. He stopped to pat Jane, which gave me the idea that he might be intending to bum a ride over to Lumpkinton with you."

Elver thought that one over for a while, then delivered. "Yup."

"You live over there, don't you? Not far from where the old soap factory used to be, as I remember."

"Yup."

"So you very kindly drove him to the lodge meeting, then offered Jim a bed for the night because he didn't have a ride home, right?"

"Nope."

"Er—any special reason?"

"Yup."

"Seeing as how my wife and I are Jim's next-door neighbors, would you mind telling us why?"

"Never came."

"Do you mean he never came at all?"

"Yup." For once, Elver waxed loquacious. "I was on my way to the firehouse with my window rolled down so's I'd be ready to give Jim the secret password an' handshake, see?"

"How fast were you going?"

"Real slow. Tryin' to remember which hand I'm supposed to shake with. I see Jim up ahead, almost to the firehouse, walkin' pretty fast. Before I could get to him, here comes this big gray Lincoln town car, a real beauty, everything electronic." His usually dull blue eyes were charged with an enthusiast's appreciation of complex wiring. "Whoever was driving powered down the front passenger window, Jim stuck his head in, and the next thing I saw, he had the door open and got inside. I figure Jim won't need any ride from me so I went along by myself."

"Did you see Jim give a password or anything?"

"Nope. Just slammed the door an' went."

"Did he show up at the meeting?"

"Nope."

"That doesn't sound like Jim Feldster to me."

"Me neither."

"Did Mirelle call you about this?"

Elver Butz thought a moment. "Nope. Nice lady, though. Jim shouldn't have worried her."

Helen and Peter stared at each other. "Nice lady? Mirelle Feldster?"

"Yup. Pretty, too." Elver Butz's eyes glowed brighter. "Did some work for them last spring. She was nice to me."

The electricity faded from his eyes as he caught sight of two men who must be his current helpers. He made some kind of grunting noise and ambled off to join them at the far-rowing barn. One was tall and fairish like Elver, one was shorter and darker. He spoke to neither of them, as far as the Shandys could tell, and neither of them spoke to him.

"Well, a nice word about Mirelle may be a first, but that wasn't much help." Helen glared after the three electricians as though what had happened to Jim Feldster was all their fault. "Who would Jim know with a big fancy car like that? Are you going to tell Mirelle?"

Peter shook his head. "I still have half an hour before my next class. I think what I ought to do first is drop over to the police station and have a little chat with Fred Ottermole."

"What will that get you? Besides a nice visit with Edmund and Fred, of course?"

"One never knows. Fred's pretty quick at spotting cars

and we don't see all that many gray Lincoln town cars around these parts."

"Then I'll leave him to you. Bye, dear. Don't let Fred stick you in the lockup."

In a time now gone, Professor Shandy and Chief Ottermole had marched to vastly different drummers. Peter had tapped the chief an officious young oaf and Fred had regarded the professor as a Grade A pain in the butt. Gradually, however, the two of them had become fast friends and forged a bond between town and gown that worked pretty well some of the time, all things considered.

Peter had remained steadfastly on Fred's side throughout a number of town meetings, never failing to raise his voice over the acrimoniously debated question of whether the town's one and only police cruiser should be replaced by a vehicle that didn't have to be held together with baling wire and positive thinking. So far, Peter and Fred had always lost; but two months ago the old hack had brought the matter to a head by disintegrating into a pitiful heap of rust and wreckage just at the junction of Main Street and Buggins Row.

The ensuing traffic jam was still a topic of fevered conversation over every supper table in Balaclava Junction. Demon reporter Cronkite Swope of the *Balaclava County Fane and Pennon* continued to crank out reams of copy highly complimentary to Chief Ottermole and bitterly critical of those rock-ribbed naysayers who were withholding their support of a perfectly affordable and much-needed piece of equipment. So far, there had been plenty of talk but not one cent had been forthcoming from the town budget. In the hope of shaming the town fathers into loosening the purse strings, Fred had taken lately to riding his rounds on his oldest son's bicycle.

Thus far, results had been mixed. Some citizens were sympathetic to the chief's one-man crusade, others sneered at him for making a fool of himself. A third faction thought the bike a neat idea and wondered what a little backwater like Balaclava Junction needed a police cruiser for, anyway. Fred's pretty wife, Edna Mae, was of two minds about the bicycle. On the one hand, she felt it somewhat demeaning for a grown man to be riding a kid's bike. On the other hand, she had to admit that the exercise was doing great things for her husband's waistline.

Peter Shandy liked and respected Mrs. Ottermole. As he approached the police station and saw her coming away from there with an empty lunch basket over her arm, he paused, regretting that he didn't have on a hat so that he could tip it. "Good afternoon, Edna Mae. What's new in the bicycle war?"

Edna Mae laughed, a bit ruefully. "I suppose I shouldn't be getting involved in town politics, but 1 do think it's pretty scroungy of the budget committee not to provide Fred with a halfway decent cruiser. What's going to happen when he runs into a case where he has to bring in a prisoner to the lockup? Does he call a taxi or strap the prisoner to the carrier rack, will you answer me that?"

"That's certainly a point to consider," Peter replied. "Knowing your husband as I do, however, I'm sure he'd make the pinch with his usual finesse and aplomb regardless of circumstances. Is Fred in the office now?"

"Yes, he's there. I told him I didn't think it was very sensible to ride the bike on a full stomach. Don't you think he ought to take it easy until he's given his lunch a chance to settle, Professor?"

"Absolutely. Tell me, has Fred said anything to you about a gray limousine that was seen last night about seven o'clock, picking up Professor Feldster near the fire station?"

"Oh yes, hadn't you heard? I thought everybody in town must know by now. It happened last night around supper time. Budge Dorkin was on the desk so that Fred could come home to eat supper with me and the boys, so he got a ringside seat. Budge says the car was a gray Lincoln, not new but still pretty classy. What really got Budge going was that the windows all had tinted glass in them. You know, the kind so dark you can't see in from the outside but you can see the outside from the inside if you ever get the chance."

"Did Budge get the car's license plate number?"

"He didn't have time. Professor Feldster came along just then; the Lincoln stopped short and somebody yanked him inside, slammed the door and took off. Budge figured it must have been some of the professor's lodge buddies practicing for Halloween. They're always thinking up some goofy stunt or other."

"And that's all it amounted to? Or would have, if Jim Feldster had shown up at the cow barns this morning as usual. Never a dull moment in this town, eh? Well, I'd better mosey along and tell Fred not to get too frisky on that bike. Good to see you, Edna Mae."

An exemplary wife and mother, but not the sort to notice out-of-town number plates. Peter hoped that Budge Dorkin, a fairly intelligent young sprout, had at least managed to get a quick peek at whoever had been driving that Lincoln last night.

Peter wasn't really sure what he was doing down here. He ought to be back in his office, bracing himself for his two o'clock class; but he couldn't get his mind off Jim Feldster. He almost wished he hadn't been so cavalier with Mirelle last night, but he was in no mood to risk another confrontation today. A chat with Ottermole might clarify the issue a little. Then again it mightn't. Since he was down here anyway, though, he might as well drop in on the chief regardless.

He glanced at his watch and hurried on to the police station: a small outer room with a beat-up desk, an unpredictable wooden swivel chair, and a wire In-basket on one corner where Edmund, the self-appointed station cat, liked to lie on the few pieces of mail that came in and think up clues to where Chief Ottermole had hidden the doughnuts.

He could get quite cross if disturbed during cogitation, had even been known to flex his claws in displeasure, although never at the chief or well-behaved visitors like Peter Shandy. Behind the office was the lockup, which took up the whole back two-thirds of the room and still was no more than a cubbyhole. The only other amenities were a poor apology for a washroom and a nominally clear space by the door that was mostly taken up by a rickety table holding a coffeemaker and a few brown-stained mugs.

Not long ago, Fred had painted the whole place a lively blue color that had been on sale at the hardware store, because he just couldn't stand the gloom and grime any longer. He'd paid for the paint and done all the work himself, but there were still a few of the townsfolk who'd jumped on him for wasting good paint on drunks and crooks. Some of these didn't think cops deserved any better treatment than their prisoners; a policeman's life was not supposed to be a happy one in the first place. Needless to say, those persons who made the biggest fuss about the chief's blue paint were also the loudest to shout down any money for a new police cruiser and the first to raise a hullabaloo when they themselves needed, or fancied they needed, any kind of police assistance.

Fred Ottermole was sticking with Edna Mae's advice about letting his stomach rest, but only up to a point. His son's bike was leaning up against the wall behind the desk where it stood a pretty good chance of not getting swiped; he and Edmund were sharing a whoopee pie. Edna Mae would have thrown a fit had she caught her husband eating the chocolate cake part and feeding the whipped cream filling to Edmund. The oversized feline gave Professor Shandy a cursory nod and went on licking whipped cream off his whiskers.

"For God's sake, Ottermole," Peter expostulated, "don't you know better than to feed that stuff to a cat?"

Balaclava's finest merely shrugged. "Ah, hell, you've

only got nine lives to live. Right, Edmund? How come we're getting squealed on by a distinguished member of the faculty, Prof? I thought you were supposed to be working."

."So did I. If you want to know, I'm not sure what I'm doing here myself. You know Professor Feldster, don't you?"

"Sure. He's that long drink of buttermilk who teaches dairy management, isn't he? When I was a kid we always called him the milkman because he carried a little milk pail home with him every night. My kids still do. What about Professor Feldster?"

"I was hoping you might know." While Fred and his buddy masticated their last bites of whoopee pie, Peter tried to explain why he'd come. "I happened to be out front after supper yesterday, exchanging a few words with Edmund's friend Jane, when Jim Feldster came out of his house, clanking as usual, and stopped to say hello. I assumed he was on his way to one of his meetings. He belongs to every lodge in the county that doesn't let in women."

The police chief snorted. "Can't blame him, can you? That wife of his is in here about six times a week raising hell about nothing in particular. No wonder he never stays home. He must belong to the Scarlet Runners, they're the guys who get out and run with the old machine every Fourth of July."

"I know. They're supposed to be a holdover from the hose cart companies back when every household had to keep a leather bucket handy and be ready to join the bucket brigade in case of fire. I don't know what they were planning to do last night. Burn down the pool hall, have a water fight; something of that sort, I suppose."

Ottermole yawned. "You planning to get to the point any time soon, Prof? I've got to go out on my rounds."

3

PETER SMILED. "THANK YOU FOR REMINDING ME, I WOULDN'T have wanted to miss waving you off. Getting quickly along with the *res gestae,* have you heard any more about the gray Lincoln with the tinted windows that picked up Jim Feldster last night?"

"Nope." Fred glanced down at his uniform and winced. "For God's sake, Edmund, did you have to smear that goop all over my uniform? Edna Mae's going to kill me."

"Too bad," said Peter. "Take a towel and sponge it off. If there is a towel. I was talking with Elver Butz just now. He told me that he'd been on the way to pick Jim up in his truck and take him to a lodge meeting in Lumpkinton last night after work, when this big Lincoln cut in ahead of him. He was all set to reach out the truck window and give Jim the secret handshake when the car stopped and Jim got aboard. They then drove away, leaving Elver nonplussed but not saying so."

"So?" Ottermole was still sponging at the whipped cream with a handkerchief on which Edna Mae had embroidered a pair of little blue handcuffs. "What's the punch line?"

Peter shook his head. "I wish I could tell you. All I know, of my own personal knowledge, is that Jim was alive and clanking when I last saw him walking down the Crescent on his way to meet Elver in front of the firehouse. Sometime after half past two in the morning, Mirelle Feldster came banging at our front door in a state of hysteria. She said Jim hadn't got home and wanted me to rush out in my pajamas and find him."

"My gosh! What did you do?"

"I have to say I didn't take her seriously. I assumed that Jim must have stayed overnight in Lumpkinton with one of his lodge buddies because his wife had left him without transportation, and was intending to ride back with Elver Butz this morning. I fully expected Jim to be on campus at the usual time but he never showed up, much to the bemusement of the entire animal husbandry department and the college in general. There's no sense in my warning you to keep it quiet because everybody in town must know by now, but I did think you ought to be officially notified."

"Damn right I ought to be notified. Thanks, Pete. But I'm not going to start raising a posse and jumping the gun, either. What about holding off till, say tomorrow noontime? Give the professor a chance to sleep it off if he's been on a toot and let his wife rest her tonsils for a while, maybe?"

"That's a very humane attitude, Ottermole. As to the drinking, all I can tell you is that I've known Jim Feldster ever since I've been at Balaclava and never once seen him under the weather. Never heard of him missing a lodge meeting either. I can't say we've ever been on particularly intimate terms, but we're as neighborly as it's safe to be, considering the circumstances."

Fred snickered. "You don't have to draw me a picture. Every time Mirelle comes bending my ear about some damn thing or other, I drop in at our house and give Edna Mae a great big kiss." He grinned a bit sheepishly, took out another spandy-clean handkerchief with another little pair of blue handcuffs on it, and wiped the chocolate crumbs off his mouth. "What do you say, Edmund? You going to mind the station while I go out and work off my whoopee pie or do you want to make the rounds with me?"

Peter thought he'd better get back to work himself, but couldn't resist pausing to watch Ottermole strap his cellular phone to his belt, hang a Back at Three O'Clock sign on the office door, mount his two-wheeler, and ride off with Edmund sitting up in the basket that was fastened to the handlebars and padded with a cushion which had blue handcuffs embroidered on it. Cop and cat obviously enjoyed each other's company. Peter wondered how Jane might take to being trundled around in a bicycle basket, glanced at his watch, decided this was not the time to try, and legged it for his classroom.

As always on the first day of classes, Professor Shandy got trapped by a steady stream of questions from incoming students. He'd hoped to be home by six o'clock but it was almost a quarter to seven when he staggered into the house. Peter's plan had been to mix a mild Balaclava Boomerang for himself and another for Helen if she wasn't still barricaded in the Buggins Room, after which he might offer to open a can or two of something or other for supper. As he opened the door, he was dismayed to hear Helen talking to another woman. Then he recognized the voice and joined the party.

"Catriona! What a nice surprise."

Catriona McBogle, Helen's friend of many years and darling of mystery fans from Boston to Tokyo with stops in between, was not easily pried out of her two hundred-year-old house in a Maine town that few people knew existed and those who did weren't any too thrilled about; or claimed they weren't because they didn't want a lot of tourists coming to strew litter along its pleasant byways.

Helen and Peter had seen Catriona not long ago in Maine, at which time she'd announced her intention of digging a moat, hauling up the portcullis, and staying immured behind her three-course-deep brick walls until she'd finished a book that she ought to have started work on three months earlier. Usually Catriona was a woman of her word, as tall women with red hair and Yankee faces tended to be. Why had she changed her mind so soon?

There was only one way to find out, and Peter was the man to take it. "What brings you here, if I may be so bold as to ask?"

"Where did I come from, Peter dear? Out of the Everywhere into the Here. If you really want to know, I came down to get cheered up. So far I can't say that you've helped much."

"Give me time, drat it, I just got home. What's gone wrong at the fiction factory?"

"That's my trouble, Peter. Nothing's gone anywhere. There I was, all fired up to start churning out the stuff that royalties are made of, when it suddenly occurred to me that I couldn't think of one jeezledy gosh-darned thing to say. Peter, I'm desperate. I need a plot."

"You've already had a plot. Lots of plots. Can't you simply dust off one of the old ones and recycle it? That's been done before, I believe."

"Yes, I know, and no, I can't. It would be like having to keep mopping the same old floor year after year after year, and you know what a rotten housekeeper I am. I don't even know where Persilla hides the mop when she's not mopping with it. I'm washed up, Peter. Finished. Kaput. Fit only for the boneyard. I should have been a pair of ragged claws scuttling across the ocean floor."

"Quit it, Cat," Helen snapped in her most librarianly tone. "You're breaking my heart. Peter, don't you think it might be a good idea to fix Cat a—"

"Balaclava Boomerang? You took the words right out of my mouth, my love. How about you, Catriona? You do understand that I make them strictly for medicinal purposes?"

"But of course, why do you think I came? Which is not to say that the hours I've spent with thee, dear heart, wouldn't still be as a string of pearls to me even if you hadn't been prepared to administer first aid. I should have made that plural, shouldn't I? Is it thees?"

"I believe the plural of 'thee' is 'ye,' " Helen murmured.

"As in 'Abandon hope, all youse who enter here'? That figures."

"If you say so, Catriona." Peter handed his unexpected guest an exotic compound that teemed with vitamins and was a standard remedy for practically everything from gallstones to glanders when taken with proper respect and discretion. "See if that's the way you like it."

Catriona accepted the glass and lifted it in halfhearted salute. "Through the teeth and over the gums. Look out, stomach, here it comes. Might you happen to have anything to eat in the house? Don't ask me what I want, just give me something to remember you by. Unless you'd prefer not to be bothered succoring a damsel in distress. I could probably pick up some edible ort or other on the ocean floor."

"I'm sure you could if you put your mind to it, Cat," said Helen, "but you really don't have to. Peter's planning to make us one of his gorgeous omelets with all sorts of wonderful stuff in it as soon as he's finished his drink. Aren't you, dear?"

"If you say so, moon of my delight. Why don't I fix a plate of cheese and crackers to bridge the gap while I try to remember which pan I'm supposed to use for omelets?"

"A splendid idea, Peter, I knew you'd think of something. Would you like to have Cat and me come out to the kitchen and egg you on?"

"I suppose I could start setting the table," Catriona mumbled through a mouthful of cheese and cracker. "That's about all I'm fit for any more."

"Bah, humbug," Helen soothed. "Say not the struggle naught availeth. This is only a phase you're going through, you'll be your own charming self again in the morning."

"How do you know I will, smarty-pants? You won't be there to see me."

"Oh yes I will. Catriona McBogle, you are not going to drive all the way home to Sasquamahoc in the pitch dark with a Balaclava Boomerang on your breath, and that's that."

"That's what? You're not expecting me to sit by the side of the road and be a friend to man, surely? I'm a bit long in the tooth for that sort of caper, wouldn't you think?"

"No, I wouldn't think and don't be silly. You're going to wallow in the luxury of that moderately comfortable fold-away sofa in the upstairs office and dream a lovely dream of poisoning some rich old curmudgeon with a tasteful and exotic potion shortly after he's willed all his earthly goods to you. And getting away with it."

"But I can't think of anything tasteful and exotic. That's my problem."

"Never mind, it will come to you. Oh, all right, I can see that you're in one of your moods." Helen gave her old friend a one-armed hug, trying not to dump saltines all over the floor in the process, and steered her into the living room so that Peter could chop and stir without hindrance in the undersized kitchen that they still hadn't got around to remodeling. "Come sit here with me. I'll fill you in on our latest neighborhood flap."

"What kind of flap?"

"Now that you mention it, we're still not sure. We only hope it doesn't turn into a full-blown crisis."

"Why should it?" Catriona was beginning to perk up a little.

"Because Mirelle Feldster seems to be determined on fomenting one."

"Mirelle Feldster being that man-eating piranha who lives next door to you, if I remember correctly."

"I shouldn't exactly call Mirelle a man-eating piranha. Though there are those who might," Helen answered after a moment's consideration. "She tears into women with equal appetite. Anyway, sometime around a quarter to three this morning, she came pounding and screaming at our front door, carrying on as though she were being kidnapped by giant scorpions. I'm sure the neighbors could hear her all the way up to President Svenson's house. It's a wonder Thorkjeld didn't come down, come to think of it. If there's any sort of row going, he generally wants to be in it. But anyway, there stood Mirelle in a hideous purple satin negligee, wanting to know if her husband was engaged in an orgy with Peter and me."

"She never said that!"

"No," Helen conceded, "but she implied it. That woman's got a mind like a cesspit. Of course Jim wasn't here. Mirelle must have known perfectly well that he wouldn't be; she simply couldn't pass up the chance to make a big scene."

"So what did you tell her?"

"Nothing. Not one single word. I just lurked in the shadows and let Peter deal with her. Which he did none too gently, I have to say, though a person could hardly blame him in the circumstances."

"Were you able to figure out what she was really screaming about?"

"What it boiled down to was that Jim hadn't come home from his lodge meeting."

"What kind of lodge does the old coot attend, for Pete's sake?"

"It could be almost any kind, except perhaps the Girl Scouts or the Bluebirds. Jim only joins lodges that won't let any women in, which is disgusting of him from one point of view but quite understandable from another. Apparently last night's fracas started with Mirelle's insisting on taking their only car to her bridge club, leaving Jim to hitch a ride with one of his lodge brothers who happens to be working at the college just now. The meeting was at the firehouse in Lumpkinton, where a group calling themselves the Scarlet Runners keep their antique hose cart and hold their meetings."

"They do?" Either the company of friends or the Balaclava Boomerang must be having a therapeutic effect on Catriona's tonsils. "So there was Brother Feldster galloping through the byways of Lumpkinton neck and neck with the firehouse Dalmation, hauling the hose cart after him? Damn! I wish I'd been there."

"You can't have missed much," Helen consoled her. "They only take out the hose cart on the Fourth of July."

"What do they do the rest of the time?"

"Sit around and play with matches, I guess. Anyway, to get back to the Feldsters, Peter thought, quite reasonably, that Jim must have stayed overnight with the lodge buddy who'd given him the lift, and would be driving back in the truck with him this morning. So the upshot was that he told Mirelle to quit making a fool of herself, or words to that effect, and she stomped off across the yard in a flaming snit."

"And you call that a crisis?" Catriona sneered. "Frankly, Helen, I'm not greatly impressed."

"Oh, but that was only the beginning," Helen reassured her guest. "It did seem odd to me last night that Mirelle should be so concerned all of a sudden about the husband to whom or about whom she's never spoken a kind word within the memory of anybody who knows them. But this morning, Jim didn't show up either at his own house or on campus, and he's never once before, in all the years he's been at Balaclava, missed being at the cow barns smack on the dot. We don't know what to think."

"Ah, now the plot begins to thicken. When did yourself last see him?"

"I honestly can't tell you, Catriona, when I saw Jim last. Sometime yesterday, I suppose. He's such a part of the scenery and yesterday was so hectic that it's hard to remember."

"Would you happen to recall what the man looks like?"

"Don't be sarcastic with me, madam. He looks like a

beanpole out for a walk. Jim's one of those tall, rangy types who can eat all day and never gain an ounce. Jim always takes second helpings at the faculty dining room and goes back later for coffee with extra cream and another piece of pie. And I know for a solemn fact that he also takes cream on his cereal and goodness knows what else because I see him bringing it home after classes in a dinky pint-size galvanized pail with a snap-on cover. Nobody begrudges Jim his little perk, they just call him the milkman. It's generally agreed that he's not a bad old scout, though I don't believe anybody goes much farther than that."

"H'm. Would you happen to have a photograph of him?"

"Good question. I believe there's a group photo of the animal husbandry staff and a few cows in last year's college yearbook. Wait a second."

Being a librarian, Helen had every book and pamphlet in the house either shelved or filed. It took her about sixteen seconds to locate the yearbook and turn it to the correct page. Two seconds later, Catriona was scowling over the tallest man in the lineup.

"I've seen that man somewhere, I know I have. Either him or his twin brother. Does he have one?"

"I have no idea," Helen confessed. "I suppose Jim must have relatives somewhere. Most people do, though I've never heard him mention any. But then he never talks much about anything, except cows and barns. I suppose we should have been more neighborly, living so close together all this time, but Mirelle's the sort who tries to swallow you whole and turns nasty if you don't let her take over your life. Fortunately Peter and I are both too busy to play games with her. And Jim has all those lodge brothers, so it's not a situation in which we feel any obligation to get involved. I must say, though, that I wish to goodness I knew who owns that gray Lincoln."

"So do I," said Catriona. "What gray Lincoln are you talking about?"

By this time, Helen had either been told or had divined by osmosis or clairvoyance the story of what might or might not have been Professor Feldster's elopement, practical joke, kidnapping, loss of memory, or any of several other possibilities, depending on who was telling which interpretation of the known facts. She could reel them all off like a newscaster. Catriona relished every detail and was avid for more.

"And you're absolutely positive his name is Feldster, Helen?"

"All I can tell you is that Jim's been known as James Feldster ever since Peter first met him, which would be approximately thirty years ago, and that's how everybody on the faculty knows him. Not to mention all those lodge brothers. Whatever makes you think his name might not be Feldster?"

Catriona shook her head. "I don't know. Do you have any other photos of him?"

"Let's see. Oh, I know, there's one of him and Professor Stott taken together, I think it was three years ago at some faculty picnic. I snaffled a copy and cherish it because it's such a perfect depiction of Feast and Famine. See what I mean?"

Catriona glanced at the snapshot and went into a fit of giggles. "How could I miss? Have you ever thought what a handsome pig Professor Stott might have been, if only he'd been farrowed in a sty?"

"Well, we all have our crosses to bear," said Helen. "I'd better go see how Peter's doing with that omelet. He gets a bit carried away sometimes."

Peter had not got carried away. The omelet, the salad, the white wine, the fresh bread from Mrs. Mouzouka's college bakery, the fruit from the college orchards and the molasses cookies for dessert, the hazelnut coffee that wound up the meal, were each of them tagged Grade A Number One. By the time the three friends were ready to call it a day, Catriona McBogle had shed all gloomy thoughts of ragged claws and ocean floors. She lay awake on the hide-a-bed for an hour or so, taking notes in her head about an antique hose cart that had turned up missing from a small museum somewhere in midcoast Maine, leaving the curmudgeonly curator dead on the floor with a fireman's helmet on his head and a leather water bucket close to his waxen hand, then gave herself over to dreamless sleep. Come morning, she made her toilette in haste and skipped downstairs singing "It's a beautiful day to be glad in, the violets budded today."

"Like hell they did," replied her genial host. "You'll have to wait for violets till somewhere around the middle of next April, if you're lucky. Were you planning to go straight home from here?"

"Perhaps not quite straight," Catriona hedged. "There's a little bit of research I thought I might take care of while I'm in the area. But I do want to get home before it gets too late because I've got a plot!"

"You do, eh? What happened to that pair of ragged claws scuttling across the ocean floor?"

"Oh, I expect they'll come in handy for something or other sooner or later. How about you two letting me treat you to breakfast at the faculty dining room?"

Peter shook his head. "Sorry, it can't be done. Non-faculty people aren't allowed to pick up the checks. Besides, I've already mixed the batter for the waffles."

"Oh, all right. Don't say I didn't try."

Catriona seated herself at the breakfast table, spread her napkin across her lap, and waited in queenly style to be served. There was little time left for chatting; she gave the Shandys a fair-sized chunk of news about their mutual friend Guthrie Fingal; Peter shared out the last of the waffles, Helen stuck the syrupy plates in the dishwasher. Then each told the other two that they'd all three better get moving. Peter and Helen climbed the rise to the college. Catriona took the downward course to the parking lot where she'd left her elderly and inelegant little car, started its motor on the third try, and drove off, with supreme confidence, in the wrong direction.

4

It didn't take Catriona very long to realize that she was not where she'd meant to go, but she didn't much care. She was bound to come out somewhere or other sooner or later. What interested her more than her present whereabouts were those two photographs of Professor Feldster that Helen had shown her last night. Just why she should get so wrapped up in a face that she'd never so much as laid eyes on in the flesh was a puzzlement. All she knew was that, somewhere along the tortuous labyrinth of her mind, a little door had opened and something hard to discern had popped out waving a tiny banner and yelling "Hey! Over here."

As she pondered this intriguing development, it occurred parenthetically to Catriona that she hadn't checked her gas gauge for some time. She did so now and decided it might not be such a bad idea to look for a service station before she found herself in the wilds of nowhere with an empty tank. The poor old car was no gas guzzler but did require something more tangible than faith and hope to run on. She kept her eyes peeled and was soon rewarded by a sign that read Texaco.

Her only problem here was that there were already two cars drawn up at the one solitary pump. From the volume of sound that came out of them, both were crammed full with long-lost relatives of the hospitable attendant. That didn't matter, Catriona still had most of the day before her. She'd find herself on the right road one way or another. On the other hand, should the way prove elusive, perhaps she should call Helen and Peter, or rather Helen and Peter's answering machine since they were both at work, and assure them of her well-being. When she returned from the pay phone, she saw that the long-lost relatives seemed to have been joined by recently found friends. Rather than sit fuming over the wait to be refueled, she picked up a newspaper that she'd bought yesterday somewhere along the way to the Shandys' and been too down in the mouth to bother looking at.

She did recall now that she'd been momentarily struck by a glimpse of a man in his later years who reminded her a little of Mount Rushmore, although the collar and tie rather spoiled the effect. Now that she had the time, Catriona became, as writers tend to do, totally engrossed in the text that went with the photograph. When her turn at the pump finally came, the attendant had to speak twice to get her attention.

"You want to pull up a little, ma'am?"

"Oh, sorry."

Even as she shut off the engine and got out her wallet, Catriona was wondering why she should be getting such a head of steam up over a dead stranger's photograph in a Boston newspaper. Her customary procedure was simply to accept any bits and pieces of potentially interesting flotsam from that boundless sea of the universal subconsciousness into which a writer of mystery fiction might dip her ever ready bucket, and draw it out either brimming with whatever she might need to work her personal alchemy or else yielding her nothing more than half a cup or so of stagnant water and one disgruntled tadpole. Even tadpoles had their uses. Catriona paid for her gas, pulled away from the filling station, and drew up under a big maple tree half a mile or so down the road, where she could finish reading her paper without being pestered to have her oil checked.

The wordage on the front page didn't run to more than a few paragraphs, but the text that came after "continued on page twelve" covered almost a full page. The face under the headlines turned out to be that of Forster Feldstermeier, an internationally known but seldom seen milk magnate whose very name had been a source of awe and admiration for many a year among dairy farmers and distributors far and wide. He had always shunned publicity. During his later years, which had reached beyond the four score and ten before he'd passed on to pastures Elysian, he'd become a virtual recluse. However, a man of his stature could never have escaped notice, either for his many achievements in the dairy field or because he'd stood only a few inches short of seven feet tall.

According to the reporter who'd written the piece, the Feldstermeier progeny, every one of them a male, were also tall enough to make up their own basketball team if they'd wanted to, which they apparently hadn't, and were clannish to a remarkable degree. They'd taken their guidance from their patriarch, never letting a bovine teat go unstripped, believing with all their hearts and souls that an honest day's work deserved an honest dollar, and thoughtfully reserving all the top jobs for themselves, their sons, their cousins, and their nephews.

There were no female descendants in the direct line; it was the Feldstermeier wives who got mentioned occasionally in the society columns as sponsors and executors of fund-raising events to benefit worthy causes such as free milk for needy children and hungry stray cats. The cats were part of a neuter-and-spay program based on the sensible premise that well-fed cats with glossy fur and no excess baggage should be easier to find homes for and would make better pets. Obviously the Feldstermeier women were all worthy mates for worthy men; nevertheless Catriona decided, as had Gellett Burgess in the matter of the purple cow, that she'd rather see than be one.

As for seeing, her visual memory was above average. She couldn't have missed the resemblance between Feldster and Feldstermeier now that she'd had a chance to compare the two photographs. If the magnate and the milkman were indeed related, that could explain why someone as yet unnamed had driven that gray Lincoln down Balaclava Junction's main street. He, or possibly she, might have been looking for the professor, to let him know that his brother, cousin, or nephew was dead and carry him off to join in the family mourning. Not stopping to fetch Mirelle wouldn't have been very polite of the driver but, from what the Shandys had let fall, it would have been the only sensible course to take.

As to whether the reporter who'd written up Forster Feldstermeier's death had got all the facts straight, Catriona could only shrug. It was not unheard of for a journalist to lay on the hyperbole in deference to an illustrious member of a family, particularly when the family was a very rich one. Not that it was any of her business. What she ought to be concerned about was the tension that was mounting between her and her editor. That beleaguered lady had been getting rather snappish as time went on and Catriona's muse was still wading around in the sea of unconsciousness.

She folded the newspaper in such a way that she wouldn't have to look at Forster Feldstermeier again for a while and restarted her car. She still had no idea where she was or which way she ought to be heading, but experience had taught her to have faith. Surely there must be a library around here somewhere. With luck, it might even have in its reference section one of those Who's Who and Why directories that could provide much the same kind of information about the moguls of American industry as Debrett's had been doing so long for the British peerage.

Who seeks may find. After another hour or so of footling around through grubby industrial towns, prim suburbs, and quaint backwaters where Catriona might, if she'd cared to, have bought a hooked rug, a pieced quilt, or somebody's alleged grandmother's purportedly antique churn, she came upon exactly the place she'd been looking for.

All libraries are beautiful to the book lover; Catriona had a particularly warm spot for those red brick and gray granite buildings that still exist in New England, exuding their literary aura after a century or so of public service. This one was a gem. It had great carved granite basins out front, one on either side of the oaken door, both of them still bright with red geraniums and clipped Boston ivy. The ivy looked as if it had been trying all summer to take over the basins but the glossy green vine wasn't going to get its own way until a hard frost had nipped the last and final geranium because there was bound to be somebody on the staff who wouldn't let it.

Obviously a well-run institution, Catriona decided; just the place to find a reasonably up-to-date version of the material she wanted to see. She left her car around back in the parking lot, picked up her handbag and the newspaper that held the article about Forster Feldstermeier, and went inside.

Yes, this was the place. It looked right, it felt right, it smelled right. Catriona made a beeline for the reference section without having to be told where it was; her natural affinity with books and librarians took care of such details. She found the book she wanted, took it to the nearest table and got down to business. In less than no time she had them all pegged: who the Feldstermeier ancestors had been, where they'd come from, where they'd settled, all the finicking tidbits that tidy-minded scholars who compile books of reference love to load on.

James, the youngest by eleven years and quite likely a miscalculation on his parents' part, had either failed or forgotten to propagate; the reference pages gave him almost no mention at all. Naturally the main focus was on Forster. Among the brothers there had been no nonsense about equality of rank. Both their father and their grandfather had believed wholeheartedly in primogeniture, and Forster had never questioned his right to exercise the family prerogative. Nor had his brothers, evidently. Franklin and George had been Forster's faithful aides-de-camp from the day their father handed him the torch; content to serve the brother best fitted by birth and ability to keep that torch alight.

If even a fraction of the information that Catriona was finding could be believed, then Forster Feldstermeier must have been the ultimate role model. It had been his acumen, his courage, and his never flagging sense of purpose that had expanded the modest local dairy cooperative which his forbears had founded into an internationally famed enterprise of the first magnitude. Forster had seemed to know by instinct when to hold back and when to leap forward. He had taken hair-raising risks and brought them off without a hitch; yet it could fairly be said of him that he had never once in his whole life cheated a customer or a competitor, reneged on a deal, or uttered a word that he didn't mean.

Forster Feldstermeier had played fair with his entire workforce, however far-flung it might be, as he'd done with his customers. While he never forgot who he was, neither had he forgotten what was due the vast numbers of employees who carried on their daily tasks in his pastures, his dairies, in great factories where a surprising number of milk-based products were made and marketed here and abroad; all of them depending on him for their hire. He had been early to see the wisdom of providing such amenities as well-run company cafeterias, paid sick leave, and in-house day care centers for young children of working parents.

At Christmastime, Forster made sure that everybody under his aegis received a handsome card signed in his own hand, containing his personal greeting and a check for an extra two weeks' pay, along with a fruitcake in a tin attractively decorated with a picture of a contented cow, to remind them of the source of their benefits. What the cows got wasn't mentioned; presumably the Feldstermeier bovines fared at least as well as other cows and probably better than most.

With all his acumen and all his wealth, there was one circumstance over which the milk magnate had no control. To Forster Feldstermeier's bitter regret, he, eldest of the line, had outlived both those brothers who had so wholeheartedly supported and assisted him throughout their sadly curtailed lives. Franklin had succumbed to a sudden massive heart attack on his seventieth birthday. George, an enthusiastic mountain climber, had died in Switzerland while on a tour of the company's holdings there. Trying to combine business with a few days' recreation, he had apparently paused in his climbing to step back and admire the view.

The newspaper story had been vague about which Alp he'd fallen from. It was even vaguer about James, the youngest and dimmest. There was no mention of his having preceded his siblings into the Hereafter, but neither was it revealed that James was still alive. Could James Feldstermeier, now sole heir to the family fortunes, possibly be the Professor Jim Feldster who for so many years had trodden a well-worn path between Balaclava Agricultural College's cow barns and his many lodge affiliations?

Catriona didn't know what to think. It seemed totally ridiculous; but then so did most things. At least, with all those begats floating around, there shouldn't be any dearth of heirs being groomed to take the places of those who had gone before. She tucked the newspaper article and the notes she'd taken from the reference book into her capacious handbag, though she wasn't sure why, carried the book back to its proper place on the shelf, and asked the reference librarian, "Is there any place around where I might be able to get a halfway decent sandwich?"

The librarian was delighted to oblige. "There's the Shoemaker's Last just around the corner and the Singing Shrimp—say, don't I know you from somewhere? Weren't you at the American Library Association's—oh my gosh! Don't tell me you're Catriona McBogle?"

"I won't if you'd rather I didn't," Catriona replied modestly. "I'm sure we must have seen each other at the convention, but you know how it is. There are always so many librarians and writers around that it's impossible to remember everybody, even with their name tags on."

"I know, Miss McBogle; it was a real mob scene. But you did sign a book for me and one for my mother's birthday present and one for the library and one for my cousin Fred, who's read everything you've ever written and keeps yelling at me to bring him some more. And to think you're right here in our dinky old library! Did you find what you were looking for?"

"Yes I did, thanks. Actually you have a very good reference department. This was just a favor I thought I'd do for some friends of mine."

"Do they live around here? Would I know them?"

Catriona laughed. "I'm afraid I can't answer that. I've been lost for the past two hours."

"Oh dear!"

The woman sounded as if Catriona's mishap had been all the library's fault. Catriona hastened to absolve her of any guilt. "Don't worry, I enjoy getting lost. I always meet such nice people along the way. Which would you recommend, the Shoemaker or the Shrimp?"

"I don't know what to tell you, Miss McBogle. I'm so flabbergasted I can't even think. I like the Shrimp myself, it's sort of English tearoomy. They do shrimp rolls and shrimp wiggle on toast, things like that. And the tea's really good. The other place is more the hamburger and roast beef sandwich type. The food's all right in its way. My problem with the Shoemaker's Last is that when they bring out the beef it always makes me think of somebody in the kitchen resoling boots."

"I know just what you mean," Catriona sympathized. "I don't suppose you'd care to join me at the Shrimp?"

Catriona wasn't much for picking up strangers as a rule, but she always felt at home with librarians of any age, shape, or condition. She'd never yet come upon one who was either discourteous or ill informed. "Is there somebody who could take over your desk for an hour or so?"

"Yes, we have four besides me on the staff but they'd all kill me if you and I went off without them."

"Then suppose I nip out for sandwiches and we can have a picnic in the staff room. There don't seem to be many borrowers around just now."

"No, they'll come piling in about half past two when we're hoping to sneak a cup of tea. I'll get the sandwiches. What would you like?"

Catriona knew enough not to decline the library's hospitality; she wasted no time shilly-shallying. "The shrimp sounds good to me. Could I have it on dark bread with lettuce and just a scrape of mayonnaise? And tea, if you're making any."

"Milk or lemon?"

"Just plain, thanks, and not too strong. What's your name, by the way?"

"Belinda Beaker. Isn't that awful?"

"No, I think it's delightful. I may even snitch it sometime."

By now, heads were appearing in doorways. Catriona knew the drill; she got Belinda Beaker to introduce her coworkers and lead the way to the staff room while the youngest and most agile member of the staff sped off to fetch the sandwiches.

Catriona took the chair that was reverently offered. She autographed an extra copy of her new novel, *The Corpse in the Coalbin,* for a retired member of the staff who was now in a wheelchair and found the McBogle stories far more therapeutic than the doctor's doses.

By the time the speedy messenger was back with shrimps for all, the teakettle was on the boil. The shrimp sandwiches were first-rate, the tea was strong enough but not too strong. The library director filled a paper plate with chocolate chip cookies that she'd baked for her bridge club before she remembered that the players were all on diets, so she'd brought the cookies along for her colleagues, who didn't have time to get fat.

A woman of Catriona McBogle's height and build didn't have to fret about excess baggage. She ate three of the director's offerings and graciously accepted a few more to eat on her way to wherever she was going. The visit had passed delightfully and her hosts all clamored for her to come again, assuming that she already knew where she was. Catriona herself still wasn't sure but didn't like to ask because she didn't want these dear people to find out what an idiot she was about following directions. It was still only a little before three o'clock; she shouldn't have much trouble finding her way north without getting into the home-going traffic, assuming she could figure out which direction north was in. Now that she had allayed Helen and Peter's hypothetical worries, she wasn't in any mad rush to get home anyway.

Back in Sasquamahoc, Maine, something had gone terribly wrong sometime earlier at the president's house; the president being her close and increasingly closer friend Guthrie Fingal, who'd been Peter Shandy's roommate in student days and now ran the forestry college just down the road from Catriona's own beautiful two-hundred-year-old farmhouse. When disaster struck the presidential premises, with the wiring shorting out because of the flooding, the woodwork catching fire because of the shorting, and the plumbing breaking down before it could get water to the burning woodwork, Guthrie had moved in with Catriona, ostensibly just for the duration of the crisis.

A crisis can last quite a while if the victim works it right. Catriona was not at all sure how she might feel about having Guthrie around on a permanent basis. Right now, however, it was agreeable to know that he was there to feed the cats and take in the mail. She'd earned this break. She'd been tied to her desk for too long a time; no wonder she'd developed a case of the mental measles. When she came to a fork in the road, she ignored the bold yellow lines that were supposed to keep her on the right track, and took the road less taken.

She should never have listened to Robert Frost. The going was twisty and narrow and pocked with holes; the farther she went, the worse it got. Catriona thought of turning around and going back but there were so many unexpected dips and rises that she didn't dare try for fear of being hit head-on or clobbered from behind, in the unlikely event that some other idiot would come along and not see her until it was too late. So far she hadn't caught sight of a single human being either riding, walking or stuck in a pothole, but surely somebody must use the road sometimes and she'd just as soon be elsewhere by the time they arrived. By way of solace, she reached into the librarian's plastic Baggie and pulled out another chocolate chip cookie.

There was something uncanny about this road, if such it could be called. She had an eerie feeling that the squirrel briars were conspiring to lash out from the underbrush and grab her. She fed the car a little more gas and began casting nervous glances over her shoulder. At first all she saw were more squirrel briars. Then, from the crown of a hill that leaped wildly into the air and fell off sharply at the sides she caught a glimpse of—what? Something too big, too elegant, too totally incongruous in this forsaken environment.

Catriona slowed to a crawl, then slammed on her brakes. She got to where she could see all too clearly the deep tire tracks on the soft shoulder and the mangled scrub through which somebody's handsome gray limousine had plowed a ragged swath clear down into the gully. It had been stopped, as far as she could make out, by a heap of granite boulders, some of which were even bigger than the Lincoln.

The car seemed to be standing on its nose, but Catriona couldn't be sure. She parked on the right side of the road where the drop-off wasn't so intimidating and crossed over to look for footprints. She saw none, either coming or going. Surely a vehicle so valuable as this one wouldn't have got dumped in a stonepit for no good reason.

And what if the driver was trapped inside? Much as she'd have preferred not to, a person couldn't just shrug and walk away. Like any sensible Mainer, Catriona had on thick-soled shoes and tough loden-cloth pants. She buttoned her heavy sweater, cussed herself and the Puritan ethic with equal vehemence, and started down.

5

<!-- faint mirror-image bleed-through text from facing page, illegible -->

"YOU HOME, HELEN?"

The front door of the small red brick house on the Crescent survived yet another of Peter Shandy's purposeful closings. Helen Shandy appeared at the top of the stairs.

"Yes, dear, I'm home. I just got here myself a few minutes ago. I'm upstairs checking the answering machine. Catriona says thanks for the visit and not to worry, but she didn't say what not to worry about. That's not much of a message from Cat."

"So what, my love? She knew we'd be going to the president's reception tonight. We mentioned it when she was here; at least I think we did. Didn't she get off some crack about not trying to reach us tonight because we'll be carousing into the wee hours?"

"Probably. I don't remember. Cat knows Sieglinde Svenson fairly well by now. She realizes how much carousing there'll be with the president's wife calling the tunes. What are you dragging out that tired old suit for? I thought you were planning to wear the nice new one you bought two months ago?"

"The one I was nagged into buying, to be more specific. What if I should spill herring juice all over it?"

"What if you shouldn't? Peter, I know you always prefer to let your new clothes mellow in the closet for a few years before you get around to putting them on, but this is a special occasion."

"So are they all, all special occasions. The only reason you're after me to spiff up is that you've bought some new designer's dream that you're planning to spring on the assembled multitudes and don't want me doddering along behind you looking like a reject from the recycling center."

"How did you ever guess? Actually I was planning to wear that nice old blue lace dress that I was married in, and the pearls you gave me for a wedding present, as a gentle reminder that we have a tenth anniversary coming up."

"I might remind you in turn, my jewel, that we're now into September and my recollection is that we were married in April."

"Yes, Peter, I remember. I just thought I might as well get in some advance reminding for next year." Helen was heading for the bathroom as she spoke. "I do wish Cat had been a tad less laconic when she left that call."

Peter was right behind her, shedding garments as he went. "What's the big deal? Catriona's a grown-up girl now, in case you hadn't noticed."

"As a matter of fact, I had noticed. I don't know why I can't stop thinking about her. I just feel uneasy."

"Among the McBogles, all things are possible. What that woman needs is to break down and buy herself a car that's not prone to hoof rot and chronic hiccups," Peter grumbled. "Do I really have to wear this suit?"

"You really do, my dear. By the way, would you care to donate one of your older and tighter suits to the fall festival at the Congregational Church? They're running a rummage sale for the church roof."

"I was under the impression that the church already had a roof. Maybe we could start a fund to buy Catriona a new roof for her car. Would you care to join me in a small tot of whiskey as a spine stiffener for the festivities to come?"

"The roof of Cat's car is the only part that's still in reasonable shape and no, I do not care to stand in the receiving line with a breath on me like a barfly's. The church roof, as I was about to remark, leaks like a Swiss cheese."

"Swiss cheeses don't leak, my love."

"They might if anybody tried to shingle a roof with them," Helen pointed out. "But nobody ever does, as far as I know. I'm sure the church mice would prefer cheese to asphalt shingles. I'll have to take it up with Edna Mae Ottermole, she's the one who's spearheading the drive. She's having some flyers made up for Fred to carry in his bicycle basket and hand out to people along the way."

Peter shook his head. "He'd better not, if he values his badge. Taking on errands for one special group would constitute a breach of Fred's duty as a public servant for the whole town. This could start a revolution. The Baptists and Methodists would be down on him like a ton of Swiss cheese, not to mention the Swedenborgians and the Monophysites."

"I don't believe we have enough Monophysites in town to make much of a protest," Helen demurred.

"Then maybe we ought to send out for some. Why the Monophysites?"

"You mentioned them first, dear. I don't know why the Monophysites, though I do think it's an interesting word that doesn't get many chances to be used in general conversation. Zip me up, will you?"

"Do I get to unzip you after the ball is over?"

"I'll think about it and let you know. I wonder whether Mirelle will show up at the reception."

"And have to answer questions about her errant spouse?"

Peter was buttoning a clean white shirt and casting a thoughtful eye at his tie rack. "What do you think? That gray one matches the suit fairly well, doesn't it?"

"It might land you a job as one of Harry Goulson's part-time pallbearers."

Like just about everybody else in Balaclava Junction,

Helen had a warm spot, located not far from her funny bone, for the jovial neighbor who preferred not to be called a funeral director. "Undertaker" had been good enough for Harry Goulson's father and his grand-sire before him. "Funeral Director" sounded too businesslike and citified, "Mortician" too ambiguous. The old-fashioned name still evoked an image of somebody who'd known you and liked you, who could be trusted to do what needed to be done and get the human clay settled into its appointed resting place while the everlasting spirit went on to its next stop, wherever that might be; Harry Goulson did not consider it his province to second-guess the angel at the gate.

The Goulsons, along with other prominent members of the community, had of course been invited to the reception. Harry might or might not be able to attend, depending on whether he got a last-minute call for his services, but his wife would surely be there because she was the stringer who wrote up the society notes for the *Balaclava County Fane and Pennon*. Among the hostesses, by decree of Mrs. Sieglinde Svenson herself, would be Helen Marsh Shandy; naturally Helen had to give solemn thought to her husband's choice of neckwear.

"Here, darling, why don't you wear this handsome dark red one with the paisley design in green and gray? Then I can switch to my green chiffon and we'll be birds of a feather." Helen was already shaking the filmy gown out of its garment bag. "We'll have to hurry a little. Sieglinde wants the hostesses all present and cranked up to be charming fifteen minutes early just in case. Grace Porble's going to wear her new apricot satin."

"Do tell." Peter was contemplating the handsome tie as though it were some bizarre apport from another world. "What's Phil Porble going to wear?"

"A supercilious smile, I suppose," Helen replied. "What's the matter, Jane, don't tell me you've eaten your supper already? Or did I forget to feed you? Just hang on a moment, you poor little orphan of the storm, and we'll get you something nice. Do hurry with that tie, Peter. And don't forget to change into your good black shoes."

"What kind of shoes is Phil wearing? I ought to have checked with him sooner."

"Honestly, you men! Am I zipped?"

"To a zee. You look ravishing. Go feed the cat."

"Come on, Jane. Men are all brutes. I'll be downstairs scrubbing the scullery."

"Atta girl. *Arrivederci.*"

Precisely seven minutes later, Jane having been placated with a special tummy rub and a bowl of chopped chicken, Peter impeccably shod and necktied, Helen a vision of loveliness in her green chiffon and a wonderful stole that she'd bought during the summer from a weaver in Maine, it was on to the festivities.

This year's President's Reception was much like all the previous years' receptions. The old farmhouse on the crest of the hill behind the college was known as Valhalla for a number of reasons, and was kept in impeccable order through the expert management of Sieglinde Svenson. Tonight, the spacious front and back parlors were glorious with magnificent arrangements of late-blooming flowers and foliage. The hostesses were gracious, the alcoholic content in the punch was expertly calculated to exhilarate but not to inebriate, the food prepared by Mrs. Mouzouka of the restaurant management department and members of her class was superb. Best of all was a vast and wonderful smorgasbord that had been put together by Mrs. Svenson herself, aided by however many of her seven beautiful daughters had not yet flown the coop.

As to the conversation, while it didn't always sparkle, it certainly was rife. Nobody came forth with any dependable information about the missing dairy management expert, but everybody had a theory. It was particularly noted by all and sundry that Mirelle Feldster had not shown up. Some of the guests were outspoken enough to count her absence an advantage. Others who didn't actually detest Jim Feldster's acid-tongued wife were exchanging guilty glances and wondering whether they ought to drop by with a baked custard or a potted plant, or at least give her a call on the phone.

Among those conspicuously present were Dr. Melchett, looking slightly underdressed without his black bag, and Coralee, his wife, dressed up enough for both of them in a gown none of those present had ever seen before and probably never would again, since it would go back on the rack at the flagship store in Hoddersville tomorrow morning. Normally, at such an affair, Coralee would be off in a corner with her friend Mirelle, swapping unpleasantries about the other guests. Dr. Melchett would be making his rounds of the party, working his bedside manner for all it was worth, particularly among the younger and prettier lady guests. Jim Feldster would be off in a different corner from Mirelle's with a plate of smorgasbord in his hands and a speculative eye on the chafing dishes. But not tonight.

It was axiomatic around Valhalla that Sieglinde Svenson was constitutionally incapable of putting a foot wrong. Therefore, she must have known what she was doing when she'd asked Helen Shandy and Grace Porble to be co-hostesses, notwithstanding the fact that the Shandys to the south and the Porbles to the north were the Feldsters' closest neighbors. Normally Helen and Grace should, by campus protocol, have been first to arrive on the Feldster doorstep with consolatory offerings. After Peter's blowup on the night Jim Feldster had failed to come home, however, Helen had hesitated about paying the usual courtesy call, knowing that Mirelle would not miss the chance to give her a royal snubbing.

Grace Porble, as Helen's closest friend among the faculty wives, would be tarred with the same stick and subjected to the same brush-off. Of course everybody around the Crescent had known immediately about that disgraceful late-night scene because they'd all been hanging out their windows so as not to miss a word. Naturally they'd told their own particular friends, who in turn had passed the word to anybody who'd cared to listen, which by now must include approximately three-fifths of Balaclava County.

Phil Porble was the only one among the peccant four who found the situation in any way amusing. It was he who decided after his third glass of punch that the thing to do would be for the Porbles and the Shandys to pay a visit to the Feldster house as soon as Grace and Helen had got through with their hostessing stints. They'd go in style, carrying a trayful of leftover delicacies and one of Grace's exquisite floral arrangements from the buffet table. They wouldn't be able to leave the party until about half past ten, but that would not be too late for Mirelle; they and everybody else in town knew that she was an inveterate night owl.

Mirelle would have spent a lonesome evening watching some old movie on television, most likely, feeling sorry for herself and bitter toward her partying neighbors. How she might be feeling about Jim by now was anybody's guess.

The reception wound down; the musicians who'd been playing soft background music at intervals through the evening swung into a pretty loud rendition of "Good Night, Ladies." Helen and Grace arranged their offerings, handed over the trayful of goodies and the mammoth bouquet for their husbands to carry, and said a warm good night to the Svensons, wondering how or whether they'd be received by the temporarily bereft Mrs. Feldster.

At least they all hoped that Mirelle's bereavement would be temporary, especially Peter Shandy. Sometime between the herring and the dessert table, President Svenson had backed him into a corner and spoken to him in what was meant to be a whisper but sounded more like a grizzly bear growling through a mouthful of somebody's Sunday trousers.

"How, Shandy?"

To Peter the how was obvious enough, as were the when

and the where of Jim Feldster's last appearance in Balaclava Junction. The what for and the with whom were what the president wanted to know, and he wanted those answers pretty goddamned soon, before the animal husbandry department found itself heading for the last roundup. This was no time to sit around waiting till the cows come home; why the yumping yellybeans hadn't Shandy come up with a plan of action by now? The obvious fact that Peter had hardly got time to breathe, let alone teach so early in the new term, was irrelevant. Now, by yiminy, was the time for all good men to come to the aid of the party.

Peter could hardly disagree, partly because it would have been rude to gainsay the college president at his own reception in his own house, and partly because Svenson was twice his size. And partly, Peter's inner self confessed to his outer self, because a number of other untoward happenings during the past several years that had been related in one way or another to the college had only whetted his appetite for more. By the time Dr. Svenson had gone back to playing host, Peter was already planning how to weasel out of various professional duties and dump them on the increasingly capable shoulders of a young teaching fellow in horticulture called Knapweed Calthrop. So long as he could get out into the hinterlands every so often and commune with the lesser bedstraw, Knapweed wouldn't mind a bit taking Professor Shandy's classes until Professor Feldster could be located.

Calthrop had made an appearance at the reception early in the evening but had soon flickered off, murmuring something about his thesis. No matter; Calthrop could wait until morning to be briefed. Right now, Peter was more concerned for the safety of the peace offering that Phil Porble had trapped him into carrying down from Valhalla to the Feldsters' front door. He was already in the doghouse with Mirelle; he only hoped she wouldn't pelt him with cream puffs and spoil his elegant paisley tie.

None of the group seemed any too sanguine about how

Mirelle would greet them, if in fact any greeting would be forthcoming. On the way down the hill they essayed a few quips about boiling oil and such-like nonsense but nobody was really amused. As they approached the Feldster house, Phil Porble was inspired to mutter, "Abandon hope, all ye who enter here." That was before, his vision partly blocked by the wide-spreading foliage he was carrying, he became aware of a dapper little Cadillac Seville, carelessly parked in front of the house contrary to Crescent protocol, making it next to impossible for any other car to squeeze by.

"We seem to have come at the wrong time," Grace Porble murmured, glancing over at her own house and trying not to act as if she'd rather be making a bolt for it. True to the Balaclava code of etiquette, however, she stuck with the pack and sailed up the front steps in her apricot satin, Helen beside her trying to control her own billows of green chiffon now that the night wind was rising. The two men brought up the rear with their laden trays, like a pair of medieval servitors.

Phil Porble was hidden from knees to eyeballs behind his wife's splendiferous floral creation. Peter wished he'd got to carry something equally concealing, such as a peacock pie with all the late fowl's feathers spread out in a fan. But it was too late to think of peacocks now. Anyway, Balaclava's poultry department didn't run to anything fancier than hens, turkeys, ducks, and geese, none of which were relevant to the current situation. The doorbell had to be rung; it must be left to the women to ring it. None of them, come to think of it, had ever rung that doorbell before and would prefer not to be ringing it now. Duty must be done, however, and Helen elected herself to do it. As she raised her hand to perform the deed, she paused.

The night was still relatively mild, the front windows were open an inch or so from the bottom. Those standing outside had no trouble hearing a deep, authoritative voice giving Mirelle what sounded like a farewell exhortation to keep her chin up and hang on to her sanity until the present appalling situation could be resolved. She was carrying a terrible load of anxiety, she'd done nobly so far, everyone was counting on her to pull through. Mirelle was plainly eating it up. Helen decided she'd better ring the bell before the fortitude wore off and the visitor, whoever he might be, caught them all huddled together on the stoop.

The door opened. Mirelle appeared, wearing a long purple velvet hostess gown and a necklace of gold and silver discs that clanked when she moved. Phil Porble, who could rise to any occasion, stepped over the threshold and presented his armload of flowers along with a few compassionate words from the Svensons. Peter proffered his heaped-up tray of pastries.

Mirelle, all of a hastily improvised flutter, declared herself overwhelmed by her neighbors' solicitude and grateful to the Svensons in absentia for their generous thought. She was all set to begin a round of introductions; but her visitor, a tall, blond, rather heavyset man who Peter thought might resemble Elver Butz quite a lot if it weren't for his tailor-made suit, his custom-made shoes, and the fact that he didn't have a cud of chewing tobacco in his left cheek, seized the neighbors' appearance as a chance to make his own graceful but speedy escape.

6

CATRIONA FOUND THAT DESCENDING THE SLOPE WAS MORE A stumble than a climb. Ruts that the car had dug on its way down had helped some, but nowhere near enough. She was close enough to the bottom now to see that the vehicle, so dreadfully mistreated, was in fact a Lincoln town car of fairly recent vintage, with tinted glass windows. She turned for a look back over the way she'd just come down, and was appalled by its length and steepness. A lighter car such as the one she herself drove would have been totally wrecked; anybody inside must surely have been either killed or terribly injured. This car would need heavy equipment to lift it out from among those gigantic boulders, but there was nothing she could do about that. So large a vehicle could take a great deal of punishment and come out relatively undamaged. She couldn't even see any broken glass so far. She'd have to get closer.

She slipped and slithered the last few yards, tripped over yet another root, stumbled forward, and stopped herself by sprawling against the rear end of the car. At least now she could get a good look at the inside. The backseat was empty. The heap in the front passenger seat was a man strapped in by his lap and shoulder belts. He was not moving.

This was horrible. His door was wedged too tight against the boulders to open and the rear door was locked. She

pawed her way from right to left, cursing the ingenious tech-
nocrats whose bright ideas could imprison hapless passen-
gers. She was scrabbling around for something to smash a
window with when it dawned on her that the front door on
the driver's side might not have been properly closed.

One up for impropriety. Any mystery fan, and most certainly any mystery writer, could figure this case out in no
time flat. The wreck had been deliberate and carefully
thought out. Whoever drove must have left the car in gear
with the engine running and hopped out just before the front
wheels hit the slope, relying on weight and momentum to
carry it down into the gully. The gas tank had most likely
been all but empty. Too much fuel aboard could have started
a blaze that might easily expand into a forest fire, calling attention to whatever might remain of the expensive car and
its dead passenger.

The front door must have got wrenched in the wreck; she
couldn't budge it more than a few inches. The window had
been rolled all the way down, however; that driver hadn't
taken any chance of getting mured up inside with whoever
was still hanging against the dashboard. Catriona squirmed
in through the window, which was her only access and likely
her only escape, hoisted herself across the steering wheel,
past the deflated air bags, and steeled herself to touch a
corpse.

It was not a corpse. At least Catriona didn't think so. It
was a man and, horrid thought, he put her in mind of Forster
Feldstermeier.

But could that be? This one was not young by any means,
but he was certainly decades short of being a nonagenarian.
His hands and cheeks were cold but not stiff and icy. He
could hardly have been in a more awkward position; he
must have been strapped into both shoulder and lap belts
while he'd been seated in the normal way. Now he was
hanging free of the upholstery, face down against the padded
dashboard. He must be hideously uncomfortable; why hadn't

he released the heavy belting that had him caught there like a fly in a spiderweb?

Because he couldn't, Catriona surmised. He was either too exhausted, heavily drugged, or in shock. She'd have to manage alone, somehow. She fought the seat buckle frantically, as though a matter of a few seconds one way or the other might save him or sink him. Either was possible, God alone knew how long he'd been hanging there. She tried to calm down, managed to brace his flaccid body against her side to take his weight, shoved the release button, and the lock parted. Now what? Was the man really alive or had she been fooling herself? She laid two fingers of one hand on his wrist and slipped the other hand inside the tweed jacket he was wearing, praying that she'd find a heartbeat.

He clanked.

"My God!" In sudden panic, Catriona snatched her hand away. Could this poor devil be wired with a bomb?

No, of course not. If this were a terrorist act, what would have been the point of dumping him out here where nobody would notice? She gritted her teeth and tried again to find some sure sign of life.

He grunted.

Was it possible that a man in such a dire position had simply been asleep? Not knowing what else to do, she gave him a pretty smart slap on the left cheek. Hearing another faint grunt, she slapped him again.

"Wake up, please, whoever you are. Say something, can't you?"

"Hose cart."

"What?"

"Hose cart."

At least it sounded like hose cart. He was hoarse and mumbling, perhaps he'd worn out his vocal cords calling for help. He'd have had nothing to drink, his mouth could be too dry to function, like the Ancient Mariner's.

"I bit my arm, I sucked the blood, and cried 'A sail! A sail!'" Ugh! Catriona hoped he'd never read Coleridge.

As to drinking water, there was a thermos jug full of it in Catriona's own car. Guthrie was always at her not to barge off unprepared with essentials such as a compass, a Scout knife, a shovel, a distress flag, matches, a bag of trail mix, a candle in a tin can, a bag of the cheapest cat litter, and a jug of water because a person never knew when she might be in desperate need of something she hadn't thought to bring along unless she had a thoughtful friend to remind her. She'd better climb back up to her car and get the water. Unless there was a creek or a brook down here. But would the water be safe to drink?

And would it be safe to leave her find? He'd slumped down now on the floor beneath the dash. He looked to Catriona as though he might be slipping back into unconsciousness. She took him by the shoulders and shook. He clanked again. She pulled the front of his jacket fully open and found the source of the clanking. It was a shiny brass chain hung with copper medallions shaped like miniature firemen's helmets and old-style leather fire buckets. The big one in the center was supposed to represent a hand-drawn hose cart.

So this was why the man who called himself plain Jim Feldster had never got home that evening. Catriona had hoped he'd say "hose cart" again; but he didn't say anything. He was trying to help himself, though, making feeble attempts to get his arms and legs back in working order. While he struggled, Catriona fiddled with the doors, trying again to make one of them let go. None worked, so she slid feet first out the window on the driver's side and stuck both hands back inside for her patient to grab. He was clumsy and fumbling, but he managed eventually to get out. She found him a stick to serve as a cane; it helped a little with the climbing. She still couldn't get another word out of him but he tagged after her up the scree, using his long legs to advantage but having to rest every few steps.

By the time they got to the top, they were both worn out. Catriona had just about strength enough left to open the gallon jug of water that Guthrie had insisted she keep in her car for emergencies. She allowed herself one paper cup full, then handed Feldster the jug. He drained it dry without pausing for breath. She didn't think it would be sensible to give him that chewy trail mix yet, but he must be starving; she held out her bag of chocolate chip cookies. He ate them all, shook the crumbs from the bag out on his tongue, curled up on the back seat, refused a seat belt, for which Catriona could hardly blame him in the circumstance, and went back to sleep.

Now what to do? She needed desperately to find a telephone and let Helen and Peter know that she'd found Jim Feldster alive and hungry; but where could she come upon one in this godforsaken wilderness? It was all Robert Frost's fault. If she hadn't swapped the high road for the low, she wouldn't have this albatross slung around her neck now.

And Professor James Feldster might have been dead in a few more hours. Carl Gustav Jung hadn't believed in the merely coincidental; neither did Catriona McBogle. Surely this terrible road must lead her somewhere, otherwise she wouldn't be on it.

Doggedly, Catriona drove on; wishing she hadn't been so self-sacrificing about those cookies; wishing her higher self had lent her lower self a road map. Or at least asked for directions at a filling station. That was wishful thinking to the ultimate degree; there hadn't been a filling station in ages, much less a working pay phone.

There hadn't been anything, except bumps and potholes. She didn't dare speed up; the road was even more tortuous in the fading light. She could only hope that whoever had ditched that gray Lincoln so efficiently wasn't planning now to come back to check the remains.

It was pitch dark and getting on for eight o'clock when she heaved a great sigh of relief and pulled out at an intersection where there were actual road signs. Each pointed to a different place, none of which she could recall ever having heard of. This didn't mean that any or all of them wouldn't be a good place to go; almost anywhere at all would have been better than where she'd just been. She did go so far as to ask her inert passenger whether he recognized any of the names on the signs. He didn't even grunt.

But that didn't matter so much now. She'd spied a little convenience store where a customer was just leaving the outside telephone with a smile on his face and a hot dog in his hand. She pulled up at the pump, asked the young person who appeared to be the sole attendant to put four each of whatever was in stock on the grill, and dialed one of the few numbers that she could dial without ever having to look them up.

"Hello," she said when she'd got her quarters lined up. "Are you there, Helen?"

Helen's voice answered, but Catriona belatedly remembered that Helen's body was scheduled to attend the President's Reception tonight. She could hardly call Information and ask for the number of Valhalla. Nor could she begin to tell the Shandy answering machine anything that wouldn't sound as if she'd partaken of aquavit or something equally potent from a Viking drinking horn.

At this point, Catriona felt as though she could use a good cry, but what would be the sense in bawling? Unfortunately, a tiny sniffle escaped as she told the answering machine that she would call back later.

Better to save her tears and her quarters until she could count on finding the Shandys at home. Since that could be a few hours, maybe she'd better find a place to roost for the night. Food first, though. She went inside to see how the burgers were coming along. They smelled like manna by now but needed a bit more grilling; she was always leery of rare meats in untried places. The counter looked clean enough, as such places went; there was coffee in the dispenser. Heaven knew how long it had been brewing; nevertheless she got two of the largest size Styrofoam cups, left hers black, and doctored the other with cream enough for two or three.

She took that one out to her passenger and sipped at her own while she waited for the food, adding a newspaper, a road map, a few bottles of fruit juice, and a handful of candy bars for emergencies. Having done all that, she asked the young person tending the grill to point out to her on her new map exactly where they were standing now, which he or she did after careful thought and taking time out to scoop the burgers and dogs into a carryout box.

"Oh, thanks," she said. "Now could you tell me if there's a halfway decent motel around here somewhere?"

"Sure, no problem. See that sign over there, the one with the arrow? You just turn left at the arrow and keep going till you see the motel. They keep the sign lighted all night, you can't miss it. My mother works there as a maid part-time; they keep it pretty nice. Tell whoever's on the desk that Fentriss sent you."

"Thank you, Fentriss. Do I pay you for the gas along with the food or separately?"

"Doesn't matter. We can take Visa if you want."

That was not a bad idea. It might be wise to husband what cash she had with her, which wasn't much by now. And there would still be the motel to pay for. She handed over her card, wondering if she was making a mistake by using her right name. No matter. At this point, Catriona didn't care about anything except that the last of the Feldstermeier brothers was still alive and clanking.

The motel was right where Fentriss had said it would be, nothing to write home about but it would serve. Catriona asked for two adjoining rooms, ostensibly because her brother's hearing aid had gone haywire and they would only be able to communicate by tapping on the wall between them in Morse code. That was perfectly all right with the desk clerk so Catriona collected her luggage, the food, and her newly adopted brother and settled them in one of the rooms, all but the overnight bag that held her own necessities.

Feldstermeier, as she now was sure he must be, waded into the hamburgers, the hot dogs, and a few tuna fish sandwiches with a zeal that didn't waver until he'd eaten everything that wasn't moving, except for a single hamburger, half a sandwich, and the cup of coffee that were all Catriona wanted. He then, to her amazement, picked up every bit of debris, put it all in the carryout box and then in the wastebasket, and made a beeline for the bathroom.

This was when Catriona thought she'd better leave her charge to his own devices. She left the key to his room on the dresser, picked up the newspaper, the road map, a bottle of apple juice, and one of the chocolate bars in case she got hungry during the night, and took them into the adjoining room where she'd left her own meager luggage. A few minutes later she heard through the thin wall the sound of a shower running. Then it went off and a creaking noise told her that her charge had got into bed.

He snored, but not loudly; she'd know easily enough whether he was all right. Catriona slipped outside and tried his doorknob to see whether he'd locked himself in. He had, he was doing all the right things except he couldn't or wouldn't talk. That would come, no doubt; it was only a matter of time.

7

"WE HOPE WE DIDN'T COME AT AN AWKWARD TIME," HELEN said after the driver of the Cadillac had pulled away from the Feldster house and the Svensons' unwieldy gifts had been coped with. "You must be worn out with worry."

"Not quite."

Mirelle was not gushing now, but neither was she showing any sign of imminent collapse. Somebody at the reception had remarked that Mirelle's first move after she'd made sure Jim was definitely missing had been to phone Gladys at the Curl and Twirl Beauty Shop and demand an appointment for a touch-up and set. Nobody doubted it for a minute. Her hair had been naturally reddish blond back when she'd come to Balaclava as a young wife back in the sixties, her college cheerleader's sweater packed in with her trousseau. By now her coiffure was the color which a hunter would call blaze orange, and showing too much scalp from so many permanents and colorings

Mother Nature had her ways of compensating; what came off the top had slid down around the hips. Mirelle couldn't be called fat, though; she kept the avoirdupois down by doing her own housework and minding other people's business. Or so Helen Shandy had heard from Grace Porble and a few others; this was actually the first time in all their years of being neighbors that she had ever been inside the Feld-sters' house.

This wasn't to say that Helen and Peter had never got an invitation from the Feldsters. Mirelle's usual way of enter-taining was to give a lawn party once a year with tables and chairs borrowed from the faculty dining room, then com-mandeer a few unlucky wights from Buildings and Grounds to clean up afterward.

Now that Helen was actually inside the house, she could see why a house-proud woman might boggle at letting un-expected visitors into a room such as this white-carpeted front parlor. It was in such a state of perfection that Helen wondered why Mirelle hadn't put up red plush ropes on pol-ished brass stanchions to keep the company away from the breakables. A full service for twelve of green and gold Minton was displayed in a handsome but glassless china cabinet, a Spode coffee service on a fragile-looking tier table. Everywhere one turned, there was porcelain: Royal Doulton figurines, Lenox swans, Limoges patch boxes, all on display, every one sparkling clean, nothing less than ex-quisite, everything breakable and expensive as hell. It was terrifying.

With one accord, the Shandys and the Porbles herded to-gether and froze. Mirelle didn't even blink.

"Sit down, won't you? What can I get you to drink? You need something to take away the taste of that ghastly punch they always serve. I've got a good Moët & Chandon if you like champagne. I'd got it all chilled and waiting for Florian, but he was in a rush, as usual. And of course he wouldn't dream of driving after he'd had a drink. That whole crowd are so damned uptight about sticking to the book." She shrugged. "Well, what can you do? Relatives!"

Phil Porble never missed a chance to squirrel up any piece of information that pertained, or might pertain in any way to the college or those persons, places, or things associated with it. "Would these be your relatives or Jim's?" he asked.

"Oh, Jim's, of course."

"You surprise me very much, Mirelle. It was always my impression that Jim had been taken in as a boy by elderly farm folks who needed somebody to milk the cows."

"That's what he wanted you to think, Phil. My Jimmy's not the simple hayseed he tries to pretend he is. He's a game-player, he never grew up and never wanted to. All those different lodges he belongs to, all that garbage about what he really loves is to be perched on a milking stool with a can of bag balm in his overall pocket and a pretty little heifer making goo-goo eyes at him while he squirts a stream of milk at the barn cat, that's a bunch of horsefeathers. Who's for champagne besides me?"

Helen looked at Peter, Peter looked at Grace, Grace was already looking at Phil. Clearly Mirelle had already lifted a glass or three this evening. Phil raised his eyebrows, Grace shrugged. "Well, if everybody else is having some, I wouldn't mind just a sip or two. What about you, Helen?"

"Why not? It isn't as though anybody has to drive home. I was so busy hostessing all evening that I never did get to try the punch. Did you, Grace?"

Grace hadn't. The upshot was that they all had champagne in glass flutes thin as paper and nobody broke one, perhaps because the flutes didn't hold much, perhaps because Mirelle drank up about half the bottle herself on her way back from the kitchen, and what was left wouldn't go far among five people. However small their shares, however, the guests could hardly just gulp the stuff and run. Phil Porble, always ready to keep the conversational ball rolling, gave it a gentle push.

"I'm intrigued by what you say about Jim's being so many-faceted, Mirelle. He's always struck me as the archetype of the real old New England farmer."

"You and a lot of other people." Mirelle drained the last of the champagne into her own flute and drank it down. "I gave up trying to figure him out years ago. Every so often I get to wondering if he's a real nut case, then he pulls one of his little funnies and I know he's laughing his fool head off inside, though he never shows any sign of it that you'd notice. He's a deep one, all right. Sometimes he scares me."

"How do you mean?" Grace put in. "Surely you don't mean that he ever—"

"Well, no, but I get that feeling every so often that sometimes he might."

"Might what?" Peter was too fed up by now to be amiable.

"That's what I'm trying to say. I never know what. It wouldn't surprise me one iota to find out that he'd just gone out to the airport and chartered a plane to Brazil without even letting me know he was leaving."

"Oh, I'm sure Jim would never pull a stunt like that," Helen demurred. "For one thing, it would take an awful wad of money to charter a plane to Brazil. Or anywhere else, fares being as they are these days. Unless you happened to be the pilot's wife or something."

"Oh that wouldn't faze Jim. He could buy his own plane and fly from here to the Fiji Islands, any time he took the notion. He can afford it."

Phil Porble wasn't about to let a statement like that go unexamined. "Why do you say that, Mirelle? No, Grace, you needn't make faces. I'm not being nosy, I'm just intrigued. Here we've been living next door to Jim all these years and never knowing a great deal about him except that he's an excellent teacher of dairy management and belongs to a remarkable number of different lodges. Now we find he's a man of mystery. Or should I say a man of means, or of both? What are we supposed to think? Mirelle, you don't actually believe that Jim would take off for parts unknown without at least giving you some sort of hint as to what he had in mind?"

This was not the optimum minute to ask. That half-bottle of champagne, along with whatever else she might have been nipping at before the impressive figure she'd addressed as Florian had visited her a little while ago, was catching up with Mirelle. She was yawning like an alligator, not making any attempt to cover her mouth, slurring her words when she tried to talk. Clearly this was the time for a mass exit, but the hostess still was not ready to call it a night.

"No, Phil, Jim never hints. He just goes and does what he feels like doing and to hell with anything I want to do. How am I supposed to know where he's gone off to? He never tells me anything that isn't about cows. I'm so damned sick and tired of cows I get queasy every time I see one of those blasted students eating a hamburger. Hold on, I'm going to get some more champagne."

"None for us, thanks."

The Porbles and Shandys spoke in chorus although they hadn't intended to. All four had the same excuse: they had to work tomorrow.

"As you wish," Mirelle told her unexpected guests and draped herself over a Victorian-styled chaise longue upholstered in rose-patterned needlepoint with a frame of grape-carved walnut all around. Helen Shandy, who was sitting opposite her on an armless chair of a similar pattern, thought she must have been a pretty girl when she was young, the type who'd have been a cheerleader in high school and Homecoming Queen at a small college somewhere. Just now, with her purple velvet robe tucked up around her legs, her eyelids half closed, her face flushed a brilliant magenta, she was no treat to look at. What a shame it had been to exchange that early bloom for a roomful of breakables and too much champagne.

It was time to go. When Mirelle realized they were leaving she waved them a careless good-bye without even trying to sit up and straighten her skirt. They let themselves out, careful to avoid all those expensive bibelots, taking special pains as they left to make sure the door was locked.

Like the other houses on the Crescent, the Feldsters' had

a small front yard with a brick walk leading from the steps to the road. Once the Shandys and the Porbles were out on the asphalt they paused, as friends do, for a windup chat.

"She'll fall asleep on that chaise and wake up stiff as a boot," Grace fretted. "We should have taken time to help her upstairs and put her to bed properly, Helen."

"Oh, I don't think so, Grace. She's not that far gone. She'll sleep a while, then rouse herself and get into a nightgown. Anyway, it's her house, she might as well do as she pleases. But what an eye-opener that parlor was. I don't know about you, but I've never set foot inside that house before, except once when I took over a letter that had been put in our box by mistake and handed it to her at the kitchen door. I don't recall her asking me in, but I was on my way to work and couldn't have stayed anyway. That's probably why she tells her friends what a snob I am."

"And you cry yourself to sleep every night over it, right?" said Phil.

"Absolutely. Poor woman." Helen laughed at herself. "Poor, indeed. There must be thousands of dollars' worth of porcelain in that one room alone. I was scared to death I'd brush something off one of those dinky little tabourets with this long skirt I'm wearing. How do you suppose Jim's stayed sane all these years, living among so much expensive clutter?"

"And being nagged about it every time he sets foot on that white carpet, no doubt," Peter snarled. "If that's all the poor fish has had to come home to, no wonder he gets out of the house whenever he can find a place to go. This disappearance of Jim's looks to me like a clear-cut case of one too many simpering figurines. He was bound to break out sometime, or else just make himself scarce and let her do the breaking. Not that she would, I don't suppose. Well, I'm sorry for them both, but it's none of our business what they do with their money."

"Of which there must be a damned sight more than we

ever thought there was," Phil added. "Jim certainly can't have managed to wrest that kind of loot out of the college coffers. It's too bad that chap with the customized Cadillac didn't hang around long enough to be introduced to us. Or us to him, more likely. Mirelle would have been more than happy to do the honors, that was obvious. I only wish she'd been more forthcoming as to whether he's really a relative or the man about the insurance."

"I expect we'll find out, one way or another, after Mirelle sobers up," said his wife. "I thought at first he must have been one of Jim's lodge brothers, but he was much too well dressed."

"And he didn't clank," Helen couldn't help putting in.

"No, there's that," Grace agreed. "My personal guess is that this is some kind of distant cousin who likes Jim well enough to be concerned about him but isn't thrilled by Mirelle. As to all the ruffles and flourishes she was getting off about Jim's having scads of money at his disposal, I expect that might have been the champagne talking. Don't you think so, Phil?"

"Never having seen Mirelle plastered before, I can't say I'm in a position to pass judgment. However, I'm inclined to think you're right as you so often are, my dear. And I'd have to say you look pretty special tonight if praise to the face weren't open disgrace. What are your views on the subject, Helen?"

"I'm all for the praise and pooh to the disgrace. Grace always looks marvelous but tonight she almost outshone Sieglinde. How's that for praise?"

"Adequate. I'd say something nice about you too, Helen, if it weren't against our great preceptrice's code to inject personal feelings into professional relationships. All right, everybody, let's genuflect three times in the direction of Valhalla and call it a night."

"I'll buy that," said Peter. "See you in the morning."

Sieglinde Svenson's attempt to bring a little sunshine into

Mirelle Feldster's gloomy situation had not worked out quite the way it had been intended. Grace's beautiful arrangement had been left parked outside the door; Mirelle had taken the pastries out to the kitchen when she'd gone to get the champagne and probably stuffed them into the freezer rather than pass them around.

The two couples went their short ways, respectively right and left, all of them eager to shed their party clothes and get into bed.

Jane met Helen and Peter at their doorway and daintily expressed her need for a discreet visit to the coral bells. Peter volunteered to wait for her on the stoop while Helen continued inside. In only moments, both his females returned, Jane complacently, Helen less so.

"There's the oddest message from Catriona. Do come and listen, Peter."

Jane came, too, but her reaction to the stifled sob in Catriona's voice is unknown, for the telephone suddenly rang and startled all three of them.

8

Now that her enigmatical passenger was safely tucked away for the night—at least she fervently hoped he was—Catriona herself was wide awake. She'd told Peter and Helen's answering machine that she'd call back as soon as she thought they'd be home; she picked up the telephone, put her call through, and waited for somebody to answer.

Peter answered on the very first ring. "Cat? We just heard your message. What's happening? Are you back from your travels safely?"

"Not yet. I'm still in Massachusetts." She was keeping her voice as low as she could and still be heard. "I've picked up a passenger."

"Are you crazy? What do you mean, a passenger?"

"I mean a milkman who'd evidently been trussed up inside a wrecked car with nothing to eat or drink ever since you got into a hair tangle with your next door neighbor. Does that ring a bell?"

"Good God! Where are you?"

"Somewhere between Gehenna and a place called Beamish. I stopped at the public library there and had a shrimp sandwich with the folks, then I took the road less taken. Don't ask me why, I just had to. I'm praying now that he'll last the night."

"Shouldn't you take him to a hospital?"

"I wouldn't dare. What I've seen is barbarity, plain and simple. Somebody wants your milkman dead. He's safe at the moment, though. I found a place for us to sleep. Two places actually; he's not very good company. You wouldn't be either, if you'd been hanging from a tangle of seat belts for the past two days. The only words he's spoken to me are 'hose cart.' An interesting topic, no doubt, but not one of great fluency for me."

"All right, Catriona. I'll believe half of this and you can take care of the other half. But why should anybody do such a horrible thing to an inoffensive dairy professor?"

"Peter, dear, don't you ever read the newspapers?"

"Not lately. I haven't had the time."

"Then listen to this. Monday morning, two days ago, a world-renowned dairy magnate died, one Forster Feldster-meier by name. He was the eldest of four brothers, two of whom had died before him. This leaves only the youngest brother, James, current whereabouts unknown, who gets along fine with cows but never took any interest in the family business. Notwithstanding that fact, he is now, according to inviolable family custom, head of the clan and therefore high panjandrum of the whole international shebang. Unless, and please note this carefully, he dies before he can be installed, in which case the next in line takes over."

"Catriona, you're dreaming. Such things just don't happen in real life."

"Then why is my impossible dream snoring on the other side of the wall from me this very minute, stuffed with hamburgers, hotdogs and tuna fish sandwiches I've paid for? Would you kindly answer me that? He's eaten all my cookies and drunk almost a gallon of water at one gulp. He was not only starved, but terribly dehydrated."

A click on the line announced that Helen had tired of sharing an earpiece with Peter and had picked up the downstairs extension.

"Cat, have you really found Jim Feldster?"

"Feldster, Feldstermeier, a rose by any other name, dear Helen, would not smell half so fragrant as when I pulled him out of that wrecked Lincoln this afternoon."

"But he can't talk?"

"No, but he can snore. That ought to count for something, don't you think?"

"He must be dreadfully tired. Was he hurt? Is he sick?"

"Judging from the supper he ate tonight, I'd say he's doing pretty well; he must have the stomach of a crocodile. The only problem I can see is a big hematoma on his left wrist; I noticed it while he was wolfing down his third hot dog. You don't suppose, by any chance, that he does drugs?"

"I can't imagine he ever would," Helen replied, "but nowadays one never knows. Peter?"

To the best of Peter's recollection, Jim Feldster had never in his life made use of any drug, potion, or medicament except bag balm, and that only on certain portions of cows' undercarriages. Jim had to exempt the last named because sometimes his own hands got dry and chapped during the colder months of the year. His solicitude, however, was not for himself but for his bovine charges.

Catriona did her best to stifle a yawn, but failed sadly. "That's very interesting, Peter, but do you think we might get around fairly soon to thinking about what we're going to do with Professor Feldster/Feldstermeier? I don't suppose there's any sense in trying to hide him somewhere not too far from the campus?"

"We could reopen Winifred Binks-Debenham's old Hobbit hole," Helen volunteered.

"No, that wouldn't wash," said Peter. "Jim's too damned tall. He'd want to take his cows with him and it just wouldn't work. Isn't there someplace up your way, Catriona? You were complaining that you had nothing to write about—maybe this is your answer."

"A fugitive milkman who may be a missing heir?"

"Why not?" Helen wanted to know. "And should he prove but a lowly herdsman after all, there are scads of cows in Maine; this could be the start of something beautiful."

"For whom?"

"Oh, Catriona, we're only trying to help. Guthrie likes it up there, doesn't he? Surely he wouldn't mind having another boarder in that big house. Would you, Catriona? I shouldn't think it would be for more than a few days. Just till we can decide what's safest for Jim?"

"I'll have to think about it."

She was too tired to say what she thought, which was probably just as well. "As for Guthrie, I'm supposed to be phoning him right now and I have to be back in Sasquamahoc by eleven o'clock tomorrow morning. I forget why, but it will come to me. I'll call you back."

Hanging up on one's friends was not the kindly thing to do, but Catriona did it anyhow. She was all set to start in on Guthrie as soon as she heard his voice but he beat her to the draw.

"How's it going, Cat?"

"From bad to worse. I'm stuck with the fourth Feldstermeier. For God's sake don't tell anybody except the Shandys, and they already know."

"How can I tell anybody but the Shandys?" Guthrie demanded. "I don't even know what you're talking about. Or what I'm talking about, if it comes to that."

So she told him.

Neither Catriona nor Guthrie could show any except Highland Scots blood in their pedigrees but they both enjoyed talking Canadian French. As their vocabularies had grown, they'd slung in some high school Latin, scraps of German Portuguese, Icelandic, and a few more. By now, nobody else could either understand or speak their private patois, or would have wanted to. Usually the two spoke it for fun; occasionally it came in handy for serious purposes, like this.

"Ja, so? Maximus schemozzle, n'est-ce pas? Quando heimlich arrivederci maminka?"

They agreed in various tongues that Helen and Peter were right about Jim Feldster. It would be irresponsible and even cruel to take a man in his condition back to Balaclava and just leave him with that harpy Jim had been callow enough to marry before he'd learned the hard way. Not to mention leaving him a sitting bull's-eye for any nefarious schemes any nefarious pretenders to the Feldstermeier dairy throne might be hatching. At least they ought to keep tabs on him until he was able to say something more uplifting than "hose cart."

The upshot, after a couple more expensive phone calls to the Shandys and back again to Guthrie, was that Catriona should get some sleep, start off in her own car not later than half past four in the morning with the professor as ballast, and head straight for Portsmouth, New Hampshire. There Guthrie and Catriona would meet and swap cars in case she and her mute passenger were being followed. None of the four thought it likely that they would be, but all of them agreed that there was no sense in taking unnecessary chances.

Guthrie's willingness to join in the action was nothing short of noble. Like Peter, who'd been his college roommate, Guthrie was already up to his ears trying to get the fall term properly under way. Driving down from the forestry school in Sasquamahoc to the landmark rotary in Portsmouth would take him a couple of hours even if he didn't run into heavy morning traffic or have to keep an eye out for possible trouble on the road.

Once he and his regrettably venturesome landlady had swapped cars as planned, he'd have to drive back by himself in Catriona's old doodlebug, which he hadn't thought much of back when she'd bought it new without asking his advice, and thought a damn sight less of now that it was in the sere and yellow leaf.

Guthrie did tend to drop arboreal allusions into his conversation. The habit was quite understandable in the president of a forestry school. He honestly did not believe that he would ever see a poem lovely as a tree, but that didn't mean he never gave a thought to the spreading chestnut under which the village smithy used to stand, nor showed a fleeting inclination to hang his heart on a weeping willow tree. Catriona caught a somewhat willowish nuance in his voice tonight. She thanked him for his solicitude even more warmly than she'd intended to, and wished him happy dreams. She then left an early wake-up call at the front desk, took a warm shower to get the kinks out, and got into the clean bed that she'd been craving ever since she'd slid down into that loathsome ravine and found herself saddled with an albatross.

Tired as she was, Catriona had a hard time getting to sleep. Her mind kept dwelling on that terrifying moment when she'd eeled her way through the one open window of a luxury car that had been wantonly dumped on its hood to get at the stiffening corpse she'd expected to find. She couldn't just lie here in the dark. She turned the reading lamp back on, picked up the newspaper she'd bought along with the hot dogs, and flipped through its pages, wondering why no mention was made of the late Forster Feldstermeier. Finally it dawned on her that the paper was a local weekly, and a last week's weekly at that.

Catriona read the paper through anyway, even the classified ads, some of which were worth a chuckle. She worked the crossword puzzle, which took her about four minutes. At last she dropped off with the light still burning and the newspaper smearing printer's ink on the beautiful blue nightgown that Helen Shandy had given her for an un-birthday present.

*   *   *

After Catriona's telephone call, Peter and Helen agreed that a drop of Winifred Binks-Debenham's organic home brew was definitely called for.

"Should we call Mirelle and tell her where her wandering boy is tonight?" asked Helen.

"After all that champagne, I doubt that it would register."

"It might if you said that he's registered in a motel with Cat."

"What a nicely evil mind you have. Which reminds me; didn't you promise earlier that I could unzip you?"

He gave her a leer and Helen leered right back at him. "I said I'd consider it. And I have. Shall we go upstairs?"

In their bedroom, after an interesting interval, Helen stepped out of her unzipped green chiffon and discovered that some dolt had dribbled herring juice on the left sleeve. Peter's tie, at least, had escaped undribbled. As he hung it with proper solicitude on the tie rack that somebody had once given him for Christmas, Helen went over to pull the curtain across the window as usual. Then she smiled and stayed her hand.

"I don't think we need bother about the curtains; Mirelle won't be doing any bird-watching tonight. Come on, Jane, you get to sleep on papa's side of the bed tonight. Poor Mirelle. Peter, do you suppose all those porcelain figures might be her way of sublimating her feelings about the children she never had?"

Peter grunted. "My personal feeling is that Mirelle prefers what she has now. Those china dolls represent a good deal of hard cash, they're hers and nobody else's, and they can be shoved around at her slightest whim. And if that's being cynical, who the hell cares? Move over, Jane. How the hell can one medium-sized cat take up two-thirds of a double bed?"

"Self-esteem, grounded on just and right?"

"Milton at midnight," said Peter. "The reward for bedding a librarian."

"One of the rewards." Helen was dozing off as she spoke; a few minutes later they were all three asleep. The fact that Jane was taking up more than her fair share of space didn't bother her two humans a whit.

9

CATRIONA HADN'T REALLY EXPECTED THAT WHOEVER SHE'D talked to at the desk would remember that wake-up call she'd requested. If anyone was there now, he or she either hadn't got the message or didn't give a hoot. Not that it mattered, because another patron left the motel at half past four in a car with its muffler in desperate need of being replaced and a radio turned to the ultimate decibel level, emitting sounds that made Catriona think of baboons throwing coconuts at a pack of howling jackals and eliminating any possibility of snatching another short nap.

Getting dressed was no big deal; all Catriona had with her were some clean underwear and the heather tweed suit she always wore when she traveled. She put on the suit, tied a scarf around her unruly hair, and pounded on the wall of the adjoining room, hoping to goodness she wouldn't have to go and confront her alleged deaf brother in his bed or in the bathroom. She opened her own door and peeked. To her relief, Professor Feldster was already up, showered, dressed, and waiting to be led from his room. His shirt was clean; he must have rinsed it out and hung it to drip-dry overnight. His tweed jacket and trousers didn't look much worse than any absentminded professor's garb is apt to look. He'd made some effort to get rid of the twigs, burs, and dead leaves he'd accumulated yesterday in his excruciating struggle to get up out of that precipitous ravine. He still hadn't uttered so much as a grunt, he showed no expression either of pain or of relief; but he followed her docilely enough to her car, got into the backseat, and flinched only a little when she reached in to fasten his seat belt and shut the door.

The two rooms had been paid for in advance, of course; motel managers did not take chances on being stiffed of their due. Catriona had learned last night from the desk clerk that the motel did not serve meals but that there was a pretty good truck stop over by the turnpike which stayed open around the clock. Thanks to the briefing session she'd had with her new map, she was able to locate not only the turnpike but also the eatery. She parked between two white cars, went inside to give her order, watched through the front window to make sure her passenger hadn't taken a notion to roam, and soon came back out carrying a Styrofoam trayful of breakfast.

Cups of strong coffee and fried eggs on English muffins helped quite a lot. The little car's gas tank still registered almost full. After the muffins were eaten and the coffee drunk, Catriona let her passenger fasten his own seat belt. It took a while, but he managed.

Maybe this was a favorable omen. Catriona had been raised on omens; she was relieved that they'd be heading northward instead of south, though she'd forgotten why she should be. The pre-dawn mist was still thick enough to cast an aura of mystery over the billboards, the fast-food restaurants, and the long ribbons of asphalt.

Driving on a divided highway would be simpler than on the one-lane country roads that Catriona was used to, she'd thought; she wouldn't have to worry about oncoming cars. Now that the strong black coffee was beginning to take hold, it occurred to her that oncoming cars might be the lesser evil.

Assuming there was a very important somebody riding in one's car whom somebody else wanted either to kidnap for ransom or kill for some other reason, it might be easier for the pursuers to speed up, pass the car which had the intended victim inside, then slow down and wait up ahead for the crucial moment to pounce or to shoot. What did a nervous driver do now?

A fertile imagination is a writer's blessing. An overactive one, goosed up with caffeine, is a curse when that writer takes to rescuing potential murder victims.

Along with its many dents and scrapes, Catriona's old car had accumulated a good deal of junk that was always going to be cleared out but never was, as old cars never were. She scrabbled among the odds and ends in the back and came up with more than she'd expected; notably one of those shapeless cotton hats that could serve as a parking place for trout flies, a holdall in which to put fresh-picked berries or wildflowers, a holder for a hot handle on an iron frying pan over a campfire, and various other purposes, most of which had been consumer-tested by both herself and Guthrie Fingal in times of need. She set the grubby hat on Professor Feldster's head and a pair of Guthrie's drugstore sunglasses on his nose; he didn't seem to mind.

The driver of the white car on their right came out carrying a tall cup of steaming coffee. He did a double take at the sight of the professor wearing sunglasses before the sun was up, this not being Hollywood. Or even New York for that matter.

Catriona gave him her haughtiest stare. The man quickly turned his head aside and gave his whole attention to his morning paper. She would have wondered how he could read in such poor light had she not been too busy wondering how to alter her own appearance.

She took off her suit jacket, hid it under the front seat, and found a faded green cardigan over which Emerson and Carlyle often fought and a head scarf that should have been chucked away ages ago but might be of some practical use now. Anyway, it was the best she could do, and there was always hope to fall back on.

It was still not quite five o'clock; there weren't many cars on the road yet. Was that good or bad? She darted back into the eatery, bought four more doughnuts in case of emergency, darted back to the driver's seat, and turned the ignition key. It caught on the first try. She made up her mind to accept this as an omen, and nosed the car out of the parking lot.

The car was behaving remarkably well; she was astonished when she dared take her eyes for a moment off the road and the rear mirror to see she'd been doing sixty-five. Was this another omen? No, it must be that Professor Feldster's weight was making an appreciable amount of difference; and no wonder, considering how he'd been cramming in the calories ever since she'd found him.

Not surprisingly, the professor was showing signs of discomfort. Dawn had not fully broken; the road was still pretty clear. Catriona pulled over to the side, looked around for a possible antagonist, didn't find one, and punched the button that released his seat belt, hoping he wouldn't take off into the unknown or stop a bullet from some hidden sharpshooter. He did only what came naturally, climbed back into the car, fastened his seat belt this time without prompting, and made sure his door was locked. Catriona guessed he'd fall asleep again before long, and he did.

She drove at a steady rate, pacing herself by a set of taillights four car lengths up ahead. Behind her, a set of dim headlights seemed content to maintain the same pace. Occasionally a car would pull out into the left lane and pass all three of them.

Maybe the professor ought to be seen by a doctor, she thought. All this sleeping might be due to a head injury, though it was just as apt to be no more than a normal reaction to the ordeal he'd been put through. Guthrie would know better than she, even though he was used more to doctoring trees than people. Catriona was surprised to realize how glad she'd be to see her recently acquired housemate. Having him around the house was a pleasant change; there had been too many evenings when she'd felt that two cats weren't quite all she craved for companionship.

Guthrie wouldn't be around much now, though, and neither would she or Professor Feldster if she didn't keep her mind on her driving. Without noticing, she had passed her own lead car. She glanced into her rearview mirror and saw a white midsized sedan coming at her like a torpedo. Should she try to get away from it, or just commend her soul to her Maker?

Before she could weigh the pros and cons, the white car had swung out around her. She tensed, waiting for a gun blast. The white car was almost out of sight before she relaxed. Would it keep on going, or might it sneak behind a billboard and wait its chance? She'd find out soon enough, maybe too soon. What in God's name was she doing here?

Sweating, mostly. She slowed down to fifty-five, taking deep breaths, giving herself time to get sorted out, and found herself a shade less panicky. The traffic was getting thicker; morning rush hour commuters crowded the lanes but didn't seem to be bothering her as much as she'd expected. She let her speedometer creep up to sixty. She was still keeping an eye out for that white car, but when it hadn't shown up again for half an hour, she decided it must have been on its own legitimate business. She relaxed a bit more, only to find a bright red car no bigger than her own getting ready to crawl up her back.

She was all set to panic again when she realized that the driver was in fact trying to get off at the next exit and was afraid to make the turn. Catriona pulled ahead, gave a gentle toot by way of encouragement, blocked the exit just long enough for the timid soul to get safely off the turnpike, and went on ahead regardless of toots, blares, and curses. That was all right, a woman didn't mind being cussed a bit in a worthy cause. Perhaps this was not a day for abductions. Feeling greatly relieved, she took some more deep breaths and kept going until she could swing into the appointed parking lot.

10

AND THERE WAS GUTHRIE FINGAL, BLESS HIS NOBLE HEART, sitting in his scratched-up, sap-smeared Jeep, staring gloomily into an empty take-out cup. Once he caught sight of the car he loved to hate, however, he grinned from ear to ear and back again, leaped out of the Jeep and rushed to give Catriona a genuine Maine bear hug.

"You okay, Cat? No problems along the way?"

"None to speak of. We didn't hit much traffic until we got toward Portsmouth. Who's your friend?"

"Oh, sorry. You've met Miss McBogle, haven't you, Hubert? She's the lady who lives down the road in the big brick house. Hubert's one of my top students, Cat. He's going to drive your car back from here to Sasquamahoc; I figured you'd have had enough of it for a while, after all the traveling you did yesterday."

Catriona was all set to bristle, but decided not to. So what if Guthrie did indulge in an occasional bout of chest-thumping? There was a bit of Tarzan in every man. Every Maine man, anyway. She snatched off the dreadful scarf she'd been using for a disguise, tossed the frayed old cardigan in among the backseat leftovers, put her decent gray jacket on and buttoned it up to hide the coffee stains on her not so decent white blouse.

"It's awfully nice of you to come, Hubert. My car really

does have all four wheels in working order, so don't pay any attention to the squeaks and groans."

Hubert was probably blushing; it was hard to tell. He said he wasn't scared because however bad Miss McBogle's car was, his would have to be worse. He made a brief feint at refusing the twenty-dollar bills that both President Guthrie and Miss McBogle were trying to thrust at him, accepted the registration, absentmindedly pocketed both twenties, and left the parking lot a happy young man.

"Don't worry, Cat," said Guthrie. "Hube's the best driver in the school and that's saying something. All the kids around here cut their teeth on their fathers' number plates. What do you say about some food?"

"What is there to say? We don't have time, do we?"

"No, but that needn't stop us. I went into a place on the way down here and got some doughnuts and muffins. The guy at the counter filled my big thermos so we can eat as we go along. What about your pal?"

"Don't call him that, he has a name. Too much of a name, now that I think of it. Maybe we'd better stick to calling him Jim. I could use a rest room about now, but I'll wait till we get to the information stop. You could take him inside there, if you don't mind."

"Cripes, is he that helpless?"

"Come to think of it, no. He apparently coped all right last night at the motel—I could hear him running a shower and he must have washed the shirt he'd been wearing all that time because it looked clean this morning."

"Had adjoining rooms, did you?" Guthrie was trying to be offhand and not succeeding. Catriona only shrugged.

"Oh, we had to. I told the desk clerk that Jim was my deaf brother and we had to communicate by tapping on the wall between us so that he could feel the vibrations through the soles of his feet. I didn't know how else to cope, I was not about to sit up all night playing nursemaid to a man I scarcely know."

"It seems to me, if you don't mind me saying so, that your best plan would have been to drive your pal Jim to the nearest police station."

Catriona sniffed. "I knew you were going to start that. In the first place, I had no idea where to find a police station. In the second, I didn't want the whole Feldstermeier clan jumping down my throat just as they're getting up steam to bury their patriarch. Especially if one of them is a killer."

Guthrie shook his head. "It's hard to believe that your 'deaf brother' is some kind of connection to International Dairies."

"He's more than just a connection. You know I've been whining around, trying to get started on the book I'm supposed to be writing. When Helen told me about Professor Feldster, I thought there might be an idea for a plot that I could use. After I'd left Helen and Peter, I stopped to buy gas and read my day-old newspaper. There was a big article in it about Forster Feldstermeier's death with a front-page picture that reminded me of Balaclava's missing milkman, so I went looking for a place to check him out."

"That was still yesterday morning?"

"Oh, yes. Helen and Peter had to be at the college bright and early. I left them, too. I did manage to find a wonderful old library with a good reference section, and learned some things about the Feldstermeier family, particularly James. This was just before I took that awful back road and found him hanging there. Don't ever try to tell me there's no such thing as guidance." Catriona took a moment to steady her voice. "Anyway, unless I'm grievously mistaken, Helen and Peter's neighbor Jim is the youngest of the late Forster Feldstermeier's three brothers, and the only one in the pack who didn't go into the business. Though I suppose teaching dairy management might count as an allied profession. That's what Jim does at Balaclava, you know. You must have met him sometime or another, he always stops to pass the time of day with Jane Austen."

"Oh, that guy? The one who knows all the secret handshakes? You honestly believe he's one of the anointed?"

11

JANE WAS THE FIRST ONE UP IN THE SHANDY HOUSEHOLD. SHE had her little ways of making her humans aware that highly educated cats required to be compensated for their wake-up services with pats and gentle cooings. Cooings were not enough, however, when the inner cat announced to the outer cat that what was needed here was a tastefully served bowl of the cat food du jour, with a small saucer of low-fat milk for a chaser; both to be set on her special tray in a spot where well-meaning but bumblefooted humans were not likely to trip over it.

Usually Jane claimed and got some little extra such as a dab of scrambled egg or a lick of the cottage cheese that Helen and Peter liked on their morning toast. Jane had to ask for it more than once this morning; her humans were not up to their accustomed form.

It was not as if they'd been fresh and rested to start with; the reception and what came after it had been more than they'd bargained for. Today they had too much to do and not enough time to do it in. By the time Jane had lapped up her milk and cleaned her whiskers, Peter was ready to dash off to his office for the emergency meeting he'd arranged last night with Knapweed Calthrop.

"Listen!" said Helen. She had snapped on the little

kitchen radio to catch the weather report and the name Feld-stermeier caught her ear instead.

"—the last of his generation . . . said to be a modest retiring professor from an unnamed little college somewhere in New England . . . by a quirk of fate, now elevated to the leadership of a gigantic international dairy corporation. All he has to do to claim it is to read aloud, in the hearing of his assembled family, a message handed down from the first of his forebears. Lacking the formal consent of the new CEO and chairman of the board, even the late Forster Feldstermeier's funeral cannot be carried out. And James Feldstermeier is nowhere to be found!"

The pundit cleared his throat portentously. "The only photograph the news media have managed to obtain was snapped fifty years ago in the family compound by a dairymaid, showing James at the age of six, seated on the back of a Jersey cow. And now on to the weather. A high pressure system moving into—"

"Oh my God!" Peter groaned. "The sky is falling and Catriona can't even tell the king because he won't listen."

He glanced at his watch and groaned again. In four minutes he was going to be late for his appointment with young Calthrop. He gave Helen a hasty kiss and galloped away.

Helen didn't have to be in that big a rush; she finished her meal with Jane's help and straightened up the kitchen. She was wondering where she'd left her briefcase when she happened to glance out the window and see Grace Porble starting up the Feldsters' back stairs carrying something wrapped in aluminum foil.

Dear Grace! She must be bringing Mirelle a few fresh-baked biscuits or muffins, not for any special reason but just because it was a neighborly thing to do. She was wearing a lightweight oatmeal-colored suit that she'd worn every spring and fall since Helen could remember; it still looked stunning on her. Now she was rapping on the door, getting no answer, which wouldn't have been surprising if the door hadn't swung open when Grace knocked. As a rule, Mirelle double-locked the back door and kept the key in her pocket if she so much as stepped out to sit on the deck with her mid-morning coffee. Now that her neighbors knew what she had to protect, her compulsive locking up didn't seem so ridiculous. It did give Helen an odd feeling, though, to watch Grace step inside without being challenged on the threshold.

She'd leave whatever it was that she'd brought on the kitchen table, scribble a little note on one of her visiting cards—Grace was the only woman in town who carried them—and come out, careful to shut the door after her. Mirelle must have been even drunker last night than they'd thought she was; perhaps she'd staggered out for a breath of fresh air to clear her head and neglected to shut the door after her when she went back inside.

"I'm getting to be a regular old biddy," Helen told Jane, "spying on the neighbors when—oh my gosh!"

Grace was back on the deck, doubled up over the waist-high railing, doing what Helen had never thought to see. Without even thinking, Helen rushed across the two back-yards.

"Grace, what's the matter?"

"Don't come up!"

Of course Helen went anyway. She darted into the Feld-sters' kitchen, snatched a dish towel, poured water into the first glass she could find, and took them back outside. "Here, Grace, rinse your mouth. Where's Mirelle?"

"In there." Grace jerked her head. "I was looking for Mirelle to give her the biscuits. Oh, God!"

She retched again. Helen braced herself and made another quick reconnaissance; she came back white around the lips. "There's a phone in the kitchen, Grace. I'm going to call Security. You stay out here and watch for them."

Helen couldn't seem to get her fingers on the right numbers; she gritted her teeth and tried again. This time, thank heaven, Silvester Lomax answered over the roar of a motor.

"Security."

"Silvester, this is Helen Shandy. I'm at the Feldsters', we're in big trouble here. Please hurry!"

She hung up without waiting for an answer; she still didn't know what the trouble was. All that had registered with Helen so far was that purple-clad horror sitting in one of the tapestry chairs, clutching the carved walnut arms, and the dark red stains on the all-white carpeting at Mirelle Feldster's feet.

News always traveled fast at Balaclava. Today Silvester Lomax traveled even faster. He must have been mowing the near campus lawn with the big riding tractor and had answered her call on his portable phone. He charged down the hill with the blade up, parked the machine next to the back stairs, and was up on the deck practically in one movement. Less than a minute later, his brother Clarence arrived in one of the college pickups.

"What's the matter, Helen? You okay, Grace?"

Grace was not okay. Helen had got her to sit in one of the deck chairs but she still wasn't up to talking; she was lying back with her eyes closed and the dish towel still clenched in her hand. Helen took it on herself to explain as best she could; she wished desperately that Peter were here and felt some relief that he wasn't.

The Lomax boys were no great talkers. The best they could do was "Better get Fred Ottermole up here. He'll be along."

"How soon?" Helen didn't know how much more of this she could take. She might have known that the police chief and the college security guards had each other's schedules down cold; it wasn't more than another three minutes before Fred came whizzing up the Crescent on his bicycle. He and the Lomaxes were boon companions, there'd be no one-up-manship here. Fred Ottermole had learned a lot about policing from Peter Shandy; he got straight to business.

"What's the trouble, Helen?"

"Mirelle. She's in there." Helen could only point, she knew better than to go near the gruesome tableau in the parlor. "It's bad, Fred."

The Chief disappeared inside and Helen said, "Look, would one of you mind helping Grace over to her house and letting Dr. Porble know what's happened? She's the one who found Mirelle, she shouldn't be left alone until she's over the shock. And Fred will probably want you to ask Dr. Melchett to come examine Mirelle."

Clarence Lomax said he wouldn't mind taking care of those items a bit. He took Grace by the elbow and eased her out of the deck chair. She demurred feebly but seemed relieved to have a strong arm steering her down the stairs.

"You want me to take you in the truck, Mrs. Porble?"

"Oh, no, Clarence, I'm not that far gone. I do feel a bit woozy, though. Maybe the walk will do me good."

"I'll be over in a while, Grace." Helen watched to make sure Grace was up to walking the short distance. Chief Ottermole came back, his face pasty. "What happened here, Helen?"

"I don't know, Fred. All I can say is that Grace came over just a few minutes ago, carrying a plateful of—I don't know. Biscuits or muffins, I expect, for Mirelle's breakfast. Both of us had been feeling rather guilty about not being nicer to her since her trouble, and of course there'd been that dustup between Mirelle and Peter the night Jim disappeared. You know how it is."

"Yeah. I know. Damned if you do and damned if you don't."

"Well, anyway, I was in my own kitchen just now, filling Jane's water dish and getting ready to leave for the library when I looked over toward the Feldsters' and saw Grace on the deck, juggling her plate so that she could knock on the door. But when she went to knock, the door swung open by itself. Grace must have realized then that something was wrong because Mirelle was always so fussy about keeping everything locked up, so she went inside. I'd hardly had time to put Jane's dish down on her tray when there was Grace back on the deck, chucking up her own breakfast over the railing."

Fred Ottermole nodded sympathetically.

"I ran over as fast as I could. She told me not to go in, but I did. Would you believe, I'd never once set foot inside that house until last night after the reception? I called Mirelle's name a couple of times but she didn't answer. There was a smell. Not pleasant. I decided something must be terribly wrong, so I followed the smell, on into the front parlor where we'd sat last night. When I found Mirelle, she was slumped in a high-backed tapestry chair, the kind with wooden arms. She was clutching the two arms. Her hands were clean, as far as I could tell, but there was blood on her face and blood on the fancy purple hostess gown she'd been wearing last night, and a big puddle of it soaked down into that white carpeting. I don't know how they'll ever get it clean."

"Do you feel like talking about this now?"

"I'm all right, it was just the shock. A person doesn't expect to see—"

"It's okay, Helen. Take a few deep breaths, you'll be fine. When did you last see Mirelle alive?"

"About eleven o'clock last night, after the president's reception. Grace Porble and I had been hostessing, and Mrs. Svenson asked us to bring some of the leftover flowers and pastries to Mirelle. When we got to the Feldster house, a Cadillac Seville was blocking the drive and a man whom Mirelle addressed as Florian was just leaving."

"A Cadillac Seville?" For a poignant moment, Fred Ottermole resembled the Spartan boy with the fox tearing at his vitals. "What year was it?"

"I'm sorry, I couldn't say. Peter might know."

"Um. Where did this Florian guy come from?"

"Good question. All I know is that, as we were going up

the front walk, we heard a man's voice that none of us recognized telling Mirelle to keep her chin up, which wasn't very enlightening. When Phil rang the doorbell, this Florian left almost immediately without giving Mirelle a chance to introduce us. Other than that, I can only say that the man was tall and reminded me a little of Jim Feldster, except that he was more heavily built and a great deal better dressed. So well dressed that you didn't realize he was, if you get my meaning."

Ottermole grunted. "Sounds to me as if he might be some rich relative of Jim's, if he has any. Are you steady enough to show me how it was last night?"

Helen took another deep breath, nodded bravely, and followed Fred inside to the parlor.

Silvester Lomax remained on guard duty outside to prevent anyone from wandering into the house unexpectedly. Not that it looked like guard duty. Curious faces had appeared at the windows all around the Crescent when he arrived on the riding mower, but no one noticed when Fred's bicycle arrived discreetly at the Feldsters' back door. The nosiest neighbors lost interest when they saw Silvester begin to prune the forsythia bushes beside the Feldster walk as if that were his only reason for being there. If anything, they assumed Mirelle was taking advantage of her temporary status of abandoned wife to get some of the yard chores done that Jim perennially neglected. No doubt Clarence Lomax would soon return to his truck and help his brother pick up the lopped branches.

Inside the house, the carpeting in both the hallway and the parlor was such a pristine white that the globs of wet-looking blood contrasted even more sickeningly. It had puddled around the tapestry chair in which Mirelle was still sitting and her slippers were soaked. By now, rigor mortis had probably set in and perhaps passed off as well, for all Helen knew. Fred Ottermole could touch the body if he needed to know. That was a policeman's job, not a librarian's.

Was it possible that Mirelle Feldster had just sat here calmly watching while all the blood drained from her body, not lifting a finger to stanch it? Was that why her hands looked so clean when the rest was so dreadfully otherwise? The blood wouldn't have come in a single great gush, Helen thought, unless there was a big wound of some kind underneath that purple robe. More likely there'd have been a steady flow for so long as the heart inside her amply padded ribs kept on pumping. Dr. Melchett ought to know. They mustn't try to move the body until he'd seen it and photographs had been taken.

As precisely as possible, she described for Fred where each of them sat, what they had drunk, and how they left Mirelle, bowed but definitely unbloody, on her chaise longue.

"I'm surprised President Svenson hasn't shown up," she said because she had to keep talking. "Maybe no one thought to let him know what's going on."

That was silly. Thorkjeld Svenson always knew. He'd be along in his own time. Fred wondered aloud whether he ought to be taking fingerprints, just to show he was on the ball.

"Oh, I don't think so," Helen told him. "Mirelle was too good a housekeeper. Even in her state last night, you can see that she cleared away our champagne glasses and I bet she washed them and wiped the kitchen counter, too. With all these porcelains, it's like a museum in here." The museum analogy somehow helped calm her. She could almost tell herself that the body in the tapestry chair wasn't real; it was just one more exhibit.

Fred must be feeling much the same. "It *is* a museum, isn't it? What do you think of it?"

Helen shook her head. "I don't know what to think, Fred. Right now I'm hardly daring to breathe for fear of breaking something. You do realize, don't you, that all this fragile porcelain must be worth far more than the Feldsters have paid in rent for the house over the years?"

"Holy cow!"

"Of course college rents are low, considering, and we're not allowed to buy, much as Peter and I have wanted to."

"But don't you think this is a funny sort of way for a guy like Jim Feldster to be living? Him being in the dairy barns all day and going to so many lodge meetings at night. It's—funny.

"Oh, I don't suppose Jim's in the habit of spending much time in this room. He must have some kind of den or office to himself, wouldn't you think?"

"We can go look." Fred turned to lead the way out and stopped short.

"My gosh! Did I do that?"

He pointed to an overturned tier table and the small heap of broken figurines that had been obscured by the back of Mirelle's chair and her trailing robe.

"Don't panic, Fred. You couldn't have done it. You'd have heard the table fall over and felt the crunch under your feet when you tried to dodge the breakage. I'd have heard it too."

12

NOW IT WAS HELEN'S TURN TO PANIC, BUT SHE MUST NOT LET that happen. The possibility that somebody carrying a bloodstained knife might this very minute be lurking upstairs under a bed or inside a closet was not one that she cared to think about. Luckily Fred drew a different conclusion.

"The Feldsters never had a dog or a cat or anything, did they?"

"Not even a goldfish, so far as I can tell." Helen was still trying to pull herself together, and failing dismally. "I'm sure there was no broken porcelain around last night while Peter and I and the Porbles were here, much less an overturned table. And that chair wasn't pulled out into the middle of the room, the way it is now. And I cannot for the life of me figure out why her hands are still clean, what I can see of them, anyway, while the rest of her is—I just don't understand it at all. I do wish Peter would come."

"You and me both. Look, Helen, I know you folks and the Porbles are good friends and I don't want to get you sore at me, but would—did—oh dammit!"

"What are you getting at, Fred?"

"Well, see, I was just thinking. Suppose for the sake of argument that Grace and Phil had gone home after you'd all left the Feldsters', and Grace had got back up after Phil was asleep and sneaked over here while Mirelle was still up, and they got to fighting, and—"

"Fred Ottermole, what in heaven's name are you blethering about? Grace Porble is not the sort of person who sneaks around in the dark and murders her neighbors. You'd better quit reading those lurid paperbacks that Budge Dorkin smuggles into the station when he's on night duty and can't find anybody to pinch. Wherever did you hear that stupid nonsense about Grace? I'm sure it can't have come from Edna Mae."

Having thoroughly squashed poor Fred, who decided it was perhaps time he searched the house, Helen wondered whether she ought to give the Porble house a ring. She was on her way across the yard to her own house when Peter came flying down the hill.

"What's going on here, Helen? Phil Porble claims Grace told him Mirelle Feldster's been murdered but nobody's supposed to know. Melchett's given Grace a sedative."

"Good," said Helen. "Maybe he'll give me one. It's true, Peter, I still can't believe this has happened."

With Peter's arm around her, Helen felt less wobbly in the knees. When he asked her, "Where's Mirelle?" she managed a sensible answer.

"In the parlor, surrounded by a puddle of damp blood. It's awful, Peter. Poor Grace had the worst of it."

"How so?"

"I was in our kitchen, almost ready to leave for the library, when I saw her come up the Feldsters' back stairs carrying a plate wrapped in foil. I thought it must be something she thought Mirelle might like for breakfast, in accordance with our new 'Be nice to Mirelle' policy. At first I was rather amused, then I realized that Grace had opened the door and Mirelle wasn't behind it."

"Was anybody?"

"No, that was the weird part. Grace waited a minute or two to see if Mirelle was coming, then went in, leaving the door open behind her. It wasn't more than a few seconds later till she came running back out to the deck, leaned over the railing, and vomited. Grace Porble, of all people!"

"So what did you do?"

"Naturally I rushed over to see what was the matter. Grace begged me not to go inside, but of course I couldn't leave her to tough it out alone. I did manage to keep my breakfast down and call Security from the kitchen over there. The Lomax boys came right along, then Fred Ottermole on his bike, bless him."

"My God! How many are there?"

"Just Fred, Silvester, and me at the moment. Clarence took Grace home. He was supposed to call Phil and Dr. Melchett. He probably sneaked a call to Thorkjeld, too. Oh, Peter, I feel ghastly."

"Don't faint yet, I can feel the ground trembling."

Whether or not the ground actually did shake as the college's resident Viking thundered down from the campus and into the Crescent was a question that never did get properly answered. That Dr. Svenson was quite capable of stirring up a whirlwind, a simoon, or even a tsunami was axiomatic. That the dauntless president would never create such a ruckus except for good and sufficient reason was equally axiomatic, if not more so. He was not in a mellow mood this morning.

"Talk, Shandy."

Peter gave his wife a look. Helen sighed and retold, in the fewest possible number of words. "Dr. Melchett must have stopped by Grace Porble's first. Maybe you ought to catch him before—"

She was about to add "he messes things up at the crime scene," but Svenson was already halfway to the Porbles'. Seconds later, he had Melchett's upper arm in a gorilla grip and was hustling him along to the Feldster house. Peter gave Helen a quick kiss and jerked his head in the direction of their own house. Helen took it as a husband's thanks and hurried to get the camera that he'd be needing very soon, whether he knew it or not. She made sure there was plenty of film in the camera bag, called Fred to pass it on to Peter, picked up Jane Austen for company, and went upstairs to lie down. She'd done her deed for the time being. Whether or not it was a good one remained to be seen.

For Peter, fresh on the scene, there could be no backing away, even though Mirelle dead in her bloodstained robe and drenched slippers was the last sight he'd have chosen to look upon so soon after breakfast. By the time he, Melchett, Ottermole, and President Svenson had squeezed themselves into that overstuffed parlor, there was hardly room left for the corpse. For a second or two, nobody knew what to do. Then Melchett picked up a sofa cushion, plopped it down over some of the bloodstains, hiked up his pant legs just a smidgen at the knees, and knelt on the cushion with his stethoscope at the ready for no discernible purpose that any of the others could see.

"Get her out of that chair, Ottermole, and lay her out on the carpet," he ordered.

Peter had often wondered what the doctor used for brains. "Hold on there, Melchett. I've got my wife's camera here. Chief Ottermole will need some photographs taken before anybody touches the body. Right, Ottermole? We don't want Dr. Melchett to be asked any embarrassing questions by the county medical examiner. Or anybody else."

"Yesus, no," growled Svenson. "Bad for the college. Least said, less trouble. No ambulance, Melchett, no flashing lights, no sirens, no anything."

It was obvious to Peter that Melchett hadn't so much as thought about an ambulance, until this moment. "If you say so, President. Step back, Ottermole, give Professor Shandy room to work. Unless you'd rather get that fellow from the *Fane and Pennon*? He's a professional photographer."

Thorkjeld Svenson made a noise in his throat that made

Peter think of what the crocodile had for breakfast. Melchett ought to know what a blunder it'd be if he let Cronkite Swope, demon reporter for the daily *Balaclava County Fane and Pennon*, find out that the wife of the missing Professor James Feldster was now dead in her own front parlor under mysterious circumstances.

On the other hand, Swope himself would have sense enough never to explode a bombshell on the college premises without getting President Svenson's permission first, last and always. Melchett quit trying to arrange his profile so that the extra chin wouldn't show up in Peter's pictures and faded into the background. It was Peter Shandy who took the photographs that might save Melchett's face with the medical examiner.

The face Peter had to record on Helen's film was a gruesome thing to see, coated with dried blood almost to the eyeballs, the nostrils clogged, the hair that had been so many times to the Curl and Twirl now in loathsome clots that stuck to the bloodstreaked cheeks and forehead. The purple robe in which Mirelle had queened it with her flute of champagne last night was saturated; the amount of blood that had flowed was amazing, though much of it had been sopped up by the deep-piled carpet. Even President Svenson had a hard time hiding a moment's queasiness.

Dr. Melchett, having got back his aplomb, was eager to flaunt it. "I know, it's not a pretty sight. Too bad. Mirelle used to be quite a good-looking woman when she was younger. I can't say offhand exactly what happened here; we'll have to wait for the autopsy report. It may be less dire than you think. I don't see a wound, but in her case, even a superficial cut might have triggered a massive hemorrhage; she'd been on Coumadin ever since she developed phlebitis two years ago."

"Urgh!" said Svenson.

"Yes indeed, President. As you of course know, Coumadin is a powerful blood thinner and a drug that requires careful monitoring. Mirelle wasn't always as aware of this as she should have been. If Jim were at home, he'd have made sure she got the proper dosage, but with him away—if she started drinking—" Melchett shrugged again. "She could easily take a week's worth of pills in one day. It's one of those things that never should happen, but what can you do? Naturally we doctors get the blame regardless."

He looked at his watch and pursed his lips officiously. "Well, I'll tell the hospital to send an unmarked van for her. I'm sure the medical examiner will agree with my diagnosis. The death certificate will be a mere formality, President. I can tell Goulson—"

Thorkjeld Svenson snarled his mightiest snarl. "Forget it, Melchett. Do it myself. Go poison your patients. And not one word to anybody!"

13

"DAMN YACKASS." SVENSON WAS STILL BOILING AT MELCHETT'S officiousness.

"I couldn't agree with you more," said Peter Shandy.

Ottermole stayed until the coroner's plain, unmarked van arrived and Mirelle's body was discreetly removed. Afterward he felt redundant. "If you two want to take over here, I'd better go finish my rounds. I'll catch hell from half the town if I don't stay to protect all their uncles and aunts and grandmothers and the family cat and the pet goldfish. And I'll get the same in reverse if I waste time pedaling around on my bicycle when I ought to be back at the station figuring out who killed the goldfish. If you think there's one satisfied customer in town who figures I'm probably doing the best I can with what I've got and doesn't give a damn one way or the other, you've got another think coming."

"Want to borrow my car?" Svenson offered.

Ottermole cringed. "Thanks, I'll stick to my bike. With four kids and a mortgage, I'm in no position to risk my life in that hunk of junk. I wouldn't mind borrowing one of your Balaclava Blacks and a wagon, though."

"Arrgh!"

Dr. Svenson didn't mind hearing his horrible old clunker reviled by the police chief; he reviled it pretty often himself. The Balaclava Blacks were, however, no targets for ill-advised japery. Those magnificent workhorses ranked only behind the president's beautiful wife, his seven beautiful daughters, and his several equally beautiful grandchildren in his affection. His sons-in-law came half a length or so after, depending on how well they handled the college horses. Getting behind even one of the Blacks for a short stint with a horse-drawn plow in the potato field would give any Balaclava student something to brag about for the rest of his, her or their life; the "their" referring to a pair of Siamese twins who'd been graduated summa cum laude fourteen years ago and had by now established themselves near the top as breeders of double daffodils, double hollyhocks, and many other doubles, several of which had never been doubled before. Svenson replied to Ottermole with a snort of derision.

"Might as well ask for the whole team."

"You don't mean that, but I wish to heck you did." A sly smile crept across the face that Edna Mae considered the handsomest in Balaclava County. "How about it, President? We could get up on that big wagon you always drive in the annual workhorse competition and ride around town with big banners all around it saying 'Let's get out of the horse-and-buggy days. Buy Chief Ottermole a cruiser.'"

President Svenson snorted again, this time a moderately genial snort. "Right idea, wrong time. Nag me later. Go."

Unlikely though it might seem, there was a genuine rapport between the college president and the small-town cop. Peter cherished a fond memory of one busy evening when, having rounded up most of a gang of big-time malefactors, Ottermole had constituted himself a one-man cheering section for Thorkjeld Svenson. He'd perched on the back of a sofa upholstered in the Buchanan tartan, watching the president and another behemoth fight a duel with antlers and horns from various large ruminants as their weapons, wishing aloud that he'd brought the kids and a bag of popcorn.*

*Something the Cat Dragged In

Svenson was not the sort to forget a fellow gladiator. Ottermole, who would get his new cruiser when the time was right, mounted his bike with a new spring in his calves and sped off. President Svenson, having made it plain who was running the show, went back to his office. Peter was left alone with that dreadfully stained carpet and a roomful of expensive china.

Now that Mirelle's body was gone, the room felt oddly empty despite the plethora of collectibles. He wondered how many of them had been smashed underfoot when that too dainty tier table had got knocked over. It was feasible, Peter supposed, that Mirelle herself had caused the damage when she came back to give the parlor a final tidying after clearing away their champagne flutes. Say she was unsteady on her feet, over goes the table, she tries to get one of her precious shepherdesses, steps on another, then cuts herself badly.

Peter thought of past cuts on his own hands. Even a small wound could produce an appalling amount of blood. But Mirelle's hands were clean, there was no apparent wound on her face, yet it was smeared with blood. If Mirelle's hands hadn't done the smearing, whose had?

Or maybe she'd simply washed her hands before sitting down in that chair to bleed to death? Peter would have breathed easier at the sight of a red-stained napkin or a wad of luridly smeared tissues.

He went and looked in the downstairs bathroom. What Mirelle would surely have called her powder room was in perfect order. The wastebasket did contain a few lavender-tinted paper tissues, but none of them showed any bloodstains.

He went upstairs and found out nothing except that Mirelle had been a crackerjack housekeeper. If someone *had* killed her, it hadn't been to ransack the house for valuables. Not a drawer was open, not a door stood ajar.

Standing here like a stuffed emu wasn't going to accomplish anything. At least he could sweep up this broken china before somebody got cut on it. Peter blundered around Mirelle's kitchen until he located the closet where she'd kept her cleaning implements, found a stash of grocery bags, a broom and a dustpan, and carried them back to the parlor. He saw no sense in fussing about fingerprints on the shards; he'd checked the soles of Mirelle's slippers while he'd been taking photographs and found nothing on them but blood, which hadn't surprised him any because she'd shed enough of it to make a puddle big enough to cover half the floor. There was so much furniture crowded into the room that the switch from sofa to chair wouldn't have been more than a step or two. She might have got some blood on her feet before she moved but that wouldn't have made any difference because the red tide would have spread over the prints as the body was drained.

Somebody must have walked through the china that had been spilled from the fallen table, though. All three tiers had been crammed with porcelain figurines, but the small objects had landed next to the baseboard on that deep, soft pile and should not have broken. Knocking the table over might have been an accident but now that he was down among the shards, its fragile cargo appeared to have been given a quick but enthusiastic stomping. Whoever did it had to stand next to the wall because the shards were not out in the middle of the floor. What he really needed were the shoes or boots of the stomper, and a fat lot of good it would do him to go looking through every closet in Balaclava Junction.

So far, neither Ottermole nor Svenson had uttered a yip about getting the state police in. This was understandable. Svenson was bent on keeping the college out of the news, insofar as that might be possible. Ottermole wanted to prevent those ginks with the snappy uniforms and the nice, shiny cruisers from hogging the glory, if there was going to be any. That was fine with Peter; all he wanted was to get on with the job, settle the mess, and go back to his classes.

He was meticulous as possible about sweeping up the broken bits of what was now only expensive trash. He hung Mirelle's broom and dustpan back on their respective hooks with utmost care, as if to placate the shade that might already be walking and thinking up a forceful murrain to wish on these meddlesome louts who'd ruined her beautiful white carpet and smashed her entire flock of Jemima Puddle-Ducks.

It was a ticklish situation to be in. Peter decided that he'd better take the bits and pieces someplace where they wouldn't get spilled or thrown away in case they needed to match the shards to those on a suspect's shoes. The safest place he could think of was his own cellar, where there was an old-fashioned jelly cupboard but no jelly.

As he swept and collected, he wondered how Catriona was making out with Jim this morning. This carpet looked like the college abattoir, no fit place to bring a man in shock.

14

OVER IN SASQUAMAHOC, THE SETTLING IN HAD BEGUN WELL enough in Catriona McBogle's newly expanded household. Upon returning home shortly before nine A.M., she and Guthrie had made up a bed for Professor Feldster/Feldstermeier on the pull-out sofa in the den and all three of them had gone to their separate beds for well-deserved naps after their long drives.

Fully intending to toss and moan for an hour, Catriona had put on one of the serviceable long-sleeved but attractively embroidered and lavishly lace-trimmed nightgowns that she'd succumbed to at a lingerie outlet in Freeport not long after Guthrie had moved into her second-best bedroom. She had washed her face, brushed her teeth, and got into bed all set to worry. Three minutes later she was fast asleep and didn't wake up until the barnyard Pavarotti that belonged to the farm down the road let loose with a midday cock-a-doodledoo that might perhaps have awakened the dead in the old town burying ground if he'd tried just a little bit harder.

Catriona had never met that rooster in person; nevertheless she thought of him as a pleasant acquaintance and hoped he wouldn't wind up in somebody's stew pot. She moved to get up, and found herself pinned by Carlyle on the left and Emerson on the right side of the comforter.

She glanced at the clock on her nightstand and found to

her amazement that it had somehow fiddled its way around
to eleven o'clock. She picked up her bathrobe, shook out
some of the cat hairs, found both her slippers after a few
minutes' hunting, and padded downstairs decently covered.

The vivifying aroma of coffee filled the kitchen. Guthrie
was there; he'd fed the cats and turned them loose for the
blue jays to cuss at. And, wonder of wonders, James Feldstermeier, wearing one of Guthrie's flannel shirts, was
standing beside the stove flipping pancakes and fielding
them in Catriona's grandmother's iron spider with the
aplomb of a logging-camp cook, even though the hour was
more suited to lunch than breakfast. Breakfast was always
more comforting though, so Catriona approved.

A place for the lady of the manor was already set. As
Guthrie pulled out a chair for her, the silent flipper sent a
pan-sized griddle cake spinning clear across from the stove
to a perfect landing on her plate.

"Where the dickens did you learn to do that?" she demanded.

He didn't answer or even look at her. He just poured another thin layer of batter into the griddle, waited until the
bubbles finished popping, did a little fancy wrist work, and
flipped her another. She buttered and syruped and took an
experimental bite. The pancakes were magnificent, she said
so. The new boarder went on pouring and flipping until the
batter was used up; only then did he sit down and finish off
what the others hadn't been able to find room for.

This was not to say that Feldstermeier left the table hungry. His enthusiasm for food was at least as keen as it had
been before he'd eaten up the librarian's chocolate chip
cookies. But he still wasn't talking. Guthrie didn't make any
scholarly attempt to draw the professor out, he just dropped
a few favorable remarks about the pancakes and added an
anecdote or two about great pancake flippers he had known.
Feldstermeier didn't appear to be listening; nevertheless he
didn't get up from the table until Guthrie had finished both

his pancakes and his story and galloped off to the forestry school.

Catriona went back upstairs and threw on some daytime clothes because it didn't seem quite the thing not to in these circumstances. Normally she would have gone into her workroom still wearing the nightgown and robe that were her accustomed morning garb, and remained so dressed until something or other interfered with her writing, as something or other invariably did. Some days she never got to do any work at all, at least not her own definition of work. It became clear that this was going to be one of those days.

When she got downstairs in corduroys and a sweatshirt, she found her self-appointed cook at the sink. The dishes were all washed and the drain board wiped clean; now the new head of International Dairies was standing like a sheep waiting for a collie to nip at his heels and get him moving. It was heartening to know that Feldstermeier could make himself useful in the kitchen but Catriona would have felt a darned sight happier if she could somehow get him to talk. The prospect of a whole day without a single word from this human statue was daunting. She'd have to keep him moving and hope he'd stub his toe and say "ouch." Anything would be better than nothing.

Rather than sit and sulk, Catriona led Feldstermeier on a tour of the house, hoping he might show a flicker of interest in something, but he didn't.

The house that Catriona had bought was on a rural route, set back from the road. Since coming back to Sasquamahoc, she'd been too absorbed in her own work to do much socializing with her neighbors. She couldn't even recall the name of the family, if it was in fact a family, that owned the farm with the dark green shutters; although she did exchange an occasional wave, nod, or toot if she happened to pass their driveway while somebody was either putting letters into their mailbox or taking mail out.

Now that Catriona had time to think about it, why hadn't

she made any effort to get to know her neighbors? She'd always liked people, sometimes even people whom nobody else could endure. Down in Massachusetts, she and Ben had been happy suburbanites, making friends right and left, though more left than right, going to dinner with neighbors, inviting the neighbors back. They'd taken some interest in community affairs; Catriona had even served two terms as a library trustee.

All that had been before Catriona had got the telephone call from Ben's distraught secretary and felt her life being ripped in two. Her friends had been kind, she'd valued their support, she'd stayed on in the house until she knew she wouldn't be able to stand another winter of lonely nights. Thanks to Ben's forethought and to the publishers who'd begun taking her seriously as a moneymaker for them even though the yarns she spun were anything but serious, Catriona McBogle could have gone almost anywhere without having to count her pennies. But where would she go? One day while she'd been trying to come to some kind of decision, she'd happened to drop in on a friend who was a numerologist. The numerologist was entertaining a house guest who was a clairvoyant; the clairvoyant said Maine.

Oddly enough, that was the penny that dropped. Catriona had spent summers in Maine as a child, she'd ridden her bike past the old brick house that her Uncle Clewitt had told her was haunted by the ghost of a widow who'd kept a team of malamutes in her front parlor and played hymns on a musical saw to them on Sunday nights at the full of the moon. He'd claimed to have gone past the house one midnight when the Hunter's Moon was high in the sky, and heard the dogs all singing "Throw Out the Lifeline" in close harmony.

Catriona had been deeply disappointed when her father told her what an awful liar Clewitt was; nevertheless she'd kept ticking off on her calendar those full moons that came on Sundays. But nothing had ever happened and she'd come to the bitter conclusion that Uncle Clewitt was full of moonshine. Her father said Clewitt generally was, when he could get hold of any.

Notwithstanding that early disappointment about the spectral malamutes, Catriona had bought the old brick house for a relative pittance, moved in with her typewriter, her many cartons of books, her earthly goods and chattels, as well as two Maine coon kittens. The kittens had been cats for quite a while now, but Catriona hadn't regretted her move for a single day despite the plumber's bills, the carpenter's bills, the bricklayer's bills, the yardman's bills, and all the other bills that people who buy antique houses on a whim fall heir to.

Not having to wear a stiff upper lip all the time had made life easier. Not knowing people, she didn't have to entertain them. Nobody made anything special of Miss McBogle's being a writer, Maine was full of writers. Catriona had chosen well, at least for now. Time would have to tell.

She suddenly realized that they had wound up back in the kitchen and that she could use some fresh air. Rather than leave Jim sitting like one of the granite rocks that must still be guarding that gray Lincoln, Catriona handed him the floppy cotton hat that he'd worn yesterday on the way back to Sasquamahoc. "Come on," she said. "Let's take a walk. Just down behind the house. We won't go far."

She was right. They wouldn't. If Catriona McBogle thought her new boarder was going to leave the spot where the food came from, she could think again. James Feldstermeier just stood there staring at the cookie jar. She had no recourse other than to take off the cover and hand him the crock.

What to do now?

Then she remembered the telephone. If she couldn't work, then she could darned well play.

As Peter let himself in at the cellar door, he heard Helen's voice in the kitchen over his head. Who would be calling her here when everybody ought to assume she was at the library during her usual working hours? No matter, this was a crazy morning anyway. He stashed his probably useless bag of possible useful evidence in the jelly cupboard and went upstairs empty-handed.

Helen had barely got settled at the telephone when her husband popped up from below like the devil in a Punch-and-Judy show.

"Hold on, Cat, he's just come in. I'll put him on, if you don't mind, I've got to go and look in on Grace Porble and then get to the library. It's Catriona, Peter. I told her about Mirelle. You'd better talk to her, she says it's important."

Something more important than a possible murder? There was too damned much importance floating around here all of a sudden, but what could a man do? Helen handed over the phone. Peter took it with some trepidation.

"Hello, Catriona. What's up?"

"Good question," said Catriona, who was still too bemused by her latest discovery to fully absorb the fact of Mirelle's death. "For one thing, you might be interested to learn that the gray Lincoln with the tinted windows will never again serve as a torture chamber for helpless milkmen."

"I'll be damned. How did you find that out?"

"I have my methods, Shandy. Actually, I was driven to it. Your old buddy Feldstermeier is not the most fascinating house guest I've ever tried to entertain, in case you've been wondering. I tried taking him for a little walk around the back forty but all he wants to do is sleep and eat, so I've left him to it. That means having to keep myself handy in case he might take a fit or something, so I decided to call that nice librarian in Beamish. I thanked her for letting me butt in and disrupt her schedule, then we got to talking. You know how one does."

"Two do it better."

"All right, if you say so. Anyway, she said something

about hoping I'd got home all right after our little party, so I gave her a carefully expurgated account of having got out on a back road that ran along a deep ravine and she went into a tizzy. Most people in Beamish, except the really crazy ones, avoid the ravine road like a plague of rabid rattlesnakes. Just last night, however, a bunch of rowdies came along that road in an old pickup. They stopped where they could see that big Lincoln sticking up among the boulders and began drinking beer they'd brought with them and smashing the empties against the trees. That wasn't exciting enough once the beer was gone, so they ran down into the ravine and began trying to break the windows with chunks of granite. Then some idiot ran up to the truck, came back with a deer rifle that he shouldn't have been carrying out of season, and the bullets started to fly. Luckily somebody must have heard the shooting and alerted the state police. A police car did come along with its sirens at full screech, but the road was horrible, as I'm here to testify, and it was a long way in so it was either drive carefully or risk landing down among the boulders with the Lincoln. That left the idiots time enough to go down and pour gasoline over the car, lay a long fuse, and set it alight before they climbed back up to the truck and made their getaway."

"Good lord!" said Peter. "Was there anything left of the car?"

"Only the car's ID number, according to Belinda Beaker. She's the Beamish librarian, in case I forgot to say so. They think it was stolen from a car-hire place in Hoddersville, Royal Rentals. Maybe Chief Ottermole can find out more details. Belinda's husband's a volunteer fireman; both the police and the firemen came in force but there wasn't much they could do except block off the road to keep sightseers away and try to keep the fire from spreading. What particularly interested Belinda was that her husband noticed four champagne bottles that had been thrown quite a way from the car, all landing pretty much together. None of the four was broken; there was even a little bit of champagne left in one of the bottles. Champagne bottles are extra thick and strong, of course; they have to be."

"Um," said Peter. "Did he notice the label? Was it a good brand?"

"Oh, yes. The very best, according to Fireman Beaker."

"Wait a minute, Catriona. You mentioned high-priced champagne but you've described the sort of Yahoo who wouldn't even know how to get the cork out of the bottle. Those birds in the pickup truck were just out for what they considered a good time, with a few six-packs of beer to grease the wheels? Four definitely upper-class champagne bottles all tidily laid out not far from a big expensive limousine strike quite a different note, wouldn't you say?"

"How would you define different?"

"M'well, macabre as it may seem, I shouldn't be surprised to learn that whoever drove Jim Feldster out to that godforsaken ravine where he was left for dead might have stayed out there long enough to celebrate a bad job ill done with a few flagons of the bubbly that they'd brought along for kicks. This is all conjecture, of course, and you know more about it than I do because you were there at the crucial time, but weird things do happen."

"I can certainly grant you that," said Catriona. "Helen described how Jim's wife seems to have been completely drained of blood. It must have been horrible for all of you. For Mirelle Feldster, too, of course. But you'd started to say something about expensive champagne?"

"Yes. After the president's reception last night, Mirelle was swigging it down as if it were Pepsi-Cola. Apparently that Sheik of Araby in the Cadillac Seville had brought it to her. She gave us each a tablespoonful or so and drank the rest herself. I wouldn't have minded another glass or two myself but she wasn't sharing."

"Poor woman. I remember some faculty ladies' tea that Helen conned me into speaking at that Mirelle said she'd been a cheerleader and Homecoming Queen at some little college once upon a time. But she wasn't a cheerleader any more when I met her, just a woman past middle age who ate too much sweet stuff at bridge parties and, from what you now tell me, evidently drank too much expensive champagne."

There was a long silence on the line; then Catriona sighed and said, "Peter? Are you still there?"

"Sorry, Cat, I was thinking. Helen says she told you about the hullabaloo Mirelle raised on our doorstep when she discovered that Jim didn't come home. Add that to the known fact that Mirelle was a thoroughly experienced though fairly wild driver, that she was in the habit of spending more time on the road than she did at home, and that everybody around the Crescent knew for a fact that the Feldsters hadn't had anything remotely resembling a relationship for the past quarter-century or so, not that most of us gave a damn. Does that say anything to you?"

"I suppose it would if I lived where you do."

"There must have been at least two people involved," said Peter. "They'd need a second car to get away in after they'd trashed the Lincoln. How much do you want to bet that the driver of the Lincoln was the one who did all the yowling after she'd got back from trashing her husband along with the car?"

"And was then herself killed? Why?"

"Too soon to know, Cat. Maybe Jim can tell us. How is he?"

"I thought you'd never ask. He appears to be doing reasonably well, so far. He still isn't talking, but he's starting to do a few small chores around the house. He's a great tidier and not a bad cook, although so far he hasn't cooked anything except flapjacks, which he fielded quite deftly. They even tasted pretty good. Now ask me how I feel."

"Okay," said Peter. "It's your nickel. How do you feel?"

"Harried, I believe, is the mot juste."

The sigh that Catriona heaved came through loud and clear. "I'm afraid for that man, Peter; but I do have a life of my own to cope with. I can't even think about my book because I'm too busy feeding cookies to the new pet albatross. If only he'd talk! And you've got classes and there's Guthrie to think about. It's a rotten thing to ask, I suppose, but can't you give me some advice? Maybe if you and Guthrie and I put our heads together—"

"M'well, if it makes you feel any better, President Svenson's already stuck me with getting Jim back to the cow barns dead or alive, preferably the latter. Obviously something's got to be done. Why don't I just drive up to Sasquamahoc and collect Jim?"

"How soon?"

"As soon as I can find my car keys."

"Peter, you're an angel! What can I do to help?"

"Just sit on a cushion and sew a fine scheme. Sounds to me as though you've done more than enough already. By the way, have you gone through Jim's things just to make sure he really is James Feldster, with or without the Meier?"

"We did think of that. Guthrie did a search but the poor goof's pockets were all empty, his clothes didn't have any labels in them, and his wallet was gone. It might have fallen down inside the car somewhere, seeing as how he was practically standing on his head in that cursed spiderweb they'd strapped him into. I didn't think of that at the time. All I can say is that the man I've got here looks just like the photographs they've been running in the media of his elder brothers. You'll know, of course, as soon as you see him. When did you say you were planning to start?"

"As soon as you hang up the phone. Is there anything you want me to bring?"

"Yes, clothes for Jim to go back in. The duds he had on when I found him are out in the woodshed; I don't expect he'll ever want them again. He's wearing Guthrie's but they don't fit very well. Will Jim have any trouble getting into his house, do you think?"

"Considering the state it's in, he may not want to. I doubt if he'd care to stay with us or the Porbles, but there's an inn nearby that he could go to. The college has someone guarding the place. Dr. Svenson doesn't want to involve the state police if he can help it."

"That's understandable. If the Feldstermeiers are involved, I don't suppose they would want the publicity either. What about you, Peter? Are you sure you're up to driving here and back in one day? That's a lot of hauling, particularly with a passenger who needs to be fed about every twenty minutes. We could put you up on the kitchen cot if you don't feel like going back tonight. Will Helen mind your coming on such short notice?"

"Not a bit, she's used to it. See you in four hours or so."

"I'll have a hot meal waiting, unless Jim eats it all before you get here."

"Kiss Guthrie for me, and likewise to you." Peter hung up before Catriona could get in another word. His first call was to Fred Ottermole, to bring him up-to-date and to relay Catriona's information about the rental car place in Hoddersville. Fred was astonished to hear that Jim had been located and promised to call Royal Rentals immediately.

Next, Peter dialed President Svenson's private number. "I thought I'd better let you know that I'm on my way to collect your wandering cowhand, President. He's at Catriona McBogle's in Maine; I'll tell you more later. Any news for me before I go?"

"Not my problem. Keep me posted."

"Right." Peter made sure he had his key to the Feldster house, found Silvester Lomax still standing guard duty, and stayed just long enough to collect one of Jim's suits, a clean shirt, and a change of underwear. His last stop before going to ransom his car from Charlie Ross was the library; he'd meant to pause for a quick word and a fast getaway but his kiss lasted so long that Phil Porble caught him and Helen in the act.

"So, me proud beauties! Is this how you waste the library's time?"

"Oh shush," was Helen's insubordinate reply. "You and Grace did all your prenuptial smooching in these very stacks, and you needn't try to wiggle your way out of it because Grace told me so herself."

Not wanting to get further embroiled, Peter picked up the overnight bag he'd packed for Jim, gave Helen another quick one for the road, and went to get his car. As always, Charlie had the pampered vehicle gassed up and ready to go. Peter handed Charlie's minion a twenty-dollar bill and was off.

The ride was not boring; he had plenty to think about. Catriona's plaint about Jim Feldster's bidding fair to eat her out of house and home rang true enough. Peter had watched Jim Feldster plow through enough second and third helpings at the faculty dining room; he'd wondered how in Sam Hill anybody as skinny as Jim could stay that way despite Mrs. Mouzouka's excellent cuisine. Not to mention the cream Jim had taken home every night in his little tin pail.

Peter was a good driver. He'd learned on tractors and combines whiie still a boy. He'd made this run a number of times since he and Guthrie Fingal had renewed the ties that had been allowed to go slack once they were no longer college roommates and Helen's longtime friend Catriona McBogle had bought the old house just down the road from the forestry school. He knew exactly where to go and how to get there, which was more than he'd ever heard anybody say about Catriona McBogle.

Peter had thought sometimes that the writer's penchant for the road less traveled was the penchant of a screwball; but he was going to have to reassess his thinking in view of what Catriona had achieved without making any fuss about it. How many women would have had the gumption to tackle that precipitous ravine on their own? How many men, for that matter?

Peter hoped Catriona had saved some of those newspaper stories about the Feldstermeier dynasty that she'd got so hung up on. Not that he doubted her word; but he was having one hell of a time rearranging his personal estimate of a man he'd lived and worked with cheek by jowl for thirty years but never really bothered to know. Maybe he should stick to the turnip fields, where he at least knew one when he saw one.

It was too bad Helen hadn't been free to ride along with him. Four hours at a stretch did get to be monotonous when one was driving along a highway all alone. Peter hoped Catriona hadn't been kidding about that hot meal, and that she'd thought to hang a padlock on her stew kettle before Jim Feldster got at it.

He'd made good time all the way. He was glad of the chance to rest once he reached Sasquamahoc and got his feet under Catriona's kitchen table. She did have the hot meal waiting, bless her: a thick soup with plenty of carrots and a plate of hot corn bread, with a man-sized wedge of apple pie to follow. He was a little surprised not to see Jim, but drew up the chair in which he always sat when he came for a meal, picked up his eating tools, and got down to business.

"Where's your star boarder, Catriona?"

"In the back room. He still sleeps a lot. You're not planning to turn around and head back right away, are you? Maybe you'd like to lie down for a little while yourself."

Peter raised a hand to indicate that he was still chewing, and shook his head. "I'll think about that when I get to it. This is great stew, Catriona."

"Grab it while you can."

Catriona took a piece of the corn bread to keep Peter company while he ate.

"Where are those newspaper stories you were telling me about?" he asked when he'd eaten his way to the pie.

"I figured you'd be asking that about now."

Catriona handed over a sheaf of newsprint, which reported pretty much what she'd told him over the phone. It even mentioned the last of Forster Feldstermeier's brothers, a man of mystery who'd chosen to teach at a small agricultural college somewhere in the Northeast rather than take his rightful place among his illustrious family. There was quite a bit more; Peter got through another piece of pie and a second cup of coffee before he quit reading.

"Have you shown any of this to Jim?" he asked.

Catriona shrugged. "I've tried, but nothing happened. He just stared blankly at these papers for maybe ten seconds, then turned away and looked around to see whether there was anything more to eat. I suppose it's funny, in a way. You're sure you don't want to take a nap?"

"I don't dare; you'd have another Rip Van Winkle on your hands. What I need to do is get up and walk around the yard awhile to get the kinks out. Your phone's ringing."

"I know, it's my editor. Tell her I've just taken off for Seattle, will you?"

"You don't really want me to."

"Fine pal you are." Catriona heaved a sigh to beat all sighs and left the table, taking another piece of corn bread with her for comfort.

Peter stacked his dishes in the sink, ran a little water over them as a gesture of goodwill, and stepped outside. This was much too nice a day to be dawdling around the house; he noticed one of those old-fashioned double swings with surprisingly comfortable slotted wooden seats that faced each other, and made himself comfortable in one of the seats. Emerson and Carlyle were already occupying the other side; neither of them showed any inclination to hop across into the visitor's lap. That was probably just as well, coon cats being the hefty critters they were.

The sun was warm but not hot, the apples on the tree under which the swing was sitting were showing red cheeks and smelling the way apples ought to smell. Peter did doze off, not for long, just long enough. He stepped away from that too-tempting swing, did a couple of stretching exercises that he copied from the cats, and strolled around behind the house to see how Catriona's perennial beds were doing.

They were doing fine, thanks largely to plenty of free advice and various donations from Peter himself. Emerson evidently had his mind on higher things; he snubbed the professor and went back to his feline musings. Carlyle was more sociable; he didn't mind playing the cicerone so long as Peter didn't attempt any unwanted liberties. The two of them made a pleasant tour of the flower beds and were just coming back to the front doorstep when Jim Feldster stepped out, smiling.

"Hi Pete. Walking the—"

That was as far as he could get. Peter took the leap. "That's right, Jim, I'm walking the cat. How's it going?"

Not well. The smile was gone, the face was blank, the mouth was open but nothing was coming out. They couldn't let that happen.

"It's nice to see you, Jim. Spotted me right off, didn't you. You ought to, seeing that we've been neighbors for so long. I'm Pete, sure enough. Pete Shandy from next door."

Feldster was showing a little animation now, staring around at the flowers, the apple tree, the two big cats, and finally at Peter himself.

"You're Pete? And I'm—what am I? Where is this? Are we dead?"

"Nope. We're just visiting Catriona. You remember Catriona, Helen's friend from Maine."

"Why?"

"Because she saved your life."

"That so?" Jim sounded as if he didn't much care. Maybe he didn't. "Is she dead?"

"No, she's alive. So are we. Come on, Jim, what do you

say we sit down in that swing over there and just talk a while."

"Talk? Can I talk?"

"You're talking just fine right this minute. What made you think you couldn't?"

"You sure we're not dead?"

"Take it from me, Jim, you're as alive as you ever were."

Which still wasn't saying a hell of a lot. Peter took Jim very carefully by the elbow and steered him toward the swing. "My grandparents used to have a swing like this," he said, for want of anything snappier.

"Are they dead?"

"Yes, they are, but we're not. Got that, Jim? You and I are still alive, remember? You've just been having a hard time, that's all."

"Hard time?" Jim puzzled over this for what seemed to Peter like a long time. He tried moving the arm that Peter wasn't keeping hold of; it didn't come off. Peter let go of the other one; it didn't come off either.

"Hard time, Pete. Is that why I hurt?"

"Yes, Jim, it is. Do you want to tell me about it?"

"About what? I'm hungry."

This was the damnedest conversation Peter had ever got into. He wanted to press Jim to talk about the ordeal in the Lincoln but he didn't dare. That "I'm hungry" must have been a cover-up, although Jim would not have consciously realized it as such. He was not ready to remember, maybe he never would be. That must remain to be seen. For now, Peter could only try to keep hold of that fragile thread of recognition that still ran between himself and the neighbor who knew the Shandys' cat better than he knew the Shandys themselves.

15

IT WASN'T MUCH OF A LEAVETAKING. PETER KNEW THAT Catriona was itching to get rid of her good deed. Once she'd seen Jim in his own lackluster gray suit and shirt and heard him actually speak aloud, even though all he said to her was "Nice cats," she packed him and Peter a picnic basket for the road and handed it over with nothing more than a smile and a wish for a pleasant drive back.

As for what they'd be riding back to, Peter wondered but didn't ask. It wasn't until the two men and the picnic basket were in the car with the motor running and their seat belts fastened that Jim flung open the door on the passenger side and blurted "Were you her?"

Catriona didn't even get a chance to say yes, he'd already slammed the door and started to cry. Peter didn't know what to do except pass Jim the box of tissues that Helen always kept handy in the car and drive off as planned. It was better to leave a man alone with the words that he hadn't been able to get off his chest while he'd had the chance. There were still the telephone and the post office.

Peter did know that there was a filling station about twenty miles up the road; he'd better tank up while he had the chance. Neither he nor his passenger had said a word since they'd left Catriona's. All he said now was "Fill it with the regular, please." Then, remembering that they had provender aboard in quantity, he asked Jim, "How about a sandwich?"

"No, thanks. I'm not hungry."

Too bad Catriona wasn't here, she'd never have believed this. "Want to use the rest room before we leave here?"

"Nope."

"Want me to shut up and let you rest?" he asked, pulling out of the gas station.

That got a rise out of him, anyway. "Huh? Sorry, Pete. Guess I'm not being very good company. I just don't know what to say. My head isn't working right. Do you think I've gone nuts?"

"No, Jim, I don't. Can you remember anything at all about these past three or four days?"

"W-what days?"

"M'well, for instance, do you remember the last time you spoke with me? It was three nights ago, Monday, one of your lodge nights. You were on your way to a meeting of the Scarlet Runners over in Lumpkinton. Does that ring a bell?"

"When we ran with the old machine! Yes, I remember. You were out in your front yard, walking the cat. Jane! She let me pat her."

"Which she doesn't allow from just anybody." This might not be so tough as Peter had expected. "You got that part right on the nose, Jim. Which way did you go from there?"

"Straight down the hill. Mirelle wanted the car, as usual. I thought maybe Elver Butz could give me a lift."

"Great, Jim. Do you recall what you did next?"

"Was it something crazy?" Feldster was getting nervous again.

"It's okay, Jim. Something crazy did happen, but it wasn't through any fault of yours. Elver told me that he'd seen you walking down Main Street toward the fire station where you'd been planning to meet up with him. Were you walking fast or slowly?"

"Fast, I guess. I know I didn't want to keep Elver waiting."

"But you were still ahead of him?"

"If he says so."

"You didn't look back to see if his van was coming?"

"Nope. I just kept walking."

"Anybody try to stop you before Elver got to you?"

This was the bad one. "I—there's something about a car. A big gray one. It came along and I—I can't remember!"

It was a while before he spoke again. Peter had begun to wonder if a sandwich might help, but Jim managed to get himself back in hand, more or less.

"Sorry, Pete. It's as if for a while I died or something. I was just—nowhere. Do you know what happened?"

"I know quite a lot of it, thanks to Catriona McBogle."

"The one back there?" For the first time so far, there was real warmth in the passenger's voice. "How does she know?"

"Because she saved your life, if you really want to know. She'd stayed with us the night after you went missing and started to drive back to her house yesterday morning. She's got a peculiar way of getting lost in odd places. She calls it guidance and I've begun to think she's right.

"Anyway, she'd managed to get off on some misbegotten byway in the middle of nowhere that didn't deserve to be called a road. She said it was all straight up and straight down and one pothole after another; and not a sign of anything human until she happened to spy some kind of structure. She was picking her way along the top of a ridge that fell away sharply on both sides, so she was driving at a snail's pace and keeping a sharp lookout in case another car might come along because there might not be room to pass.

"Fortunately or not, depending on how you look at it, she had the road all to herself, so she stopped to see how that big gray thing down in the gully, which was very deep and almost precipitous, had got there. She was flabbergasted to see that it was in fact a Lincoln town car balanced on its nose in a tumble of boulders, with the tail end up in the air and you inside, not moving a muscle."

"Me? For God's sake why?"

"Good question, Jim. I was hoping you might know. Can you think of anybody who'd like to see you dead?"

"There's Mirelle. She gets pretty mad sometimes but she'd never waste a Lincoln town car on me. I suppose there'll be hell to pay as usual when I get back. If I go."

"Better wait and cross that bridge when you come to it."

Peter was not about to bring in Mirelle until he was forced to. He was relieved that Jim seemed far more interested in Catriona and the Lincoln. Had he been wearing his seat belt? Had he been driving the car?

"Far from it," Peter told him. "You were penned into the passenger seat with lap and shoulder straps. Catriona said you looked like a fly caught in a spiderweb. At first she thought you must be dead, but she got you untangled anyway and was trying to drag you out of the car when she realized you were still alive. What with the way they had you trussed up, whoever they might have been, and the angle the car was pitched at, you were practically standing on your head. No wonder you've been feeling a bit foggy these last couple of days. Not many men could have lived through such an ordeal."

"Are you telling me the truth, Pete?"

"Oh yes. If that gray Lincoln was the same one that picked you up, you were most likely driven straight to where Catriona found you and left there to die of hunger and dehydration. She said you were in desperate straits by the time she got you out and boosted you up that precipice. Or you boosted her, she still isn't sure which. Most likely you each helped the other. She doesn't know how you managed to survive."

"And she didn't even know who I was? That's something!"

Jim sounded both awed and pleased, but mostly pleased.

Peter decided it was safe enough to carry the discussion a step further.

"Actually Catriona had a pretty good idea who you were," he said. "I don't know whether you've been in touch with your family lately?"

"What family? What do you mean?"

"Mind telling me the rest of your name, Jim? It wouldn't be Feldstermeier, by any chance?"

"Oh, cripes! What the hell did you bring that up for?"

"Because you'll have to know all the bad news pretty soon, and I seem to be the one stuck with telling you, though I'm hardly the right person to do it. In plain words, your eldest brother died the same day you were kidnapped."

"Forster died! Don't give me that baloney. He'll outlive the whole damned family, grandchildren and all."

"Doesn't look that way, from what the media's been saying all week. The only reason the family hasn't been able to go ahead with the funeral is that his only surviving brother isn't around to sign and read aloud in the presence of his assembled relations a code of ethics drawn up and written down by the first of the Feldstermeier dynasty to set foot on American soil. He must then append his own signature after that of the demised head of the family, thus taking upon himself the headship with all its duties and all its perquisites. I'm afraid that means you, Jim."

He groaned. "Why didn't she leave me inside that Lincoln?"

"Come on, Jim. You don't mean that."

"Don't I? You ever tried being the unwanted youngest son of an avalanche?"

"No, I can't say I have," Peter admitted. "Tell me about it."

"Later, maybe. How about that sandwich you mentioned a while back?"

It wasn't much over half an hour since they'd left the gas station. Peter wasn't the least bit hungry himself and he wanted very much to hear about the avalanche, but they still had three hours or so of driving and he wasn't about to start anything yet that might be awkward to finish. He pulled over into the breakdown lane, hauled the picnic hamper out of the backseat, and opened the half-gallon thermos.

"Want some coffee, Jim?"

"Sure."

"How do you like it?"

"Any way I can get it. Cream and sugar if there is any."

There was. Catriona had put some cream in a separate little jar and included some of those handy sugar packets that people swipe from eateries on general principles. Peter wasn't interested in Jim's cream. He'd been taking his coffee black ever since Helen had offered to take his Sunday pants over to the tailor in Hoddersville and have them let out a couple of inches.

It was a first-rate picnic. To begin with, there were four hard-boiled eggs; Catriona considered it irreligious not to put the egg before the chicken. There was a good-sized wedge of cheddar cheese and a bag of common crackers to go with it. There were apples and a slab of dark chocolate. The sandwiches were hearty slices off the tag end of a pot roast that Guthrie had cooked the day before. Jim was eyeing those four pot roast sandwiches much as Romeo might have ogled Juliet before they'd been properly introduced. Which, come to think of it, they never were. Peter had an uneasy feeling that his passenger was scheming to snaffle the lot for himself; no wonder Catriona had pushed the panic button once she'd realized that she'd saddled herself with a human tapeworm.

So that was what became of heroines. Woman's work was never done because there was always some man hanging around getting in the way. Peter decided he might as well take one of those sandwiches now since there might not be a second chance. He offered Jim a refill of coffee, noted that Jim's first sandwich was now on its way through the tortuous windings of Jim's alimentary canal and persuaded Jim to try the hard-boiled eggs. Jim ate all four like peanuts, one to a gulp.

It was time to call a break in the supply line. Peter finished his own sandwich, put the hamper back in the rear seat where it couldn't easily be reached and eased his way back onto the highway without asking whether or not Jim was ready to go. He did make a vague noise to the effect that they might stop somewhere after a while. Jim didn't say anything, but cast an anxious backward glance at the repacked hamper to make sure it was safely braced as before. Having it there seemed to reconcile him to the expectation of more food in the offing. He juggled the passenger seat into a more relaxing angle and settled himself for a nap.

Peter let Jim doze for a while, but not for too long a while. It had occurred to him that sons of avalanches appeared to require a damned sight more waiting on than ordinary sons of the soil, and he found himself resenting it. He hit the button that brought the passenger seat back upright.

"Awake, Jim? You started to tell me about the avalanche."

"Did I?" Jim showed signs of going back to sleep; Peter was having none of that.

"Yes, you did. Or words to that effect. I thought Catriona might have been talking to you. She's taking a great interest in all the information that's been coming out about Forster Feldstermeier."

"That's peculiar, Pete. She struck me as being a sensible woman."

"Aren't you being a tad caustic?"

"I expect so. Anything the matter with that?"

"I wouldn't know, Jim. Perhaps you might care to tell me. A little while ago, you described yourself as the unwanted youngest son of an avalanche. This was shortly after somebody, or maybe a couple of somebodies, tried to kill you in a particularly outlandish way. Don't you have anything to say about that?"

"Pete, I know you're trying to help me. I'm just not sure I want to be helped."

"M'well, I guess that's up to you, Jim. We're going to be in this car for another three hours or so, maybe longer if you decide not to go back to the Crescent."

"Any special reason why I shouldn't?"

Oh, drat! Why couldn't a person have had sense enough to keep his mouth shut, at least until they'd eaten the rest of the sandwiches? There was nothing for it now but to tell the truth.

"The thing of it is, Jim—" It was no use, he couldn't do it.

"What's the matter, Pete? Not—my God! Not a fire in the college barns?"

"No, the barns are still standing, or were when I left this morning. It's—oh damn! It's Mirelle."

"What about her?"

"She's dead, Jim."

"That it?"

"Isn't that enough?"

"Yup, that's enough for me. Did someone kill her?"

"My God, Jim, is that really all you want to know?"

"How much more do I need? All I want is to shake the bugger's hand, whoever he may be."

How was a person to answer that one? "If you'll take a hint from me, Jim, it might not be wise to—er—voice that kind of sentiment around the cow barns. Or anywhere else, for that matter, assuming you want to stay out of jail."

"Jail? I should worry about jail. My brother—"

"Your brother is dead, Jim. You're going to have to sign the family pact or whatever it's called, before you can get on with the funeral. It's already had to be postponed, I told you that before. Don't you remember?"

"No, but it's a great idea. So Forster's kicked the bucket. Now you're telling me Mirelle's dead too. Are they all dead down there?"

Jim was wandering again, Peter thought. Maybe he was having some kind of delayed reaction from whatever drug he'd been shot up with before he'd been left to die in the Lincoln. Or was he putting on an act? Had this whole big shemozzle been a carefully staged farce?

This middle-aged man sitting beside Peter now, this man who'd been Peter Shandy's next-door neighbor for three decades, this teacher who had steered God knew how many would-be dairymen and maids along the paths they needed to go, who was always surgically clean but never more than adequately dressed; who was he? Had Peter made a horrible mistake in not heading straight for the state police barracks once he'd got Jim into the car?

16

No, Peter Shandy could never have done that. In the first place, if Thorkjeld Svenson ever got wind that Peter Shandy was going behind his back to embroil the college in a public scandal, he'd skin Peter alive and nail his pelt to the chapel door in accordance with ancient Viking protocol. As for a second place, there wouldn't be one so there was no sense in bothering his head about that. He might as well just keep on driving. If Jim wanted to ask questions, Peter would answer.

There was already one question on the table; this was as good a start as any. "In response to your question, Jim, no. They're not all dead down there. You're not, for one. According to Catriona's research, your brother Forster was in his nineties and died mainly because his time had run out. As for your wife, you know as much as I do and probably more. She was found sitting on a chair in your parlor with a pool of blood at her feet that had run into the carpet pile and dried there. Melchett had to call for an autopsy, of course. He said he'd been treating her with Coumadin for blood clots, and that you'd been supervising her medication. Is that right?"

"If you mean sorting out the pill with the right dosage and handing it over to her because she was too ornery to go ahead and take it herself when she had somebody around to pester into making a soap opera about it, yes, I did, though I often wondered why I bothered. So she wound up bleeding to death on that idiotic white carpet she'd insisted on buying with Forster's money. Huh! Serves 'em both right."

"What am I supposed to read into that?"

Jim shrugged. "Not a hell of a lot, I guess. I'm just letting off steam. It's so seldom I get the chance, so I might as well make the most of it."

"You've really got it in for your brother, haven't you? Any special reason you'd like to talk about?"

"How do I know why I felt the way I did growing up? Because he was the big cheese and I was only a mouse in the wall? Maybe. By the time I was ten, Forster was twenty-three, married to an heiress with a pedigree even longer than her nose, and practically running the business. I'd see him maybe once a month for about thirty seconds. He'd be carrying a big bouquet of flowers for his mother, who also happened to be mine, though she wasn't keen on having it generally known. He'd say 'Hi, Jimmy, how's it going?' and keep right on walking. Every so often he'd send me a big box with some expensive toy in it that his secretary would have been delegated to pick out. Once, when I was eight, Forster bought me a pony. But it was the stable hands who taught me to ride. And all I really wanted was for my big brother to sit down with me just for a little while, as if we were two real people talking together."

Peter didn't know what to say; he fudged. "Then Forster was more than ten years older than you. Would it be impertinent of me to ask how much older than Forster your father was?"

"I honestly don't know, Pete. All I can say is that he married late and made up for lost time. My mother was a great deal younger than he, but it wasn't unusual then for a rich old man to marry a beautiful young woman and start a family when he was practically in his dotage. Father was sharp enough right to the end, though, except that he never did manage to remember who I was. What he'd do was just lump me in with my brothers' kids; I suppose by then he just didn't give a damn."

Jim looked as if he'd been chewing on something bitter. "Neither did my mother. She'd borne and nurtured three fine sons, all of them big and handsome, two of them obedient. Forster didn't have to obey anybody. He was the young god, the rising sun. When my father was dying he gathered Forster, Franklin, and George around him, completely forgetting that I was in the room too. So I slipped out and went for a ride on my pony and caught hell from my mother afterward. Mother had her own way of handing out punishment. She just stood there like a marble statue—she always dressed in white, summer or winter—and explained why Feldstermeiers did not commit the sin of rudeness, no matter what the circumstances. I could hear the icicles dripping off the end of her tongue. I can still remember that lecture, word for word, but I don't recall one single time when she read me a story or kissed me good night. She was always too busy doing noble works for everybody else."

"Who took care of you, then?" Peter asked because he thought he ought to say something.

"Oh, I wasn't neglected; far from it. I had a nanny as early as I can remember, then a governess, then a tutor, then I got shipped off to an ultra-upscale prep school. All I remember about that was having a long series of tutors trying to cram my head full of stuff I didn't want to know."

"Then what did you want?"

"I knew what I wanted from the time I was twelve. That was when I started spending my summers on one or another of the dairy farms in our family cooperative. Being who I was, I got to do pretty much as I pleased, which was to learn all I could about the dairy business; not out of books but right there in the barns and the pastures."

Jim was more animated now than Peter had seen him for a long time. "You know my thesis on dairy management, of course. That was the only really useful piece of writing I ever did. I got my degree on the strength of it and also my job at Balaclava. And I did it myself, with no so-called expert breathing down the back of my neck, trying to tell me I was getting it all wrong when I knew damned good and proper that I'd got every line of it right. And now here you come, trying to tell me I ought to be sitting in Forster's office throwing thousand-dollar bills around because I'm the new king of the cats."

"Hold it right there, Jim. I am not trying to run your life. I'm just trying to be a good neighbor, damn it." Peter thought for a moment of what he'd just said, then he burst out laughing. "Could you tell me what we're bickering about? Want another sandwich?"

"Ah, why not?" Jim was grinning too, sheepishly. "I thought I'd managed to hog them all."

"Maybe you have, now that you mention it." Peter pulled over to the breakdown lane and took inventory of Catriona's picnic hamper. "No, by George. There are still two left, and plenty of cheese. Well, we can fix that easily enough. Any coffee left?"

"Seems to be." Jim sloshed the thermos jug around, nodded, and poured out another paper cup's worth for each of them. "Guess we'll have to go easy, though, it might be a long time between milkings. Shall I cut you a hunk of cheese?"

Peter shook his head. "We'll want it later, we still have quite a lot of road to get over. And you haven't yet told me where you want to go."

"Because I don't know yet. Are we still in Maine, Pete?"

"Yes we are, but not for much longer. Assuming for the sake of argument that you did decide to get in touch with your family, how would we find our way?"

"Get on the Massachusetts Turnpike, go straight on out toward the Berkshires, and turn left at the filling station."

"Any particular filling station?"

"I'll let you know when we get there, unless I chicken out. I'm scared, Pete, and I don't know why."

"That so?" said Peter. "I can think of several reasons, the first of them being that somebody has lately gone to a great deal of expense, inconvenience, and possibly personal danger in an unsuccessful attempt to kill you. Has anybody ever tried to do that before?"

"I couldn't say. Mirelle used to rant about it every so often but she never got down to business. She knew Forster would cut off her allowance if she tried any funny stuff."

"Forster seems to have been something of an autocrat."

"I'm not sure I'd go quite that far, Pete. It's just that he always knew what was best for everybody and he was always right. If Forster gave you good advice and you didn't take it, then it became your personal responsibility to run your own life. Once you'd made your own bed, you might as well lie in it, there wouldn't be any second chance. Forster was dead set against divorce in the family, but I have to say that he did try to make life less uncomfortable for any poor little lambs that went astray."

"How so, if I may ask?"

"Well, for instance, take Mirelle and me. She was pretty and lively and I married her chiefly because my dear mother didn't think poor little Mirelle would fit comfortably into the Feldstermeier ambience; which she sure as hell didn't. That part was all right, I'd never fitted into the family picture either. Neither of us wanted children. As I soon found out, Mirelle only wanted what was going for herself and I figured there were already too damned many Feldstermeiers extant. I had my job at Balaclava and my lodge buddies, I didn't need any help from my family and I refused to take any. But Forster was too damned philanthropic for me. Rather than leave us to go through a wretched life snapping at each other's throats, Forster commended me for my dedication to the cause of dairy management and made Mirelle a personal allowance; not a big one but enough to give her the satisfaction of collecting her check every month and squandering the money on hairdressers and trips to Boston."

"And porcelain figurines?"

"Oh, sure, her collectibles. Anything useless and expensive was right down Mirelle's alley. I guess you think I'm taking her death rather coldly, but whatever spark there was between us died years ago, Pete. And of course she had her little flings on the side that I wasn't supposed to know about and didn't give a damn anyway. There was a steady stream of tomcats at our back door. Mirelle really was quite pretty when she was younger, and she's still not—wasn't—bad looking. Remember that oaf whom Sieglinde Svenson got fired for moral turpitude? With a student, supposedly? Mirelle scraped through that one by the skin of her teeth; I'd have had to leave Balaclava if the whole truth had come out. Then there was that Bob somebody who wound up in jail. She really knew how to pick 'em. Lately she's been seeing some guy in Worcester, I think it is. I noticed she'd been putting a lot of extra miles on the car."

"You wouldn't happen to know the fellow's name?"

"No, but I suppose I could find out. Some of the lodge brothers are regular bloodhounds. Of course we're all sworn to secrecy about what goes through the lodge."

"Which lodge would this be?"

"Sorry, Pete, I'm sworn to secrecy." Jim sounded perfectly serious and no doubt was. "I shouldn't even be telling you now but I figure I owe you something."

"Thanks. Now I'll give you one, for whatever it may be worth. I don't know whether I've mentioned a small thing that happened last night before Mirelle died. It was the president's annual reception. Mirelle didn't go because she didn't think it would be proper, what with you missing and everything. But anyway, the Porbles and Helen and I stopped by your house on our way back from the reception and this man she addressed as Florian was just leaving. He was very well dressed and drove a Cadillac Seville. Do you know anything about him?"

"Probably my nephew Florian. He's Forster's oldest son and a bit less of a poop than most of the other nephews. With Forster dead and me missing, he probably hoped Mirelle might have some helpful information. I can't think why else he'd have picked that night to pop up on my front stoop."

"Had he ever visited you before?"

"He might have dropped in on Mirelle occasionally when I wasn't around. I'm not home much, between my work at the college and the various lodges. We do a lot of volunteer stuff, you know, and we're seriously committed to it. Some of us, anyway. What did Florian say to you?"

"Nothing. He disappeared as fast as he could, for fear she'd introduce us to him. I thought for a second he was Elver Butz."

"Florian wouldn't be overly pleased to hear that." Jim was really enjoying himself by now. Peter was still on the fence.

"You're going to talk to him, then, Jim? You're not entirely estranged from your family after all?"

"Well, no, not entirely. I inherited a share in the business from our father. Even though I don't do anything about it, I can't seem to get rid of that blasted family. They have to get my signature on various documents once a year or so in order to keep the business running. It's all very formal, old-fashioned gentlemen's agreement stuff. I told Forster time and time again that he might as well write me off the books because I didn't want to play, but he'd just give me one of those benevolent all-things-bright-and-beautiful smiles he was so good at and remind me that I was, no matter what, a greatly loved member of the family, which was a lot of pigeon piddle. I tried making rude remarks but they just rolled off his back so I quit trying. If there's one thing I've learned in this life, Pete, it's that you can't lick the system."

"That so?" Peter's mind was on not missing the signs for

the Massachusetts Turnpike. "We ought to be pretty near the pike, shouldn't we?"

"Not far now," Jim agreed. "We might as well get on, if you don't mind risking a bunch of my relatives. Or you could just dump me off wherever suits you best and I'll send for a company car to pick me up."

Peter took that one for what it was worth. "Left at the filling station, right?"

"This might make us as much as an hour longer than if we were going to Balaclava. You sure you don't mind, Pete?"

"I don't mind." Peter wasn't sure by now whether he minded or not; he might as well go with the flow. "So actually your family farm isn't such a long way from the college."

"Well, that depends on how you measure. It's back in the boonies, you'd need a pair of bloodhounds to find the way in unless you'd been drilled on all the twists and turns. The Feldstermeiers have always been fairly rabid about their privacy; that's one of the reasons why they could never stand having Mirelle around. I forget what the other six hundred reasons were, but some of the relatives will remind me, I expect."

Jim didn't say much after that. Neither did Peter. It was dark by now and he was tired; he had to concentrate on his driving and invent new insults for thoughtless drivers who kept their high beams on when there was no damned need of it. Engrossed in innovative scurrilities, Peter almost jumped out of his skin when Jim yipped, "Left at the filling station."

"You mean there really is one?" Peter wished there'd also been a stoplight but there wasn't, so he waited out two semis and a beat-up old Chevy with his left blinker counting the seconds for him and got across without scathe. "Now which way, Jim?"

"Down the road and take the next left, then a sharp right at the big boulder. I'll tell you the rest as we go."

Too bad they hadn't brought Catriona McBogle with

them, Peter thought. This sounded like her kind of driving. At least this road was in pretty good repair and less precipitous than the one she'd described back in Sasquamahoc. He negotiated the big boulder with exaggerated care because there hadn't been a street light since they'd turned off the pike. The sky was pitch black by now, and he hoped to hell there wouldn't be much more of this hide-and-seek.

He was pondering the possible efficacy of a primal scream when his headlights showed him a cow; not a real cow, but an excellent simulacrum of one. "Feldstermeier Farms" was not painted across its ribs and loins; but Peter could sense that the thought was there.

"This the place, Jim?" It was the only remark he could think of offhand except for the cow, and that was too obvious.

"Couldn't miss it, could you? Just turn up the driveway and keep going until you hear the buckshot rattling against your windshield."

"If you say so, brother. What's that up there? The janitor's cottage?"

In fact, Peter knew perfectly well what it must be; one of those family-oriented farmhouses that never gave up. What had started out in 1820 or thereabout as a simple wooden farmhouse had rambled on down through the many decades, adding an ell here, a barn there, a handsome three-story late-federal house attaching itself to a covered walkway that connected with the original structure. And so on and so on, as the begetters begat and were merry withal, except for an occasional malcontent like the one who for so long had been calling himself simply James Feldster.

How many family members might be living there now would be interesting to count, Peter thought, sometime when he was feeling less knocked out. At the moment they were being approached by a burly young man in a white coverall that had *Feldstermeier Farms* embroidered in a tasteful grass green color on the right sleeve.

"Excuse me, sir, but these grounds are private."

Peter jerked his head toward Jim. Jim rose to the occasion.

"I know all about it, sonny. I was born here. Have somebody take the car around and tell whoever's answering the door these days that Jim's back. And hurry up, we're hungry."

"Uh—yes sir!"

The chap in the white suit took off like a rocket. Peter and the prodigal son made their more leisurely way to the front entrance. At the crucial moment, the door was flung wide in welcome.

"Well, well, James! Nice to see you back. And this is—?"

"Professor Peter Shandy, a colleague of mine. Who's running the shop these days?"

"Depends on who's asking. You are, I guess, or will be as soon as we let 'em know you're here. You'll be staying this time, I hope. We need you, James."

17

THE WOMAN WHO'D ANSWERED THE DOOR MUST BE A RELATIVE, Peter thought, or else a longtime member of the staff with special privileges. She looked to be about Jim's age; maybe she'd been his childhood sweetheart. Peter was ready to believe whatever anybody chose to tell him.

"We're pretty much full up for beds on account of Forster's going," she was saying. "Things being as they are, though, I don't see why you shouldn't use Forster's own room, Jimmy. You're entitled to it, and the Lord knows *he* won't be wanting it again. As for Professor Shandy—my gosh, professor! You wouldn't by any chance be the Shandy who invented the Balaclava Buster?"

Peter never quite knew what to say at times like this. "We generally say propagated, Mrs. er—"

"Just call me Agnes, everybody does. So you're the great Shandy. To think I'd ever get to meet you in the flesh! What a pity that Forster had to go just at the wrong time. I couldn't tell you how many times he wished he could get around to meeting the creator of Brassica napobrassica balaclaviensis. And you're not even an old man. Not what I'd call old. Do you ever think of how many thousands upon thousands of cows in far places that you've made happy, Professor Shandy? And the farmers too, of course. We've been mighty gloomy around here the past few days, I have to tell you;

you're just the tonic we need. You are planning to stay awhile with Jim, I hope. It's his place now, you know. Come right in and make yourself at home. Where's the luggage, Jim?"

"Forget it, Aggie," Jim growled. "All we've got with us is a picnic hamper, and that's borrowed. Any chance of a bite to eat?"

So this was life among the bigwigs. It was not quite as Peter had envisioned it, but then things never were. He wanted very much to let Helen know where he was and that he'd be spending the night at James's ancestral pile. He was relieved when Agnes delegated a dapper little fellow whom she called Curtis to take Professor Shandy upstairs and make sure his cordless phone was working. The professor would be in the room next to Mr. James; which had been Mr. Forster's dressing room, Curtis said, until it had become necessary for a male nurse to be available at all times.

The cordless phone worked fine. Curtis handed it over to Peter with a dapper little bow and disappeared into the room that was now Mr. James's. Curtis's face was clean and close-shaven, his hair parted an exact half-inch to the left of his crown, and his outfit of gray trousers, white shirt, black coat, and gray-striped tie no doubt just what the well-dressed valet should wear.

Never having seen one before, except in a few old black-and-white movies starring Adolphe Menjou, Peter wouldn't know. Helen was suitably impressed when he told her where he was and that he was being valeted by Adolphe Menjou. As they talked, Curtis buzzed back in with a full complement of dinner jacket, black trousers, boiled shirt, black silk socks, black patent leather evening pumps, and a gentle intimation that dinner would be announced in ten minutes. Before Peter could remonstrate, Helen was off the phone and Peter was having his black tie properly tied by an expert.

The wonder of it was that everything fit. Being built short in the legs and broad in the shoulders, Peter couldn't possi-

bly have worn just any old clothes that Jim might have left
lying around. How had he been turned into a Feldstermeier
clone so fast? Maybe a layout of this grandeur maintained a
roomful of spare monkey suits to lend to visiting dignitaries
like the propagator of the Balaclava Buster. Maybe everybody was a dignitary at Feldstermeier Farms.

"You ready, Pete?"

That was Jim, coming through from the master bedroom
wearing the exact same outfit as Peter's. Peter had seen Jim
in a dinner jacket on a few previous occasions when he was
on his way to some solemn rite or other, but never without
an insignia of office, usually something around his neck that
clanked. It was disquieting, but what could a mere guest do?

"Ready as I'll ever be, Jim," he said. "Go ahead, I'll walk
behind you and steer by your coattails."

"No, you won't. Come on, we might as well get this fool-
ishness over with. At least the food won't be too bad."

There were sixteen people in the spacious drawing room.
Peter assumed it was a drawing room; he might have known
a place like this would have at least one. As soon as those inside spotted the two latecomers, the doors to the dining
room were flung open and a tall old woman with a long,
sharp nose began putting them in their places.

The men tended to be on the youngish side, Peter noticed;
all of them tall, blond, and aristocratic in their bearing.
Some of the women were quite a lot older; Peter deduced
that the three with the most pearls must be the widows of
Forster, George, and Franklin. Whether anybody realized
that Mirelle wasn't there was not remarked upon. The rest of
the older women might be cousins or aunts or possibly Jim's
sisters. Jim had never mentioned having any sisters, but then
he'd never said anything at all about his family until that
ride down from Catriona's this afternoon. Even though hypothetical female siblings might be barred from holding office in the family firm, that didn't necessarily mean they
couldn't share in the family meals.

There hadn't been time for introductions before the party sat down, which was probably just as well, Peter thought. He wouldn't be able to distinguish one Feldstermeier from another anyway, not in these elegant but monotonous dinner jackets. At least he was pretty sure he had Mrs. Forster pegged. She must be the doyenne in black lace who had supervised the seating and was now taking her place at the far end of the table.

Peter noted that the older women in the company wore much the same kind of gowns, either black, gray, or purple, top quality and made to last. No doubt they had other jewelry but tonight they were making do with simple strings of genuine pearls and modest diamond brooches. They must be showing respect to the honorably fallen patriarch, but nobody appeared to be grieving, as why should they? Forster Feldstermeier had done his work and done it well. Surely now he deserved his rest.

Jim was presiding at the head of the table, probably for the first time in his life, and managing with greater aplomb than Peter would ever have thought he could. Maybe clothes did make the man, or else those many fraternal banquets Jim had attended over the years had rubbed off the hard corners. Or maybe the ordeal that he was still going through had given him some new insights. He apologized for his last-minute entrance, explaining simply and truthfully that he'd been detained, then introduced the friend he'd brought with him.

"I expect you all know everything there is to know about the famous Balaclava Buster rutabaga that has meant so much to so many cattle," Jim began. "But I wasn't sure how many of you had ever met the horticulturist who's responsible for its existence, so I thought I'd bring him with me. His name is Peter Shandy, and I'm proud to say that he's a colleague of mine at Balaclava Agricultural College and also my next-door neighbor. You want to stand up so they can get a look at you, Pete?"

"Not particularly."

But Peter knew the protocol. He half stood, pinning a sheepish grin to his face and sending a fast and furtive glance around the table. Then he stood up straight, gave a snappy two-minute commercial on the droves of students whose lives and bankbooks had been enriched by the untiring effort and inspiration of Professor James Feldster, as he was known far and wide in the world of dairy management, and sat down. Nobody applauded because it wouldn't have been the thing; but a few of them looked as if they might have, under different circumstances. Some asked questions, which enlivened the talk until the long table had been cleared of its main courses. Desserts were brought in, and the conversation drifted back to family concerns.

Peter had been seated between Mrs. Forster and Mrs. Franklin. It was Mrs. Franklin who dropped the brick. "I must say I'm surprised not to see your wife here, James. Mirelle's not ill, is she?"

"Not now, she isn't."

Jim took his last, loving bite of a custard-filled napoleon heavily freighted with genuine home-whipped cream, laid down his dessert fork and spoon, touched his lips with his napkin, and answered Mrs. Franklin's question.

"She's dead."

Gasps were heard around the table, mostly from the women. Mrs. Forster decided she'd better handle this herself. "Goodness, James, you *have* been out of touch. How long ago did she die?"

"I don't know, I haven't been home to find out."

"I don't believe I quite understand."

"Neither do I," said James Feldstermeier. "Do you, Pete?"

"Does anybody? I'll tell you as much as I can, Mrs. Feldstermeier, but I'd better warn you that it's not exactly dinner table conversation."

"Why? What happened?"

"Our local family doctor thinks she had a massive hemorrhage. He thinks she accidentally overdosed on a blood-thinning drug, but there's also a possibility that foul play is involved."

"Surely not!"

"We saw nothing of this in the news," said Florian.

"And you won't," Peter assured him. "Not if President Svenson has his way. And he usually does."

Jim cleared his throat. "I know you're all concerned about that family pact, so I'd like to get the signing over with as soon as possible. I agree with Pete that this isn't the right way to end a meal, but it's the first chance I've had to bring up the subject of Forster's funeral. Was that what you and Mirelle were having that private meeting about last night, Florian?"

Clever Jim. Peter wondered how the man could have kept up such a lackluster facade for so many years. Maybe it hadn't been so lackluster after all; and Mirelle had for once been speaking the exact, simple truth about her husband's Peter Pan proclivities.

"Were we?"

The biggest, blondest, and handsomest of the Feldster-meiers, the fortyish man whom Peter, Helen, and the Porbles had caught so brief a glimpse of before he'd leaped into his Cadillac and vanished from the Crescent, was making an in-depth study of the green glass finger bowl that had been set in front of him.

"I did stop in, as Mother suggested I ought to, partly on account of that rumor one of our farmers let drop about your strange disappearance and partly because it seemed the decent thing to do."

"My God!" Jim reared out of his chair. "Have you been keeping tabs on me all this time?"

"Well, of course. We have a family duty toward you, Uncle James, whether you like it or not. Anyway, Aunt Mirelle seemed glad enough to see me. She'd been rather down in the dumps, I gathered, not so much because you were missing as that it was the president's reception and she'd had to stay home because you weren't there to escort her; but I may have misjudged her. You didn't exactly drop whatever you were doing and rush back when you got word of your own brother's death, did you, Uncle James?"

"That's not quite how it was, Florian. I did not know about Forster's death. If a message in any form was sent to me, I never saw it." He slumped back into his chair, holding his bowed head with his elbows on the table. "You tell them, Pete. I can't."

"Why not?"

Florian must be Forster's eldest son, hence the next after his Uncle James in line for the headship. No doubt he'd been handed the role of Crown Prince at birth, as his father had been so honored more than ninety years before. Florian had had a long wait for his crown. He must have been thinking ever since his father had begun to show signs of lying down with the cows that he had the position sewed up. Now here was this all-but-forgotten will-o'- the-wisp of an uncle barging in and taking over, leaving the favored son nothing to do but grin and bear it. It was almost painful to watch such a gorgeous, great animal struggle with his frustration.

Peter had to force himself to begin talking. He floundered at first.

"I might as well start with my cat, since she and Jim are on neighborly terms. Today is Thursday? On Monday night, around seven o'clock, Jim came out of his house, which is next to mine, stopped to pat our cat, and mentioned that he was on his way to a lodge meeting. Mirelle had taken their one car because it was her bridge night, so Jim hoped to be picked up by a fellow lodge member.

"That's all I saw of Jim that evening. It's only the beginning of the story, however. About two o'clock early Tuesday morning, Mirelle came pounding at our front door. She was in a state of hysteria, crying and screaming that Jim hadn't come home and wanting me to go get him, wherever he was.

I'm afraid I didn't respond as enthusiastically as she thought I should and we wound up having a row, but that too is beside the point.

"As it turned out, various eye witnesses saw Jim walking down our main street toward the fire station, where he and the lodge member, Elver Butz, were to meet. Just before he got there, a big gray Lincoln town car came along, pulled up barely long enough for Jim to get in, and was not seen again."

Now for the ugly part. "Jim didn't show up at the college all day Tuesday, which was totally unlike him. We now know that he spent a night and a day inside the Lincoln, held hanging almost upside down by two seat belts, without food or water. On the evidence, it appears that Jim had been given a big jab of some drug to knock him out as soon as he'd entered the car Monday night. He was driven to a deserted road, the car was driven over a steep ravine where it landed nose down among the huge boulders, and Jim was simply left there to die."

"How dreadful!"

That was one of the lace-clad ladies. Peter didn't know which and didn't see that it made any difference, so he continued his tale. "When I got home Tuesday evening, I found that my wife's longtime friend, Catriona McBogle, had dropped in on her way home to Maine and was prevailed upon to stay with us for the night. By that time, as you doubtless know, Forster Feldstermeier was attracting a good deal of attention from the media."

"Which he would far rather have done without, as would we all." That was definitely Mrs. Forster.

"M'yes, I can see your position. In any event, Miss McBogle happened to buy a newspaper and became quite fascinated by your late husband's almost incredible record of accomplishments. She's a writer of mystery novels, as you may already know; she wanted to learn more about Mr. Feldstermeier so she went looking for a public library."

"Really? How odd."

"By her reckoning, it made excellent sense. You'd have to know Miss McBogle to believe in her. She has the world's most unreliable sense of direction. She relies absolutely on guidance, which is a fancy word for blind luck, as far as I can make out; but it seems to work for her. Anyway, the librarians threw an impromptu party for Catriona, after which she headed for Maine, or thought she did. She got onto some godforsaken back road and didn't know how to get off it, so she just kept chugging along. She was at the top of a high rise that sheered off steeply into a deep ravine when she noticed what she thought at first must be some kind of silo at the bottom of it. Then she recalled the gray Lincoln town car that had been such a big topic of conversation around Balaclava ever since Jim disappeared. Catriona realized that she could be looking at the car Jim had been taken away in; she decided she'd better get down there and make sure nobody was trapped inside. Catriona McBogle is quite a person, as Jim can tell you. Want to take it from here, Jim?"

"I can't, Pete. I don't remember."

So it was left to Peter Shandy to let James Feldstermeier's assembled family learn what agonies the ill-matched pair had endured getting away from that rockbound Lincoln. He described what personal sacrifices Catriona had made for a lost, speechless, more than half-dead man of whom she'd known almost nothing, and had barely recognized at all in his dreadfully mishandled state. Only hours ago, Peter had driven to Maine to bring Jim back to Massachusetts and the magic words—"Walking the cat?"—had been spoken.

"So that's what brought him out of the shock, just those few little words." That was Mrs. Franklin, the loquacious one. "And then to learn that his wife is dead, possibly murdered? I can't believe it!"

There were one or two others who weren't believing it either, Peter noticed. He was not a bit surprised that Florian led the charge.

"Your friend did say, Uncle James, that this Miss McBogle writes mystery novels?"

Jim cast a pleading look Peter's way. What could a friend do but oblige? "Yes, she does, and quite successfully. If you're wondering whether this story might be just one more of Catriona McBogle's brain-children, I suggest that you examine the evidence. There's been, as you know, a good deal in the papers and on television about Forster Feldstermeier, all of it laudatory; but there has been nothing at all, to the best of my knowledge, about what happened to Jim. That, for your information, is because a few key people have banded together to make sure that nothing of a sensational nature leaks out until the outrage visited on Jim and the appalling death of his late wife has been thoroughly investigated."

"Very prettily said, Professor Shandy."

"Thank you, Mr. Florian. If you want to discuss this matter with President Svenson, I'll be glad to arrange an appointment for you. If you'd care to see the mess somebody's made of Jim's arm with a hypodermic needle that he or she either didn't know how or didn't care how to use properly, I expect Jim would be willing to roll up his sleeve and show you what's left of a large and nasty hematoma. However, I don't recommend that you do it here at the table after the excellent dinner we've all enjoyed and for which I personally thank you very much. Now, if you'll excuse me, I'd better change out of my borrowed plumes and drive myself back to Balaclava."

"Pete, you can't go tonight," Jim protested. "You've been driving all day."

Mrs. Forster could not be overjoyed at seeing her long-wandering brother-in-law seated in the patriarch's chair, but she was taking it like a lady. "We hope Professor Shandy will at least stay the night, James. Your solicitude for my brother-in-law's welfare and for all our wounded sensibilities is much appreciated, Professor, and I really do not think that a man of your age ought to be out driving on strange roads at this hour."

Even Florian could not deny his uncle's colleague a night's rest, particularly since he himself was no longer in the catbird seat. Peter admitted to himself that he hadn't been particularly keen on driving another hundred or so miles in the dark, even if he didn't consider himself quite the doddering gaffer that Mrs. Forster made him out to be. He yielded gracefully when the liqueur tray came around and chose a small tot of a brandy the like of which he'd never before encountered. As the warming fluid trickled down his expectant gullet at the rate of about two dollars a sip, he decided that there was something to be said for opulence, after all.

18

AFTER THE KIND OF DAY HE'D HAD, PETER WASTED NO TIME getting out of his borrowed finery and into a bed that was softer than he'd been used to and awfully lonesome-feeling with Helen not in it. He was not about to complain, however; a sleeping bag laid across a picket fence would have been paradise enough for one night.

He did have some thought of lying there for a while mulling over the day's events, but Morpheus beat him to the draw. When he woke up, Peter felt fresher and more rested than he'd felt since the night before the night that Jim Feldster had been kidnapped. That brandy must have therapeutic virtues of a special kind; he wished he could get the recipe. Winifred Binks-Debenham, his favorite bootlegger, would probably know how to concoct a reasonable facsimile out of cattail roots and burdock juice, or something along that general line; he must remember to ask her about it.

But first things first. Peter wished he'd brought a change of clothes; he was going to feel pretty scroungy skulking out of a mansion like this in yesterday's wilted shirt and wrinkled pants. At least he could be clean in body if not in haberdashery; he stepped into the shower and made good use of the opportunity. He was relieved upon stepping out of the tub to see one of those all-enveloping Turkish toweling bathrobes that he'd hitherto found only in deluxe hotels, which he didn't frequent often. There were also an electric razor and one of the do-it-yourself kind. Peter chose the latter and found it the clear old quill, as his father had been wont to say. By the time he emerged from the bathroom, shaven and swathed in the opulent robe, he was only mildly surprised to find his clothes, from necktie to socks, laid out for him, freshly cleaned and pressed and ready to travel.

Even his shoes were polished until they practically glittered. Peter glanced around nervously, wondering whether that ubiquitous valet was lurking just outside. He hurried to complete his toilette before Curtis, or whoever worked the morning shift, barged in to brush his teeth, tie his shoelaces, and check behind his ears. He finished in the nick of time; Curtis was right on the dot, making a *hem*ming noise in his throat and tapping lightly before he opened the door.

"Good morning, Professor Shandy. Mr. James presents his compliments and hopes you will join him at your convenience for breakfast in the small family dining room."

"My convenience being now?"

"If you're quite ready, sir. Would you wish me to escort you downstairs?"

"Oh, I think I can sniff it out by myself. Just draw me a map and lend me a bloodhound or two."

Curtis permitted himself the freedom of a smile and a chuckle. "If you prefer the thrill of the hunt, sir, take a sharp right at the foot of the stairs and keep straight on until you smell coffee brewing. The small dining room will be at your left. Mr. James is already down."

"Thanks for telling me. And thanks for seeing to my laundry."

Peter did not suppose that Curtis had had any hand in the laundering himself; there were likely six or eight washers and pressers hard at work in the nether regions. He did not think it his place to ask, and he did want his breakfast. Curtis's directions had been right on the button: Peter found the small dining room with no difficulty, partly because he spied a row of chafing dishes on the buffet and partly because the small dining room would have been far too big to miss even without the chafing dishes, much less the predicted smell of coffee.

And there, by golly, was James, looking oddly foreign yet perfectly at home in a well-worn but superbly cut tweed Norfolk jacket with knee breeches to match, hand-knit Argyle socks, and a pair of leather brogues heavy enough to anchor a thirty-foot sloop.

"Hi, Pete. Haul up and set, unless you'd like to browse at the trough first. Take whatever you want and yell if you don't see what you like. That's what I do."

Since when? Could this possibly be the same old Jim Feldster who'd been such a dim bulb around campus all these many years? Certainly it was not the piece of human wreckage who had crawled out of a crashed limousine, shocked into a silence that might never have been lifted without the help of one hell of a woman whom he hadn't even known.

James Feldstermeier was now, and Peter might as well get used to it, no longer the plodding old milkman trudging off to the college barns or clanking down the hill from the Crescent to spend a few hours with some of his multifarious lodge brothers. The events of last night had left no question that Jim was in fact the lineal head of a worldwide corporation. Whether he'd continue to repudiate any claim to his hereditary office and go back to his barns as though nothing had happened was yet to be seen. Right now, Peter wouldn't bet a nickel either way.

When Peter entered the dining room, Jim had been the only other one there. By the time he'd sailed into his first selection and Jim his second or third, or maybe fourth or fifth, others were coming in and making a beeline for the buffet. Evidently the Feldstermeiers kept farmers' hours even though none of them looked as if they did much, if any, of what Peter himself would call farming.

They were all being gracious as could be to their new patriarch and his friend the professor. Last night's signing of the Family Pact seemed to have lifted a pall from the entire assemblage. Even Florian, looking superb in knee breeches like Jim's, had quit sniping at his uncle now that the reality of the situation had seeped in, and appeared to be making a genuine effort to be sociable.

Forster's funeral had been set for half past nine in the family chapel. No outsiders had been invited. Peter had hoped they'd give him a hint to sheer off for home before the service began, but nobody did. Then he thought perhaps that Jim was expecting to drive back to Balaclava with him, to sort things out with Dr. Svenson about his lectures and the work in the college barns; and to make some kind of arrangement about Mirelle and the house.

As usual, things didn't work out Peter's way. Jim entreated him to stay through the service in the chapel, Forster's burial in the family plot, and the luncheon that would follow. It would have been hard to decline, considering the circumstances. Peter reconciled himself to putting a message for Helen on the answering machine and went back for a second helping.

Interestingly enough, once the dowagers had come to the table, it was the question of Mirelle's obsequies that they chose to be thoroughly worked up over. Knowing the late Forster's views on divorce, his own widow, the widows of her two brothers-in-law, and just about everybody else except James himself were all in favor of giving her a decent burial as a member of the family. Even James was finally worn down, their argument being that he had in fact remained lawfully wedded to Mirelle ever since their long-ago marriage; and had still been occupying the same house with her at the time of her demise even though he'd happened to be unavoidably detained elsewhere just then.

It was generally agreed that nobody except immediate relatives would be invited to Mirelle's burial service. These would be James's relatives, of course; Mirelle had never mentioned to them any relatives of her own. She might not have had any whom she'd cared to own, although nobody said so out loud to spare James's feelings.

The service would be kept as brief as was consonant with the solemnity of the occasion. As yet, Peter could give no information as to when and where the body would be released. Therefore, there was no sense in trying to set a date and a time, particularly considering the bitter lesson which the family had recently been given regarding deadlines that turned out not to be tenable.

What with one thing and another, this discussion went on until somebody looked at the time and realized it was almost nine o'clock. Those who had come to breakfast casually dressed, including James and Florian, dashed upstairs to change. Peter was relieved that he'd worn a good gray suit for the long drive, though of course not his new one. He didn't really suppose he'd have created any stir if he'd shown up in overalls; Curtis would inevitably have produced an appropriate outfit at a moment's notice, or maybe even sooner.

Being as ready as he could get, Peter merely stood at the foot of the staircase and watched the others come down. Nobody had taken any great effort to shine; simple daytime dresses with a minimum of jewelry were in order for the women, the men were dressed much like Peter himself. Once the family were all together, they simply walked more or less en masse from the house to the chapel, sat down quietly in the uncushioned pews, and listened while Mrs. Francis played a few of Von Weber's gentle short pieces on the relatively unpretentious pipe organ behind the altar.

While they were walking, James and Florian had evidently made an amicable arrangement between them that it was Forster's son and not his brother who would deliver the eulogy. That wouldn't break James's heart, but it might easily have brought tears to some eyes if the Feldstermeiers had been the sort who went in for that sort of thing. Florian spoke well and affectionately of his father. James had taken on that blank, stone-faced look that Catriona had found so disturbing, and kept his eyes fixed on nothing that was visible to anybody else. Finally a clergyman—Peter never found out what his denomination was and didn't suppose it mattered—said a short prayer for the repose of Forster Feldstermeier, and the service was ended.

Those who felt up to it followed the eight hardy pallbearers up a knoll to the family burying ground. The grave was dug and lined with evergreen in the old-fashioned way, the coffin was lowered into the grave. Some of the mourners cast handfuls of earth over the closed coffin. Others had brought armfuls of flowers from the family gardens to strew on the grave after it had been filled in, to hide the rawness of the exposed soil.

A few days from now, Forster Feldstermeier's grave would have been planted over with hardy chrysanthemums, ground covers, and shrubs that would bloom next spring and summer. Peter Shandy would be unlikely to see the graveyard in its glory then, or the great house exuding its hospitality from every door and window to persons of good will, or the widows in their lace and pearls. But what did it matter? Forster Feldstermeier was off in some other world by now; Peter didn't suppose those present would relish the funeral luncheon any the less because the guest of honor was no longer among them in the flesh.

It seemed hardly credible that anybody who'd partaken of that gargantuan breakfast could be hungry for yet more food now that the funeral rites of passage had been duly performed; but nobody was backing off, including Peter Shandy himself. He didn't know why; he tried to rationalize his greed on the grounds that he had another long drive ahead of him.

But he didn't, not really. According to Jim, Balaclava Junction wasn't much more than a hundred miles from here, roughly two hours' traveling time, depending on the flow of traffic and the condition of the roads. Would he be going back alone or with a passenger, and how soon could he decently raise the question? He'd thought it would be just a matter of getting Jim aside and asking him yes or no; the problem was that everybody else was just as eager as he was to get the new family head's ear.

Jim was tolerating the impromptu interview surprisingly well. He was smiling and nodding and even putting in a word or two of his own every so often. Peter had never seen Jim so affable, not even when he'd been exchanging pleasantries with Jane Austen. The mouse was definitely out of the trap.

Of course everything was different now. James Feldstermeier was no longer the lonesome little boy whom nobody stopped to remember. He was cock of the walk, king of the castle, cream of the crop. He was not a young man, though. Could he stand the kind of pressure that went with the headship of a huge international enterprise like the Feldstermeiers'? Would the day come when he caught himself wishing desperately to be back among the college cows, and would Thorkjeld Svenson take him at his word? Jim had trained so many good young dairymen and maids that surely some of them would rise like cream to the top, leaving no space for an old has-been.

But this was no time for bleak soliloquies. Now that they'd got the late, nonagenarian patriarch safely laid to rest, the party appeared to be picking up. Family relations less closely connected and some of the higher echelon executives, with their spouses, were starting to arrive. Florian had taken upon himself the genial task of presenting them to Mr. James. It would take a while for each of those who came to mourn and, no doubt, stay to be fed, to be herded through the receiving line that had formed itself as if by chance but was moving on in a thoroughly efficient manner with a little help from Florian.

Peter gazed upon the mounting wave of visitors with dismay that was working up to become unconcealed horror. How was he going to cut Jim out of the herd long enough to ask whether or not they'd be riding back to Balaclava together? Worse still, Peter was collecting a small queue of his own, thanks to the over-enthusiastic offices of Aggie, the woman who'd flung wide the door for the black sheep returning to the fold and spread the word about Professor Peter Shandy, propagator of the famous Balaclava Buster.

What price glory? Peter was heartily sick of this endless buffet, of the whole pageant, interesting as it had been for the first several hours. Now he could hear a harpist tuning up in the banqueting hall, or whatever it was called by the Feldstermeiers. He wished he could grab hold of Curtis for even a few seconds; that facile factotum would surely know how to extract a yea or a nay as to whether or not Jim wanted a lift to Balaclava. Peter had an increasingly strong feeling that the newly crowned king was not about to be parted from his guests; he had an even stronger feeling that he himself wanted to go home.

Jim was entering a new life, but his old wife was still dead and Thorkjeld had charged Peter with finding out how and why. Thanks to Catriona, this was one time the husband was not an active suspect. Jim had not moved ten feet out of her sight, or out of sight of her food supplies, since several hours before Mirelle's death, so there was no pressing need to force Jim to return to Balaclava at the moment, even if the Feldstermeiers were willing to let him out of *their* sight again so soon.

The queues were breaking up into chatty groups. The widows and their daughters, or somebody's daughters, were being gracious. The servers at the buffet were serving for all they were worth. Down in the kitchens, the cooks must be gearing up for a real sit-down dinner after the lesser orders had dropped out. As Jim turned to say good-bye to someone or other, Peter saw his chance and grabbed it.

"Jim, tell me quick. Do you want a ride to Balaclava tonight? I've got to get going."

"Oh Pete! Not yet, surely. This is almost as good as a lodge meeting."

Peter nearly said "So how come you're not clanking?" but decided it wouldn't be quite the thing in such distinguished company. "Then I'd better just slip out and go along in my own car. You can get somebody to drive you easily enough, can't you?"

"Well, sure, but why don't you sleep over again tonight? Somebody can drive your car to Balaclava tomorrow morning. Our helicopter can have us there in fifteen minutes."

The helicopter was tempting, but Peter held firm. "What shall I tell Thorkjeld?"

"I'll talk to Svenson when I've decided what I want to do."

That should be an interesting meeting, Peter thought, the formerly drab and dull milkman bearding the behemoth in Svenson's own den.

"Sorry to miss saying good-bye to your family, Jim. This has been a memorable experience and I'm glad I've been able to help a little, but the show's not over yet, not by a long shot. It looks to me as if you're going to have your hands full here for the rest of the day and half the night. Tomorrow too, like as not, and who knows after that? In the meantime, I'm supposed to be helping the president find Mirelle's killer, whatever that may mean. I assume, by the way, that you have no objection to my entering your house on the Crescent."

Not that Peter needed to ask, since that house belonged to the college; always had and always would, according to the deeds that were drawn up many years ago when a farseeing college treasurer suggested utilizing some unused land on the grounds to build a few houses for faculty people, offering them at reasonable rents and keeping them in such good repair that they were still comfortable places to live in. What would happen to the house Jim and Mirelle had lived in, so close together and so far apart?

Peter didn't say any more about that; he didn't want to sound pushy. Jim Feldster might not take umbrage at being questioned but James Feldstermeier had far more important matters on his mind. Another group of bigwigs from various European countries had just arrived. Florian was performing handsomely as aide-de-camp and hinting with just the flicker of an eyelid that his uncle might be doing a bit more in the hospitality line.

Jim barely had time to murmur "Sure, Pete, go ahead," before his sense of duty forced him to get busy shaking more hands, receiving more condolences, and telling more diplomatic lies about how kind it was of all these distinguished persons to have flown all this way in order that they might pay their homage to the illustrious Forster Florian Feldstermeier.

19

PETER SANG ALL THE WAY HOME: OLD BALLADS HE'D HEARD from his grandparents, popular songs of a later period that his mother had played on the piano while the family stood around and made a joyful if not particularly tuneful noise, college songs, kids' songs, songs that his mother wouldn't have touched with a ten-foot pole. It was not very nice of him, Peter realized, to leave a house of mourning with "Hallelujah, I'm a Bum" on his lips, but he sang it anyway. Breaking away from the luxuries of the Feldstermeier compound made him feel much as Sisyphus might have felt if he'd simply parked his rock somewhere and walked away unencumbered.

Peter wondered how Jim was making out with the foreign dignitaries. He'd been pleasantly astonished to notice how readily Mr. James, as his former next door neighbor was now being addressed by everybody who got the chance, had fitted himself back into the clan after all those years of refusal even to bear the family name. Clothes were alleged to make the man; had those tailor-made tweeds and worsteds and sleek-fitting dinner suits given Jim a new feeling of self-esteem? Maybe just the fact that Mr. James was sitting in the catbird seat had put the glow in his cheeks and the spring in his step.

How offhandedly Jim had accepted Mirelle's death; how

matter-of-factly he'd taken advantage of Catriona McBogle's goodwill and compassion. Perhaps this rather cold-blooded behavior had been due to his having been brought up by a series of caregivers who'd done their best for the child, collected their pay, and gone off to do the same for somebody else's pampered young one. Probably few, if any, of these capable stewards had gone in much for sending birthday cards or other small remembrances to the child they'd left behind.

It was strange, come to think of it, how one person could see another as not much more than a familiar part of the landscape for years on end, then suddenly become an indispensable though most likely transitory factor in that other's life. Peter was doubting more and more that Jim would come back to Balaclava College. He did feel a bit wistful about that helicopter. It would knock the socks off a lot of people, particularly those students who'd taken the milkman for a dull old stick, if Professor Feldster, who walked over from the Crescent every morning, became Professor Feldstermeier, who casually commuted to classes in a noisy doodlebug with a pinwheel on top.

Well, life was full of surprises. Peter got one himself when he'd parked his car down at Charlie's as usual, walked on up to the Crescent, and stopped short before he'd got to his own front steps. The September shades were falling a little sooner each night; Peter had naturally assumed that the Feldster house would be in darkness, with the stolid form of a Lomax lurking in the ligustrum, but how wrong could a neighbor be? Every switch in the house must be turned to "on"; each window was ablaze with light; and somewhere inside, a short but sturdy form in black stretch pants and a too-short jerkin was popping around like a pea on a hot griddle.

"I'll be damned!"

Peter could do nothing but stand and gawk until his own front door opened to reveal Helen waiting to greet him.

"If you're that snake oil salesman who's been around here, Mister, we don't want any. What's the big idea, staying out all night wallowing in the fleshpots? You know perfectly well that fleshpots don't agree with you."

"Bah, humbug. Kiss me again, Tallulah baby, but take it easy this time. I'm a shadow of my accustomed dashing and handsome self, for good and sufficient reason. What the flaming perdition is going on next door?"

"I think it may be a whirling dervish. She showed up here early this afternoon in a taxi from Claverton; or so my spies tell me, and hasn't sat down since. She claims to be Mirelle's sister. I don't doubt it for a minute. Have you had anything to eat?"

"Madam, you jest. I've eaten more in the past twenty-six hours or thereabout than I ever ate before and hope never to eat again. I fled the buffet that came after the funeral luncheon, which had been preceded by an early breakfast that didn't break up for two hours straight. The breakfast came in fifty-seven different chafing dishes, all of which people kept pressing me to eat some of so that I wouldn't faint from inanition walking up to the chapel, which is all of a hundred paces from the house. I expect somebody must have fixed me a picnic hamper of stuff to snack on while I was on my way home, but I'm afraid to look. Do we own a chafing dish, by the way?"

"No, we don't, and I have to say I've never missed it. We do have that fondue pot that you heat over a candle and dunk pieces of bread in on a long-handled fork and get them all gooked up with cheese and drop the bread off the fork. I believe you can dunk other things too, but what's the point?"

"That's a good question," said Peter. "Where did the fondue thing come from?"

"Who knows?" said Helen. "Let's pass it along to Edna Mae Ottermole. She's getting up a white elephant sale for the benefit of the Balaclava Junction Police Force Cruiser Fund. Are you exhausted from all those chafing dishes?"

"Not to mention a two-hour drive on an over-full stomach," Peter reminded his wife. "I did get an offer to stay over and get a ride back in the Feldstermeier helicopter tomorrow morning but I didn't want to. As you may by now have realized, the hours I've spent with thee, dear heart, are as a string of pearls to me."

"Is that so? What have you done with the oysters?"

"Ate them in a moment of absentmindedness, I suppose. It got so I couldn't tell a plate of Wiener schnitzel from a case of dyspepsia; not that there isn't a resemblance between them, in a manner of speaking. Now that we're on the subject, you wouldn't happen to have an old cup of weak tea and a stale bannock kicking around, would you?"

"I always thought bannocks were where the wild thyme grew. Oh dear, I must be catching it from that nice sophomore who lugs the cartons of books around for me. Wilfred, his name is. He's an awful punster but it is rather refreshing to know that we have some students around here whose vocabularies run to more than fifty words. His father is a trainer of seals."

"You don't say. Does Dan Stott know about this?"

"I have no idea, Peter dear. You could ask him but I think perhaps the best thing for you to do right now is to sit down at the kitchen table and have a nice bowl of bran flakes. Or crackers and milk. I used to like crackers and milk, I don't know why I never have them anymore."

"Tout lasse, tout casse, tout passe, as your friend Catriona would say. At least I think she probably would, but one can never tell with Catriona. Have you spoken with her since I took Jim off her hands?"

"Yes, she called around suppertime, or what would have been supper if Jane and I hadn't decided to settle for poached eggs. They're really more breakfasty, but we figured there was no sense in our waiting because we weren't sure when you'd be back. We did miss you, in case you were planning to ask. As for Catriona, she wants to know how you feel about the subject of beatification."

"You sure you didn't leave out a *u* along there somewhere?"

"The deletion was deliberate. She thinks you're a saint. What are your thoughts on the matter?"

"Oh, put me among the undecided. Unless you'd rather dump me in a turnip patch someplace where I won't be in the way. Then I can decompose at my leisure and stew in my own juice."

"Peter, that's disgusting. I'm going to poach you an egg. Or would you prefer two?"

"Two eggs are better than one, assuming they're not bad eggs. Where's Jane?"

"I think she's upstairs in the office, hiding under the couch. She happened to stroll over into the Feldsters' yard, or whatever we'll have to start calling it now, I suppose; and that woman leaned out the window and deliberately threw a whole pailful of water at her. And it wasn't clean water either. Jane and I were both deeply affronted. I'd have got under the couch with her to soothe her nerves but there wasn't room for both of us. I do hope that woman isn't going to be around here for long."

"One can always ask. How are those eggs coming?"

"They'll be along when they take the notion. Stick a slice or two of that good rye bread Iduna made into the toaster and get yourself a plate. You're not at the Feldstermeiers' now, you know. What did you do for clean clothes?"

"Put them on, of course. They have minions in the basement who toil all night over the washtubs. At least I think they must. Either minions or brownies. If it's brownies, one's supposed to set out a saucer of milk on the hearth, as I understand it; but there's this fellow named Curtis who takes care of everything so I didn't have to. You should have seen me last evening in my monkey suit and black tie, I was the beau of the ball. Or would have been if they'd been holding one; but of course the circumstances wouldn't allow for that. How do you think I'd look in plus fours?"

"Baggy. Slide your plate over here, the eggs are done. What brings up the subject of plus fours?"

"The fact that they take less time to say than knicker-bockers."

"Oh yes, of course. You had me puzzled there for a moment. Don't tell me Jim Feldster's taken to wearing knee breeches."

"All right then, I won't. You'd be amazed at how that man blossomed out once he'd got his old hand-tailored tweed bloomers on. I hope he wears them tomorrow. I can just see the president's face when Jim steps out of that helicopter dressed like Gene Sarazen."

"Peter, you don't mean it! What did you do with our camera? We should be there to take pictures before Cronkite Swope beats us to the draw. Is Jim going to let you know when he's coming?"

"Not that I know of. He was rather offhand about it, almost condescending; though I don't suppose he meant to be. Those people out at the old homestead appear to be taking Jim very seriously as the new head of the dynasty and he's falling right into the part. I got the impression that they all, particularly the three widows, feel a need to have a father figure around, ridiculous as it may sound."

"I don't find it ridiculous at all, Peter. If they've spent most of their lives following the patterns that Forster set for them, they probably want everything to go on as it always has."

"M'yes, I see your point. The atmosphere struck me as being a good deal slanted to the feudal side. You may be interested to know, by the way, that the fellow we saw leaving Mirelle's champagne party is in fact named Florian."

"Do tell. Is he nice?"

"I don't know. He looks to me as if he'd been groomed to be next in line for the robe and scepter. He was a bit snotty at first, but he's obviously well drilled in diplomacy along with everything else. Florian must know a damn sight more about the business end of milk than Jim does. He'll still be the crown prince rather than the reigning monarch, but he'll have a good deal more latitude, I should think, than he did when Forster was still alive. It may not be a bad spot for him to be in."

Helen saw the matter from a different angle. "How do you suppose Jim himself feels, now that you're not there to shore him up? Catriona's being a bit mother-hennish about how he's going to adjust to his new role."

"How's Guthrie bearing up without Jim around?"

"It sounded to me when we last talked that he's treating the situation as a case of good riddance," Helen replied, "for which I have to say I don't blame him. Guthrie and Catriona have been making excellent progress just by being themselves and treating each other accordingly these past three months. I can't imagine how Catriona and Jim Feldstermeier could ever wind up in a satisfactory relationship, even if he did start to cry when it came time to leave her."

"Maybe it was his old teddy bear that Jim was crying for," Peter suggested. "According to some of the things Jim told me when I was driving him back to the family estate, he never got much in the way of mothering when he was a kid. He was the youngest of the four sons by so long a gap that his own father thought he was somebody else's grandchild and he missed out on the deathbed scene."

"Peter, that's ridiculous."

"Oh, I don't know. It could easily happen in a house that size, with so many relatives wandering in and out. It's like living in a big lodge with a lot of ritual attached. They even lent me dinner clothes to wear last night so that I wouldn't embarrass the footmen. They fit me perfectly. Apparently they keep a regular wardrobe of extra clothes in various sizes, just in case somebody happens in without the proper accoutrements."

"How do they know what will fit?"

"Don't ask me. I mentioned that fellow Curtis. He takes care of the haberdashery department and practically everything else, as far as I could see. He's the one who trotted out Mr. James's own knickers from God knows how many years ago. I shouldn't be surprised if Curtis had kept James's first bootees and teething ring in case he takes a notion to marry again and beget his own crown prince."

"It's rather late for Jim to start begetting, isn't it?" said Helen.

"Don't ask me. I didn't notice any indication that he'd be ready to try; but he did mention that male members of the family tend to marry late and choose wives young enough to be their daughters, or even granddaughters. It's amazing what money can do."

"But not any more, surely," Helen protested. "What sort of woman would marry her grandfather?"

"A young lady of good family who goes around refraining from sneering at the less advantaged, as far as I could figure out on such short notice. It wouldn't be her *own* grandfather, of course. Is there any more tea in the pot?"

"A little, but you can't have any. You'd be tossing and turning all night. You're already overexcited, as your dear old highly paid nanny would have told you if you'd had one."

"No, she wouldn't. According to Jim, nannies are neither old nor dear. They just show up in their uniforms, snap to attention, and get on with teaching the kiddies not to drink out of their finger bowls. Once the tads have got the finger bowl principle thoroughly memorized, the nanny takes off for greener kids and in comes a governess. After her, if the child happens to be male, comes a tutor; at which point the parents ship the kid off to a highly recommended private school, assuming that they happen to think of it."

"So that's how it's done? Aren't we lucky not to have been born to the purple. Was that what they did with Jim?"

"Not entirely. Jim told me that he'd been allowed as a youngster to spend summer vacations at some of the company-owned farmhouses, living with the farm people and helping out in the barns. By the time he'd passed his twelfth birthday, he'd learned all he needed to know about the fundamentals of dairy management and had decided that this was what he wanted to spend his life teaching. Dairies and secret handshakes appear to have been pretty much all Jim ever did get around to learning. Just what he's going to do with either skill now that he's First Feldstermeier should give pause for a good deal of thought, wouldn't you say?"

Helen nodded. "Oh yes, no question. He'll also have to do something about the house next door, whether he wants to or not."

"And I have some thoughts on a different subject, my love. Shall we dance?"

20

"EXCUSE ME, LADY. WOULD YOU HAPPEN TO BE SHE WHOSE bed I've been sharing?"

Peter had wakened early, full of beans and raring to go. Somewhat to his chagrin, he found Helen up and about before him, wearing an apron over her tweed suit, taking a pan of biscuits out of the oven. "Egad, woman," he said when he'd finished kissing his wife and giving Jane Austen her ritual pat, "are there no bounds to your aspirations? Just because I mentioned that grossly over-calorized breakfast at the Feldstermeiers', you don't have to burble around like an out-of-work Easter rabbit trying to drum up a clientele. Wherefore the sudden spate of housewifery? Don't I feed you and Jane well enough right here? Should I go back to the Feldstermeiers' and run through the scenario again?"

Helen shook her head. "Not today, thank you. It's just that I'd got to thinking about that whirling dervish who's parked herself next door. It occurred to me for some reason that Mirelle had never got a chance to eat those biscuits Grace Porble baked for her; so I thought I'd make a few for her sister now that there's somebody alive over there to enjoy them. Or not, but that's up to her. Her main purpose, according to Grace, is to help out."

"Help out how, for instance?"

"Oh, dusting the doodads and snaffling Mirelle's best underwear for herself, I suppose. All she said was 'I'm Mirelle's sister, I've come to help out.' Then she whizzed off and began flapping a feather duster around like a turkey with a bad case of vertigo. Grace claims she hums like a top as she whirls and is probably a robot from one of the faster-moving asteroids, so maybe she'd prefer a basket of iron filings or something of that sort. Anyway, she hasn't apologized for throwing her dirty scrub water on Jane. I wanted to shoot her as soon as I saw what she was up to but then I decided that wouldn't be very kind, considering that she's just lost her sister. Hence the biscuits."

"I see. But how come I'm not getting any biscuits?"

"Good question, dear. You just go ahead and eat all your conscience allows. I'll be right behind you with a tape measure and the bathroom scales."

"You're all heart, Helen. Will you be dropping in at the library today, or do you think you'd better stay home and hold an umbrella over Jane in case Miz Twinkletoes doesn't care for biscuits?"

"She'd better like mine," said Helen. "Some kind soul ought to have a little chat with that woman as to what's done and what is not done around here. As you well know, Grace Porble is not a woman accustomed to making snap judgments but she did not take kindly to Mirelle's sister. Though of course Grace didn't just whirl up to her and say so."

"Um. Did Grace happen to mentioned how long the sister's planning to stay?"

"Probably till the funeral, I would think. What are your plans for the day? You're not scheduled for any classes, are you?"

"Not this semester, but I've got the president on my back. I also need to check in with Ottermole and have a few words with Cronkite Swope, if I can find him. Cronk generally knows what's either happening or about to happen. If there's anything blowing around but horsefeathers, I'd like to know.

You haven't talked to the president while I was gone, I don't suppose?"

"I've barely seen him at all; he's still up to the eyeballs and I really have nothing earthshaking to give him. Except my hearty sympathy," Helen added after a moment's thought, "and the sympathy really ought to go to Sieglinde for having to put up with him."

"Blah. You know perfectly well, my love, which of that pair rules the roost on Valhalla. How about meeting me for lunch in some secluded rendezvous, assuming I don't get ambushed by the tootsie in the tutu?"

"That would be nice, and I think we'd better leave Jane in the house. One never knows which way a cat may jump." Helen picked up the elegant little feline and gave her a few minutes' quality cuddling. "Poor Jane! Did that mean old woman in the tutu throw dirty water on you? She'd better not try it again or we'll all three go over there and give her a good, hard scratch. Have you any idea where we might find a markdown sale on backscratchers, Peter?"

"Sorry, ma'am, we only sell rutabagas here. Could I interest you in a first-rate line of Swedes?"

(Professor Shandy refers here to *Brassica* campestris, a large, yellow-fleshed turnip introduced to Britain and thence presumably from Sweden to America ca. 1781. Hence the name Swede employed in this context.)

Helen wasn't buying. "No, thank you. Why should I care for tall, handsome, blond males of Nordic descent when I already have a genuine honest-to-gosh mongrel Yankee with a bald spot on top for the brains to bulge out of? Will you answer me that?"

"How can I? You've rendered me speechless."

"Not everyone could have done it. You'll think of something sooner or later. How about a little kiss to keep me going till lunchtime?"

"Oh, all right, if you insist. Pucker up, me beauty, here I come."

"Well, that was quite pleasant," Helen remarked after she'd got her breath back. "Why don't we think to do this more often?"

"I suppose we might, sometime or other. Jane won't mind."

"Dr. Porble will mind, however, I've really got to scoot. Try to stay out of trouble. I'll look for you in the dining room."

Peter hadn't originally intended to make the Feldster house his first port of call. He'd been more inclined to nail Cronkite Swope before Balaclava County's ace reporter had dashed off to some other hot spot on the local scene. Now, however, it seemed more sensible to take the handiest first, particularly since Helen had forgotten to do anything about the biscuits she'd baked for the dead woman's relative.

Peter's first thought was to deliver the biscuits; his second was to eat them himself. He'd look pretty silly charging over there with a token of welcome if the woman turned out not to be welcome at all. He put on a professional yet mildly benign expression, the one he used when introducing himself to a classroom full of new students, walked in a purposeful way down the brick path from his own house to the sidewalk, and turned sharp left at the path to the house next door.

The vacuum cleaner was going full blast. So was the radio, so was the television set that Mirelle had spent so many idle hours watching. Whoever this woman was, she was not about to deny herself whatever was going. Peter did the only thing he could in the circumstances: he walked over to the baseboard and pulled out all the plugs.

"What do you think you're doing?" The question came out as a high-pitched squeak.

"I'm sorry to break in on your concert," Peter said, "but this was the only way I could make you hear. My name is Shandy. My wife and I live next door. Am I correct in assuming that you're Mirelle Feldster's sister?"

"Her younger sister. I'm living here. It's my house now."

This was a stopper. Peter wondered whether Mirelle's younger sister might be another borderline case who functioned well enough in certain areas and spent the rest of her time in a fantasy world that she could twist around until it met her criteria. Then again, maybe the woman was simply trying to be cute. After all, she had on a one-piece jumpsuit that featured large pink pigs cavorting through a field of purple daisies with picnic baskets balanced on their heads. What was a man to think about that?

The sister who looked like Mirelle was trying to mop around Peter's feet now, giving him a pretty strong hint to be gone; but he was not yet ready to leave.

"How long have you been here, may I ask?"

"Since yesterday." She sloshed the mop across the toe of Peter's left shoe. "Look, it's nice of you to come by, but I have a lot to do here. If you're looking for a certain kind of company, forget it right now. And would you mind keeping that disgusting cat of yours over in your own yard? I can't stand cats, they make me sick to my stomach. The door's this way."

"Thank you."

Peter was not about to get into a shouting match with this she-devil. By now he was convinced that she was in fact Mirelle's sister who really believed she had a right to live in the house where her sister had so recently died, though why she would think that when Mirelle's husband would, under normal circumstances, still be in residence was beyond him. He gave her a curt nod and left the house without having got any farther inside than the door from the entry to the kitchen.

At the campus security office, Alonzo Bulfinch was holding down the desk this morning. Lonz, as he was more generally known, had been a friend of the Lomax brothers for many years. He boarded with Mrs. Betsy Lomax, who knew even more about goings-on in Balaclava Junction than Helen Shandy did. Mrs. Lomax had the advantage of cleaning for the Enderbles, the Stotts, and the Porbles as well as the Shandys; was related to about half of Balaclava Junction and a third or so of nearby Lumpkinton, and belonged to almost as many ladies' aid societies as Jim Feldster did to his all-male lodges, though he might have to give them up now that he was perched on the top rung of the dairy business.

Sociable soul that he was, Alonzo greeted Peter like a long-lost relative, offered him a chair, and was all set to regale him with some peanut brittle that he and Betsy Lomax had together cooked up last night; but Peter demurred on the grounds that he'd been eating far too much sweet stuff lately and Helen was making nasty remarks. He did take the chair, though, and drank a cup of black coffee to be sociable. The courtesies dealt with, he got down to brass tacks.

"I've been out of town for a couple of days. I must say I was surprised when I got home last night to see a woman I didn't recognize in the Feldster house who claims to be Mirelle's sister. She was still there this morning, so I stopped by to see what the story was. She told me in so many words that the house now belongs to her, that she's living in it, and intends to stay on. Anything you can tell me about her?"

"Yup." Alonzo opened a big ledger and pointed to the most recent entries. "There she is. Perlinda Tripp. She said she was Mirelle Feldster's sister, and there was no reason not to believe her. She sure looks like Mrs. Feldster."

"How did she get here?" Peter asked.

"Came in a taxi from Claverton. All she had with her was a couple of suitcases that didn't weigh hardly anything, and a big tote bag that she wouldn't let me carry for her. I figured she must be meaning to pack up some of her sister's bits and pieces to take home with her. She showed me some kind of paper that purported to give her the right to function as the executor and the inheritor as well, being as how she was the only one of her family left alive, or so she said."

"Wonder how she heard about Mirelle so soon?" asked Peter.

"Hey, that's right!" Alonzo turned pale. "The president will have our hides if the leak came from this office."

21

BACK WHEN CRONKITE SWOPE HAD BEEN A CUB REPORTER FOR the *Balaclava County Fane and Pennon,* then a struggling weekly, he'd been awarded the post of staff photographer, developer, and printer. This was mainly because he was the only one on the staff skinny enough to fit into a wretched cubbyhole that his new boss had conned him into believing was a darkroom. Now that the *Fane and Pennon* had become a thriving daily, thanks in no small part to the efforts of Cronkite himself, its top newsman had serfs of his own to do the dog work. There was even a genuine darkroom, with a full-time attendant to process the many strips of film that the staff photographers brought in. Nevertheless, Cronkite still preferred to do his own processing when he could find the time. Knowing this and not wanting to trust the films he'd taken of the late Mirelle Feldster, with Dr. Melchett looking on, to anybody not absolutely dependable, Peter Shandy had elected to entrust his films to the Fane and Pennon's ace developer.

He'd known that Swope could be trusted implicitly not to give anybody at all so much as a peep without Shandy's own express permission; he hadn't reckoned on giving the hotshot newspaperman a bellyache. Perhaps he shouldn't have used color film for so grim a subject; black-and-whites would have been at least somewhat less grating on a young man's sensibilities. There was only one thing to do.

"Swope, when you've finished turning green, would you mind giving me your opinion as to why Mirelle Feldster would have stayed sitting in that fancy chair long enough to bleed to death without so much as lifting a finger to save herself? Look at her. Her hands are clean as a whistle while everything else looks like a reject from an abattoir. See what I mean?"

"How can I help it?" Cronkite stifled a belch. "It's pretty gruesome, all right." He gave his alimentary canal another moment to settle down, then went bravely on. "You know, professor, maybe I'm crazy; but what it looks like to me is that somebody took a paintbrush and a bucket of blood and swabbed her face with it. Then they dumped the blood all over the rug and that fancy gown she was wearing, being careful not to get any on the arms because they didn't want to ruin the chair."

Peter stared at the color prints he'd taken, shaking his head slowly from left to right and back again. "I'll be damned. That's one I wouldn't have thought of."

"That's because you don't know my mother. Last Christmas, we all clubbed together to buy her the new parlor set she'd been wanting for the past fifteen years. Now that she's got the set, she won't let any of us sit on it for fear we'll mess up the upholstery. Women get sort of goofy over their furniture, don't you think? Look at all those doodads Mrs. Feldster had stacked up on that tippy little table, for instance. She must have had enough of those china figures to start her own gift shop with, and what did she get out of them? Let 'em sit around and collect dust, or else spend half her life trying to keep the fool things clean."

"M'yes, you have a point there. Poor woman. Her sister's taken on the cleaning job, did you know that?"

"I never knew Mrs. Feldster had a sister."

"Neither did we. Yet somehow she's popped up here before anyone else knew Mirelle was gone. You didn't happen to call her for a statement, did you?"

"I told you—I never knew a sister existed. Honest."

"Sorry," said Peter. "I guess I'm clutching at jack-straws. Any other news?"

"Well, I stopped by the Lumpkinton fire station last night on my way home from the interscholastic checkers tournament. Some of those kids are pretty sharp; Balaclava Junction won two firsts and a runnerup. The guys over in Lumpkinton are still wondering about what's happened to Jim Feldster. He's been one of the Scarlet Runners for I don't know how long. They're saying something about a big gray Lincoln town car that Jim either did or didn't get into last time the Runners met, depending on who's telling the story. It gets a little nuttier every time; now they're claiming that Jim's body's been found in the woods somewhere out beyond Beamish."

"That so?"

"Who knows? Beamish is a heck of a long ride from Lumpkinton and Jim's never been much of a traveler that I know of. What do you think, professor?"

Peter would greatly have preferred not to think at all. "Has anybody actually seen the body?"

"Gosh, I couldn't say. Somebody did mention something about a wrecked car and a woman's footprints on one of those umpty-seven back roads they've got out there."

"I hope you're being careful about starting rumors. You know what President Svenson's like when it comes to anything that might reflect on the college. Perhaps if you were to drop in at his office. . . ."

Peter let his voice dwindle off. Why was he continuing this foolery, wasting time listening to Cronkite Swope speculate about Jim Feldster's bizarre disappearance when in fact the erstwhile milkman was both alive and safely ensconced as CEO and patriarch of the Feldstermeier dynasty? Jim had already agreed with Florian and the rest of the

Board of Trustees—all Feldstermeiers, of course—to ignore the media's bombast and let the newshounds bay as they might. After a day or two of yelping, they would go find themselves a new bone to gnaw on.

Couldn't the same excellent principle be applied at the college? The whole story would inevitably come out sooner or later; why not simply tell the president what he knew and let him take it from there? Peter jerked his head in the general direction of the administration building.

"Come on, Swope. The beans are bound to get spilled one way or another. I'd say our wisest course right now would be to dump what I've got in Svenson's lap and run like hell. Are you game? If you are, let's go."

"You mean right now?" All of a sudden Cronkite's voice was two octaves higher than usual and a good deal shriller.

"Why not? Quit bugging your eyes out, Swope. He's not going to eat you."

"That's what you say."

"No, it isn't. 'Say not the struggle naught availeth' is what I say."

"Oh, all right. My sole regret is that I have but one life to give to my editor. What are we supposed to tell King Kong?"

"As much as you both need to hear."

Which was what? As Peter chivvied the grumbling Swope across the campus to the administration building, he wondered why he was doing this, and what were his chances of surviving. Perhaps it wouldn't be so bad. There was, for instance, the revelation of Jim Feldster's true identity and a legitimate question as to whether there'd be any chance of James Feldstermeier's coming back to take up his familiar role in the dairy barns.

There was also the question of Mirelle's sister and probable heiress, who appeared to be under the delusion that she was in line to get the house now that Mirelle was dead and Jim had disappeared. The only way she'd ever get to live in

that house would be to marry a member of the faculty within
the next week or so, which was not going to happen, if Peter
Shandy knew his men. Anyway, the only available bachelors
just now were a few graduate students still in their early
twenties, if you didn't count the dairy expert who'd spent
half a lifetime bemoaning his marriage to Mirelle and was
not about to get stuck twice.

And was there any chance Mirelle might have committed
suicide, either on purpose or accidentally by overdosing on
that blood-thinning medication Melchett had prescribed for
her? Odder things had occurred, no doubt, although Peter
couldn't think of any offhand. He and Swope were going
into the administration building now; Peter fingered the revolting results of his foray into the realm of medical photography and braced himself to beard the president in his
den.

Peter might dramatize his superior's roars and rampag-
ings but he and Thorkjeld Svenson were close friends; as
close, at least, as protocol within the constraints of Academe
would tolerate; Academe being pretty much what Sieglinde
Svenson chose to make it. Just now, Mrs. Svenson was not
available for consultation, however. A college president's
wife has many duties and occupations of which relatively
few are ever noticed or appreciated by the persons who benefit from them. It was perhaps just as well that Sieglinde was
not in her husband's office when Peter Shandy drew out his
envelope of photographs and spread them across the president's blotter pad.

"Yumping Yehosaphat!" Svenson edged his swivel chair
back a few inches; his face contorted in horror and disgust.

He had seen the murdered Mirelle Feldster Thursday
morning after his reception, but somehow the photographs
were worse.

"What?"

President Svenson was not one to waste words. Peter

knew he was asking for a full report on all he'd learned these past two days.

"When we got to the Feldster house after the reception Wednesday night, Mirelle was just saying good-bye to a big, impressive-looking man who drove a customized Cadillac Seville and answered to the name of Florian. I know now that her visitor was Florian Feldstermeier, a son of Forster Feldstermeier, the dairy magnate. You've probably seen Forster's obituary plastered all over the papers these past few days."

"So?"

"So I'm afraid what it's going to boil down to, President, is that you'd better begin scouting around for somebody else to teach fundamentals of dairy management."

"Urgh!"

"I know, and I'm sorry, but that's the way it goes. The man we've all known and liked fairly well for the past thirty-odd years as Jim Feldster turns out to be none other than James Feldstermeier, youngest and last of Forster's three brothers, newly crowned king of the family castle and chief executive officer of International Dairies."

"Urrgh!"

"Well you may say so, President," Peter rejoined, "and a fat lot of good it's going to do the rest of us."

"Holy cow, Professor!" Cronkite Swope had been busy making up captions in his head, now he blanched. "You don't mean—my gosh!"

"It's my gosh too, and see that you remember it."

"You're saying President Svenson doesn't want the *Fane and Pennon* to publish—"

"Sorry Swope, but that's the way it is. And that's the way it's going to remain until we get this mess straightened out, if we ever do. Right, President?"

"Urf!"

Cronkite Swope was disappointed. "If you say so, honored sir."

Peter continued. "This has grown into quite a saga already and don't ask me how it's going to end. The one thing I'm completely and positively sure of is that we'd damned well better watch where we're stepping or we'll have the whole dad-dratted legal department from International Dairies beating us over the heads with milk cans full of subpoenas. I can give you a quick rundown on what's happened so far; but we'll have to keep it in the lodge, as Jim himself would be the first to tell you."

"Ungh!"

"I couldn't agree with you more heartily. You both know by now, of course, how Jim Feldster started out for a meeting of the Scarlet Runners and never got there, and how Jim's wife came pounding on our front door, yowling for me to go out and round up her errant husband. I refused, mainly because I was fed up with Mirelle's histrionics and also because I knew she'd snaffled the car in order to drive about a quarter of a mile to play bridge with her girlfriends. I assumed—wrongly, as it turned out—that Jim would stay overnight in Lumpkinton and ride back here in the morning with Elver Butz."

Svenson nodded; he knew already about Elver Butz. Peter went on. "I'm not proud of the way I handled the situation but there'd have been no point in my going to look for Jim Feldster that night. As things turned out, he'd already been forced into that big car, drugged, driven to some godforsaken dumping ground in the wilds of Beamish, if you know where Beamish is, and sent hurtling over a precipice in what was probably the same gray Lincoln that he'd been forced into when he was on his way to meet Elver."

"Police?"

The word came out like a blast from a howitzer. Knowing Svenson's feelings about dragging the college into any sort of publicity except the right kind, Peter hastened to set him straight.

"It's all right, President. We managed to get a line on the

Beamish incident without going anywhere near the state police. They know about the ditched car and they know it came from a car rental in Hoddersville, but before they could do a real investigation, the car had been destroyed by vandals."

22

The opening days of fall semester are always hectic, but since Peter already had the president's floor, and ear, he kept them.

He told how Catriona McBogle had dropped in on the Shandys unannounced, how she'd noticed a newspaper article about the recently deceased nonagenarian who had been for so many years head of Feldstermeier Farms and followed up on it at a library in a town whose name she'd hardly remembered; how she'd found her way to that wretched apology for a road which had led to the ditched limousine in which she'd found Forster Feldstermeier's only surviving brother helplessly pinned without food, water, or any hope of rescue.

There was quite a lot more. Peter didn't try to tell it all, particularly those things that James Feldstermeier had said to him during the long drive down from Maine, once Jim's voice had come back and he was no longer afraid to talk. Such confidences were only for those who had been neighbors for many years but had not achieved friendship until the time had come for them to separate.

Cronkite Swope had been chewing over bits and pieces of what Peter had been saying. "So there you four were, drinking champagne with the milkman's wife while he was trying to stay alive. That would make a tidy little sidebar. Do I really have to keep it buried?"

"Yah!" growled Svenson.

Swope didn't know a word of Swedish except "smorgasbord," but he could interpret easily enough what "Yah" meant. Peter tried the temperate approach.

"We weren't exactly holding a debauch while Jim burned, Swope. We were all tired after the reception and ready for our beds, but Mirelle insisted that we stay and have a drink of champagne with her so we figured a fifteen-minute visit wouldn't kill us. None of us had ever been inside that house since she and Jim had moved there, strange as it may seem. We were somewhat flabbergasted by the white carpeting and all those porcelain geese and spaniels. We sat down very carefully and stayed just long enough for Mirelle to serve us each one skinny glass."

"What kind of glass?" Cronkite Swope was determined to get something quotable out of all the talk, however paltry it might be, against the day when he might be allowed to print the story.

"Helen called the thing a flute, and who was I to say it wasn't?" said Peter. "What are you looking at now, Swope?"

"These photographs. Don't you think this is a strange way for Mrs. Feldster to have been sitting, smack in the middle of the room as if she were playing queen of the castle or something? Is that how the chairs were arranged when you and she and the Porbles were squeezed in there together?"

Peter took the sheaf of photographs from Swope and fished his reading glasses out of his breast pocket. "No, Swope, that's not how it was. The chair you see her in was over by the front window then, as I recall. Phil Porble was sitting in it, ready to abandon ship as soon as he could spy an opening. By the time we'd each finished our champagne, Mirelle had had two or three more; she was sprawled on that squashy-looking sofa you see there in the background. There'd been a three-tiered table loaded with china bunnies in front of it but that must have got knocked over after we left. You can see a table leg and some broken china, though they don't show up very well in the photographs. It looked to me as if somebody had deliberately stepped on them and ground them into the carpet, but that's merely conjecture."

"Ungh." That was the first sound Dr. Svenson had made in a while. "Was she drunk?"

"I'd say Mirelle was pretty well squiffed but not yet sozzled. Drat! I wish I knew why she wound up in that straight chair, and why it had been dragged out into the middle of the room. Any ideas, President?"

"No. You took the pictures."

"So I did, and was too appalled by what I was doing to think about what I was seeing. Tell me, have you spoken with Ottermole in the last two days? I'd like to know whether he's been given the results of the autopsy and if the M.E. agreed with Melchett."

"Ask."

"Yes, President. I gather it's all right to throw your name around."

"Argh."

The interview was over. Svenson was already scowling over the next item in his packed agenda. Shandy and Swope let themselves out of the office; the president didn't lift his head to see them go.

"Now where?" said Swope.

"Good question. Aren't you supposed to be somewhere else about now?"

"Is this what's known as the bum's rush, Professor?"

"In a word, Swope, yes. I want to see that autopsy report and then I want to ask Melchett a few questions that I don't think he'd want to answer in front of you, much as he enjoys seeing his name in the *Fane and Pennon*. I have a hunch that he may have missed something important when he was making his examination, but for heaven's sake don't let on that I said so."

"No, I won't. He's getting pretty touchy lately. My mother called him about changing Grandpa's medication the other day and he almost bit her head off."

"M'well, Melchett must be in his late sixties by now, he probably resents the thought of growing old. Tell you what, though—if you have time on your hands, you might give some thought to doing a piece about the college barns."

"Oh, hey! About the milkman?"

"Just keep the lid on until you've checked with me and President Svenson, in that order. Trust me, Swope."

"Sure, Professor. Thanks." Swope was off like a speeding bullet.

Peter stopped by his office and called the police station and was asked to leave a message if it wasn't urgent. If it was urgent, the machine suggested calling Chief Ottermole's home. The chief must be out making the rounds, he decided, and called Dr. Melchett's office where he heard a similar message. The doctor must still be at Hoddersville Hospital. Peter left his number on both machines and sat down with a new textbook on the cloning of tissue culture.

He got in some very useful reading before Melchett replied in person to his telephone call and offered an invitation to lunch.

The reason for Melchett's sudden cordiality toward Peter stemmed from the fact that Mrs. Melchett was not at home. She had left a casserole keeping warm in the oven, however, a tossed salad keeping chilled in the fridge, a compote of fresh fruits and some macaroons on the buffet, and the coffemaker ready to perk at the flip of a switch. The table in the dinette was set for two, Melchett explained, because he sometimes brought a colleague home while the lady of the house was absent on important business.

Mrs. Melchett's important business often meant standing in for a saleswoman who was home with the megrims, or altering a gown for a frantic bride-to-be in one of the seven dress shops that her father had established around the state and which her brother had taken charge of ever since he'd left college with a bachelor's degree in marketing and a headful of Yankee know-how. According to Helen, Mrs. Melchett was in fact itching for the day when her father would at last retire, her brother would be too engrossed with his latest top-of-the-line computer to bother his head over which styles would catch on and which would not. And she herself would fly off to New York once a month and all the big-name designers from all the best houses would genuflect when they saw her coming. Successful as the shops had been all these years, a shopkeeper did not rate the prestige of a doctor's wife; at least not in Balaclava County. Ah, but in New York . . .

While Mrs. Melchett honed her merchandising talents at her father's stores, the doctor played the attentive host with panache, setting the salad close to Professor Shandy's elbow and the hot-from-the-oven casserole in front of himself so that he could serve his guest without having to treat the guest's burns. The pleasantry—it could hardly have passed for a joke—sounded feeble with age and use but Peter managed a smile and a chuckle, mainly because the casserole was in fact quite good.

As Melchett filled his plate, Peter noticed four bright red scratches on the back of the doctor's hand. "I didn't know you had a cat," he said.

"We don't, just my wife's Pom, which fortunately she's taken with her today." He saw Peter staring at the fresh red marks on his hand. "You mean because of this? Embarrassing. When I was taking the casserole out of the oven, I burned my hand on the upper rack. It's nothing."

After a decent interval for chewing and swallowing, Peter got down to what he'd come for. "As you've doubtless gathered, Melchett, I'm here on an errand for President Svenson. He's anxious for your opinion of the medical examiner's findings. He regrets that he wasn't able to break free this noontime, but you can imagine what sort of turmoil we're in at the college. The latest drop in the bucket seems to be a sister of Mirelle's who's moved into the Feldster house under the mistaken impression that she now owns it. I don't know whether the president intends to handle the matter himself or pass it on to somebody else."

Melchett produced a shrug to indicate that his own burdens were at least as heavy as the president's and that he didn't have any lackey like Peter to do his running for him. Peter decided this would be as good a time as any to bring out the photographs he'd taken on the morning Grace Porble had found Mirelle Feldster so gruesomely dead.

"I thought you'd want to see these, Melchett, seeing that you supervised the photography."

Melchett had done no such thing, but a little bit of sugar could make the medicine go down as well for a doctor as for anybody else. Peter took the revolting color shots out of the manila envelope he'd brought them in, and handed them over.

"Here you are. They came out almost too well, I'm afraid, but no doubt you're well hardened to this sort of thing."

"Never hardened, Shandy. Inured perhaps, yet it's never easy, particularly if the victim is somebody one's known for a long time."

The doctor seemed reluctant to examine the photographs. The bloodstained effigy in the tapestry chair hit him hard.

"You know, Shandy, for the first time in my long career as a physician I feel totally baffled. I thought I'd had Mirelle Feldster pretty well under control. She was, I grant you, a difficult patient in many ways; but I'd never known her to do anything so totally insane before. I can't help wondering whether this melodramatic disappearance of Jim's could have been what pushed Mirelle over the brink."

This time the sigh came more spontaneously. "As for the Coumadin, I don't know what to say. I thought I knew pretty much all there was to know about the stuff, but . . ."

Melchett kept looking at the photographs and looking

away again, as who could have blamed him? "I just don't
know what to say, Shandy. I've prescribed Coumadin a good
many times for a variety of patients and never had anything
but success with it before. The only explanation I can think
of is that when Jim did his disappearing act, he remembered
to leave Mirelle her proper dosage but failed somehow to
enclose any directions about using it. Or else he—but that's
unthinkable."

The doctor stood up, shaking his head like a swimmer
coming up out of the water. "I'm sorry, Shandy, I shouldn't
have rambled on like this. My afternoon hours start in exactly fifteen minutes and there are a couple of things I need
to do before I see my first patient. Thank you for coming. I
was glad of your company."

Melchett was finished, but Shandy was not. "Er—President Svenson was quite pressing about that autopsy report.
Might I borrow your copy long enough to make him a
copy?"

"Eh? Oh, but I haven't seen it yet either. Ottermole told
me it arrived in the morning post, but I haven't had a chance
to go over and pick it up yet. Perhaps you could do it for me?
And then you could make a copy for Svenson at the same
time."

Melchett's pompous posing grated, but since the police
station was already on Peter's list of places that needed visiting, he merely thanked the doctor for lunch and left.

When Peter entered the small police station, he found that
Fred Ottermole was still taking his wife's advice to rest his
stomach immediately after eating. Indeed, a little more resting and he would be dozing as peacefully as Edmund, who
was curled in his usual spot atop the In-basket on the chief's
desk.

Both opened their eyes and sat up alertly. Both relaxed
when they saw it was only Peter. Edmund began licking his
left leg. Fred licked the last crumb of Edna Mae's meatloaf

sandwich from his upper lip and said, "I thought I'd be see-ing you in here today. Have you learned anything more about that man with the Cadillac who visited Mirelle the night she was killed?"

"Florian Feldstermeier? What about him?"

"He's the guy who stole the Lincoln from Royal Rentals."

"What?"

"Mr. Royal, that's the man who owns the car-hire place, said he was in looking over the selections on Saturday. He was particularly interested in the Lincoln, said his aunt needed a car while she was visiting the area and that she par-ticularly wanted one that was both comfortable and fully au-tomated." A wistful look overspread Fred's handsome face. His son's bicycle was still propped behind his desk. "He said he'd be back on Monday. And he was. Only he came before Mr. Royal opened up and must have hot-wired the Lincoln and taken it. It wasn't till Royal was closing up Monday night that he noticed one of his cars was missing. He re-ported it to the Hoddersville police right away, but it must already have been nose down in that ravine by then."

"How do you know it was Florian Feldstermeier?"

"The description fit the one Helen gave me—big, tall, light hair, blue eyes. Fiftyish."

"That description fits hundreds of men."

"Yeah, but Royal Rentals is a snooty place that only rents luxury cars. Mr. Royal said that some of his customers have so much money they don't have to dress up and that he fig-ured this guy must have had buckets because if you didn't know better, you'd swear he was wearing ordinary brogans and windbreaker. So that made me remember Helen saying that the Cadillac guy was so well dressed you didn't realize he was."

"Ingenious," said Peter. And it was. "Except that Florian Feldstermeier spent the whole weekend at his father's deathbed in plain view of numerous and assorted Feldster-meiers."

"Darn," said Ottermole, crestfallen.

"Never mind. Is this the autopsy—Ow!" Peter jerked away, more startled than hurt, though it did hurt. Edmund's claws had raked the back of his hand and Edmund still glared at him, ears laid back, tail twitching angrily.

"Edmund! What's got into you?" Fred yelled. "You okay, Peter? Gosh, I'm sorry."

"It's okay. My fault. Sorry, Edmund. I shouldn't have tried to grab that envelope out from under you without asking you first."

His bad manners had not cost him blood, only a couple of stinging red scratch marks. Peter knew the big cat could have dealt him a more serious injury had he really been trying. He spoke soothingly to the animal and Edmund's tail quit twitching, his ears resumed their usual erect posture and he lifted his chin to accept a conciliatory scratch. This time when Peter indicated that he wanted the envelope, Edmund graciously stepped out of the basket.

Ottermole was still shaking his head, puzzled. "Mirelle Feldster's the only other person I've ever seen him go after like that."

"Probably because she didn't own a cat," said Peter, slightly embarrassed that he'd been rude enough to Edmund to provoke an attack, but a little puzzled himself that the big cat had reacted so grumpily. His attention turned to the envelope with the return address of the county coroner. It hadn't been opened. "You didn't read this yet?"

"No, it's always so much medical gobbledygook that I usually wait till one of the doctors is around to translate."

"Well, I'll get it copied and see if I can't get you a translation while I'm at it," Peter said.

He left the station house and made a beeline for the library. There were several copiers for the students' use in an alcove set off from the main reading room but Helen Shandy had one all to herself in the Buggins Room. Naturally that was the one Peter chose.

"Well, hail to thee, blithe spirit." Helen looked up from the file drawer that she'd been putting to rights, saw who her visitor was, and adjusted her head to the optimum angle for a kiss. "Where were you when the lights went out?"

"Visiting Fred Ottermole after lunching with Melchett at his house, oddly enough. Mrs. Melchett was off on important business."

"Trying on a new batch of evening gowns and swimsuits, no doubt. How come Dr. Melchett? Darling, you're not sick or anything?"

"I got a little sick of Melchett after a while, but the food wasn't bad."

"What did you have?"

"A surprisingly tasty casserole, a tossed salad, and I forget what else. Cut-up fruit and cookies made with wheat germ and acidophilus milk, I think. Something along those general lines. She's quite a cook, in her way."

"Yes, dear."

"What's so funny?"

"It's just that Mrs. Melchett buys her entrees from Mrs. Mouzouka and heats them up as needed. Since when have you and the doctor been lunching buddies?"

"I don't think we ever were. We have the same sort of relationship we've always had, which isn't saying much. I thought he'd have had the results of the autopsy on Mirelle Feldster but he said he hadn't. I picked it up at Fred's and promised to make a copy and get it to him, which I'm now about to do. Is this gadget fed and watered and ready for use?"

"She's all hitched up and raring to go, provided I get to see the report first."

"Me, too, but we'd better read fast or Melchett will be on our backs. Though actually I'm not so sure he wants to know. He was skating all around that Coumadin, trying to

make a case for Jim Feldster's having purposely messed
with Mirelle's dosage before he decamped."

"You think the doctor's afraid he may have mixed it up
himself, by accident?" Helen asked.

"Anything's possible, particularly when the attending
physician's an old turkey who's better at strutting around
and practicing his bedside manner than he is at doing a
proper day's work. Could you hand me that paper knife?"

"Let me, I'm quite reliable at opening envelopes."

Helen slit with precision, laid down the paper knife, unfolded the enclosure, and started to read. Peter read over her
shoulder, and a nice little shoulder it was, too, he was thinking, until his eye fell upon a line of what had to be scientific
error.

23

WHEN SHE HAD FINISHED READING AND COPYING THE REPORT, Helen said, "Peter, did you bring those photographs with you?"

"Drat! I was hoping you wouldn't ask. You're not going to like them."

"I didn't expect to." Helen took the sheaf that had made Dr. Melchett flinch and tried the old stiff-upper-lip gambit. It didn't seem to be working very well. "It's a good thing I hadn't got around yet to eating lunch. I did think, considering that I'd already seen Mirelle so soon after she'd been— but—ugh!"

Peter put his arm around her. "Come on, then. Walk up to Melchett's with me, the fresh air will do you good. You didn't leave the original of the autopsy report in the copier, by any chance?"

"Please darling! I'm not that far gone. Here are clean envelopes for the copies, not that Thorkjeld needs one. He always knows about everything before it's happened. Oh, rats! I'm all thumbs. You fix it."

Peter folded the two copies, returned the original to the envelope it had been mailed in, and put all three envelopes in his inside jacket pocket. It would definitely not do for him to lose the reports on campus and have them picked up by some flighty freshman who'd broadcast the contents to the whole college and start a general panic.

The short walk was doing both the Shandys some good. The Melchett house was in itself a welcome distraction. Like other old New England houses, it had an air of serenity that could not be duplicated. Much of the work had been done by the present incumbent's great-grandfather, the first Melchett to become a doctor as well as a competent carpenter and a few other things, as people were in those days.

His first patient had swapped him a horse in exchange for his fee; the horse had been ugly as sin and badly afflicted with glanders. While the neighbors chuckled in their sleeves about the green kid who called himself a doctor, young Melchett had cured the glanders, curried the horse, and ridden the willing beast on his rounds for many years. He'd pulled teeth, human and equine; he'd lanced abscesses, birthed babies, ridden out in the black of night to sew up the results of a barroom brawl, set a broken leg, or sit up with an old woman whose pain was lessened more by the doctor's presence than by his medicines.

His son had gone to college for two whole quarters, had studied hard and learned what he'd needed to know. He'd prospered and made his rounds in a trim little buggy. His grandson had spurned the old buggy for a new horseless carriage which ran on gasoline instead of oats, when it ran at all. Melchett's own father had driven a Packard, later an Oldsmobile. The present Melchett turned in his car for a new one every three years; he made fewer and fewer house calls, and those only when the afflicted one was rich and prominent enough not to be inconvenienced.

Thus was the line running out. Melchett the fourth and his lady wife were childless but didn't much mind. The ancestral home would eventually be willed to the college for some purpose that they hadn't yet given much thought to except that the Melchett name must be conspicuously displayed with pomp, circumstance, and, of course, impeccable taste. Just now, Dr. Melchett had a patient and mustn't be disturbed. Peter handed over the autopsy report to the doctor's assistant, a woman neither old nor young, suitably but not stylishly dressed, courteous but not chummy; obviously hand-picked by Mrs. Melchett in person.

"Okay, kiddo," he said. "Whither next?"

"I wonder if Mrs. Mouzouka has any of that lemon sponge pie left."

The lemon sponge pie was, as always, superb. Like Great-aunt Beulah, though, it wasn't magnificent enough to take the Shandys' minds off that bizarre autopsy report for long. As they left the faculty dining room, Peter said, "I might as well mosey over and see what Dan Stott has to say about this autopsy report. You don't have to come."

"I'd rather stay with you," Helen told him. "We both know what this could do to the college. At least we can go down with the ship, if necessary."

"Oh, I hardly think it'll come to that. Come on, then, we might as well get it over with."

The animal husbandry department was mooing and quacking and whinnying along pretty much as usual but it felt rather chilly without a long drink of water in an immaculate white lab coat and white canvas shoes padding around the dairy barns. It was hard not to wonder what James Feldstermeier might be doing right now. Helen said so.

"Jim's probably trying to milk a helicopter," Peter said absently. "I hope Dan Stott's in his office."

"He will be. Iduna says he always takes a little nap in his chair after he's eaten."

"Somehow that doesn't surprise me. This way to the elephants."

Professor Stott was right where they'd expected him to be, tilted back in his oversized swivel chair, his eyes closed, his lips gently curved in a smile of repletion, his nose emitting gentle snorts and whoofles much as a particularly high-bred porker might do.

"A picture no artist could paint," Helen murmured. "Except perhaps Rosa Bonheur. It seems a shame to wake him."

They didn't have to. Persons who spend much of their time in the presence of large ruminants tend, as Stott himself had once remarked, to become occultly linked to their charges. Peter and Helen were by no means large ruminants but the occult link must be there in some degree; the man in the swivel chair lifted first one eyelid, then the other, and saw that it was good. He hoisted himself to his feet and expressed in courtly word and tone his pleasure at being visited by two dear friends.

"Sorry, Dan, but this one's not for pleasure," said Peter. "We don't want to spoil your postprandial ruminations. Er—how's your stomach?"

"Am I to infer from this query that you feel some trepidation on my behalf with regard to the digestive process?"

"You could put it that way. Not to horse around, since you and Iduna don't live on the Crescent, you may not be aware of certain—er—goings-on down at our end of the college grounds."

"Would these goings-on be in any degree related to the strange disappearance of my valued old colleague, Jim Feldster, and the subsequent sudden death of his wife?"

"They would, but I ought to have mentioned in advance that the president is very anxious to keep this whole dirty business as quiet as possible, for good and sufficient reason. Actually the reason is not good, but it's surely sufficient. You may have heard that Mirelle Feldster is dead; what you haven't heard is that there's a pretty fair possibility that she was murdered. While that may no longer be the case, something horrid *did* happen to her that night."

Peter fumbled in his inside pocket and brought out the packet of photographs and the autopsy report. "This is how she was found the morning after the president's reception, by Grace Porble, who'd taken Mirelle some biscuits that she never had a chance to eat."

"Great heavens!"

Whether it was the enormity of what Stott was seeing in those full-color photographs or the fact that Mirelle had never got to eat the biscuits that Grace Porble had baked for her, he was certainly taking the situation to heart. Never inclined to make snap judgments, he pondered over each separate exposure even though there was little difference from one to the next. He put them all back in their envelope with the greatest of care and went on to the autopsy report, reading every word and paying close attention to the punctuation, shaking his head slowly from side to side as he murmured, "Coumadin in the bloodstream at excessive levels?"

Then, all of a sudden, he shoved his reading glasses to the very tip of his nose and stared at the Shandys as though he'd been struck by lightning.

"This is monstrous! It says here—it says—I cannot believe this. Is there no limit to human depravity?"

"I've often wondered about that myself," said Peter. "Then you agree with the postmortem? It actually is hog's blood and not human?"

"Oh yes," Stott assured him. "I've done similar tests many times myself. So has my friend the county coroner. What I find astonishing, to use no more pejorative word, is that someone deliberately sat that poor woman—dead or alive, I can't say—in one of her own chairs, in the middle of her own living room, and painted her face with a paintbrush and a bucket of blood drawn from what I grimly suspect was a freshly butchered hog. If another test would be of any practical use to you, I should be most willing to run it myself."

"But what about the blood on the carpet?" said Helen. "It

looked to me as though the body must have been totally drained."

"On the contrary, Helen. You may take it from me that the stains on the clothing, the body, and also the carpet were all the same, nothing but hog's blood. If there had been a wound, she would indeed have bled quite a lot. With this much Coumadin in her system, her blood would take forever to clot. The coroner found no external wounds, but that's what did it, all right. According to this report, she bled to death internally. So how come you don't think it was murder?"

"She was taking Coumadin for her phlebitis and—

"Mirelle? Phlebitis? Who told you that?"

"Why, Jim did," said Peter.

Stott was shaking his head.

"And Dr. Melchett. He prescribed it."

"He did? For real?" Stott turned back to the autopsy report and ran his finger down the lines. "Nothing here about phlebitis. Except for carrying a few extra pounds and a slightly enlarged liver from excessive drinking, Mirelle Feldster was healthy as a horse when she died."

"Then why did Jim keep having to give her the Coumadin?"

"Sometimes a friend will help another friend."

"Melchett prescribed a placebo?"

Stott permitted himself a moment's jocularity. "Jim loved lodges, but Melchett and I were once lodge brothers ourselves several years ago. No longer, alas. Nevertheless, my lips must be sealed. Melchett will speak for himself if it is necessary."

"But he's already spoken, in a way," Helen argued. "When he examined Mirelle's body Thursday morning, he told Peter she was on Coumadin."

"And he said it again at lunch today," said Peter.

"Maybe by now she was, but my lips are still sealed, dear friends. Now, unless you'd like to come and admire the new incubators Elver Butz has just wired for us, I must go and pay my respects to Belinda, who is again great with piglets and somewhat fractious as a result."

Belinda of Balaclava had every right to throw a snit if she felt like it. The seventeen little bundles of joy she'd produced as a blushing bride some years back had brought renown to herself; to her doughty consort, Balthazar of Balaclava; and most particularly to Professor Daniel Stott, whose thirty-year aspiration to breed the Perfect Piglet had proven him a veritable Sultan of Swine. By now, the team of Belinda, Balthazar and Stott was almost legendary.

Not every one of Belinda's many offspring was perfect but most of them came close enough to delight the hearts of those farseeing pig farmers who bought them from the college to become the sires and dams of many other happy piglets, on condition that they adhere closely to the criteria set forth by Professor Stott and President Svenson, and agree to quarterly inspections by qualified veterinarians.

"Now where?" Helen asked as Peter escorted her to the upwind side of the pigpens. "I suppose I ought to pay a courtesy call on our new neighbor?"

"Are you sure you want to? After she threw scrub water on Jane and called her dirty names? After she invited me to leave this morning?"

"No, I don't, but it's something we should do. After what happened to Mirelle, I'd as soon not walk in unannounced on another slaughterhouse scene. That makes sense, doesn't it?"

"Don't ask me what makes sense, Helen. All I can think of is to keep the stewpot boiling and see what floats to the top. Do you want to ask Grace Porble to join us?"

"Too late, we've missed the bus. Grace has gone off to Boston with a group from the Claverton Garden Club. They've rented a sight-seeing bus and plan to stay until Sunday night. Grace wasn't crazy to go, but Phil thought it would do her good."

"Why didn't you tell me in time, drat it? You could have gone with them."

"No, I couldn't. I'm a working woman with half a cat to support, remember? Besides, I just didn't want to be away from you."

"Any special reason?"

"Yes, my love, a very important one. The nights are beginning to get nippy and you know how cold my feet get if you're not around to warm them for me."

"So that's all I am to you, just a stand-in for a pair of bed socks?"

"But that's not all you are, Peter, dear. You make perfectly exquisite waffles. Which reminds me, Catriona wants your recipe."

"Well, she can't have it. Woman's place is out slopping the hogs and greasing the tractor. Whatever became of the old-fashioned virtues?"

"I wouldn't know, darling; I wasn't born then."

"Very amusing. Come on. If we're going to make this house call, we might as well get cracking."

By now, they were near their own front door and Helen said, "Just a second, till I run in and freshen up my lipstick."

"What for? You weren't planning to kiss that woman, were you?"

"I can see you're in one of your moods. Perhaps we should take something?"

"I tell you what, Helen. Why don't we drive out to the Annex and dig her up a nice pot of poison ivy to remember us by?"

"That's a thought. Oh, hello, Jane dear. I'm sorry, but you can't come visiting with us."

Peter scowled and wished he had Jane's luck.

Helen plied her lipstick, slapped the top of the case down over the business end, and took a purposeful step forward.

Jane got between her ankles; Peter had to sort out his two females and put the smaller and furrier of the two inside the house. Jane did not take it with her usual calm; it almost seemed that she didn't want them to pay this visit. But with or without feline approval, the Balaclava banner must be held high; Helen and Peter walked up to what had been the Feldsters' front door and rang the bell.

24

"WELL! I'VE BEEN WONDERING WHETHER ANYBODY WAS GOING to lay an egg on my doorstep. You're a real hospitable bunch around here, aren't you?"

Presumably the woman thought she was being funny. Helen pretended not to notice the sarcasm that Perlinda Tripp was laying on with a trowel. "We'd like to be good neighbors, but we just don't have the time. You're Mrs. Tripp, I believe?"

"Miz."

"Certainly, if you prefer it. This is my husband, Professor Shandy."

"We've met. What are you?"

"Just call me Dr. Shandy."

"Well, lar de dar. You coming in or staying out?"

"Perhaps just for a minute. We have to get home to our cat."

"What would anybody want of a creature like that? Just so you don't bring it in here. I've been working all afternoon on that big stain in the parlor carpet."

"That was very kind of you."

"What do you mean, kind of me. It's my carpet, isn't it?"

Peter cleared his throat. "Er—actually, no, it isn't. Anything that's fastened to the house, such as a nailed-down carpet, automatically becomes part of the dwelling and may not be removed without the owner's permission. I suppose you might try to strike some kind of bargain with the college if you happened to be one of the legatees."

"What the hell are you talking about? I own this house. Me, myself, and nobody else."

"Ms. Tripp, I'm afraid somebody has, for some unknown reason, grossly misrepresented the facts in this matter. This is, always was from the day it was built, and always will be a faculty house for so long as it stands; owned and leased but never sold by Balaclava Agricultural College to bona fide members of the faculty, of which you are not a member. Being sister to the deceased wife of Professor James Feldster, as he is named on the college rolls, does not in any degree qualify you to assume your late sister's position."

"That's not what Florian said."

"Florian who?" Peter snapped. What sort of game was this woman playing here?

"What do you mean, Florian who?" she snapped back. "He's Jim Feldster's nephew, as you ought to know if you're so smart. Jim deeded the house over to Florian before he died."

"This is nonsense. Jim could not have deeded the house to Florian or anybody else because, like myself, he's never been anything but a lessee. I doubt very much whether he'll want to renew the lease now that Mirelle's gone."

"I just told you, for God's sake! Jim's dead. Florian said so. He's going to deed the house over to me. Can't you get that through your stupid head, Mister Professor?"

"I've got it but I refuse to accept it because it's a pack of lies. How long have you known this person who calls himself Florian?"

"None of your damned business. Leave or I'll call the cops."

"Do, by all means. The telephone number is 101-2233 and the chief's name is Ottermole. If he's not around, ask for

Officer Dorkin and tell him Professor Shandy recommended
you."

"For what?"

"That will remain to be seen. I should perhaps warn you
that the station cat is quite large and—er—opinionated."

"Oh, great! Now you're siccing those goddamned cats on
me. If you think I'm going to knuckle under to you,
egghead, you can think again. I'm not budging from this
place until I've got my rights."

"What I think is that we may as well postpone this discussion since we're obviously not getting anywhere
tonight," Helen said in her most no-nonsense tone. "I hope
you have enough groceries in the house to tide you over, Ms.
Tripp. You must be tired from all that scrubbing; it's a shame
that you've been victimized by some practical joker who
thinks it's funny to spread lies and make trouble. Is there
anything you need for tonight?"

"Forget it, *Doctor* Shandy. You needn't try sucking up to
me. I've got your number and don't you think I haven't. See
you in court."

Having a door slammed in one's face is never a pleasant
experience. Helen didn't like it any better than the next one;
but she couldn't help feeling some compassion for that pathetic woman who'd come to Balaclava trailing dreams of
affluence, only to be handed the bird. "Peter," she said, after
they'd gone into their own house and he'd made them each
a Balaclava Boomerang for therapeutic purposes, "you don't
think you made a mistake leaving Jim in the hands of that
Florian person, do you?"

"I think Ms. Tripp may have got the whole thing bass-
ackwards, as your great-aunt Beulah may have remarked at
some point in her career." Peter essayed a sip of his drink to
make sure nobody had been messing around with the essen-
tial ingredients. "Tastes all right to me. That business about
Florian— Come to think of it, Miz Twirlybird never once

mentioned the Feldstermeier name. Either somebody's a mighty good actor or—"

"Or what?" Helen prompted.

"That's where I'm stuck. It stands to reason that Number One Nephew must have been taken aback when his uncle showed up all in one piece just as he thought he had the cat in the bag, but that doesn't necessarily mean Florian had anything to do with the kidnapping or that he'd have been stupid enough to take it out on Mirelle or have anything to do with Perlinda Tripp. When I was at the Feldstermeiers', it looked to me as if Florian was pulling himself together and preparing to make the best of what was still a pretty sweet deal. Drat it, I'd begun to like the fellow."

"Yes, dear. You must be as sick of those gruesome photographs as I am; but would you mind handing them to me just one more time? I know the autopsy said Coumadin, but I keep having a feeling that there's something we still haven't caught. Not that it makes much difference now, I don't suppose; except that we still don't really know whether Mirelle was murdered or just having a little frolic with her current boyfriend and forgot to quit when she should have. Furthermore, we also don't know who the boyfriend was, assuming there was one."

Wisely, Peter sipped his drink in silence while Helen sorted through the grisly sheaf yet again, pondering as Dan Stott had done over each separate exposure. The difference between them was that it took Helen exactly fifty-seven seconds.

"Here we are, Peter; I think we may have something. Look at the way Mirelle was sitting, stiff as a broomstick; and look at those clutching hands. Doesn't she remind you a little of that Antonio Moro portrait of poor old Bloody Mary, hanging on to the arms of that brocaded armchair with all her might, sitting out there in the center of the room trying to look regal and scared stiff, like a timid child bracing herself for her first solo ride on the flying horses. Being

Mirelle, though, she'd have been right in there waiting for her reward, whatever it might be, while whoever it was watched his chance to slip extra Coumadin into a final drink."

"Mirelle would have sat still for that, would she?"

"Oh, absolutely, provided a reasonably willing and good-looking man like Florian was in the scenario. In this case, though, I expect anything male would do, she being already drunk enough not to be fussy. You see, Peter dear, that's the trouble with you eggheads. You think too much; such thoughts are dangerous."

"If you say so, my love. The trouble with you librarians is that you remember too easily. I had a pretty clever idea all worked out on the basis of something or other that seemed like just the ticket to explain all that blood, but I find myself a trifle perplexed over the wiring."

"Maybe you should ask Elver Butz for a few tips."

"And maybe I shouldn't. Elver Butz may not be much of a talker, but you can bet that he's right there on the dot with his bills all worked out down to the last turn of the final screw three and a half minutes after the job is done. Besides, you heard him. He liked Mirelle. Probably the only person in Balaclava Junction who did besides Coralee Melchett. It'd be wrong to show him those pictures and spoil his memory of her. Anyway, if I can't remember what my invention is for, there doesn't seem to be much sense in building it, is there."

"Well, dear, I hate to stifle your initiative but we really should pause and consider before you decide to build a pipe organ or an ark. And I really don't think Jane would feel comfortable with all those other animals around."

"Scratch the ark, then. Maybe I'll just get out my old mouth organ and practice awhile on that. By the way, did I ever get around to mentioning the china doodads that got trampled into that white carpet while Mirelle was either dying or being killed? Anyway, I swept them up and brought

them over here and stashed them away in the jam closet.
They're still there, as far as I know, in a little brown paper
bag that I snaffled from Mirelle's bottom kitchen drawer. I
don't know why I did it but there they are if you should happen to want them."

"And why not, my dear? We never know when our new
neighbor might come cavorting over to borrow a cupful of
shards, do we? Peter, do you suppose there's any chance that
Mirelle actually didn't have phlebitis? Why didn't the autopsy report have anything about it?"

"If you want my opinion, that autopsy report's about as
useful as a pickle fork in a blizzard," Peter grunted. "It
doesn't say much of anything about anything, except that
disgusting reference to hog blood. Just internal bleeding
from too much Coumadin. Melchett might as well have
written the report himself." Peter was taking a last look at
the scorned document; he slipped it back into the plain envelope and stood up.

"You have your keys to the library?"

"Of course. Do I need them? The library doesn't close
until nine on weeknights, you know that. Are you looking
for something special?"

"Not really. I just want to play with the copier a little and
I'd prefer to do it in the privacy of the Buggins Room, if the
librarian will let me."

"The librarian wishes only to serve. Knock and the door
shall be opened unto you. Peter, what are you thinking?"

"I'm thinking the unthinkable. Want this fuzzy thing to
put around you?"

"Does that mean I get to come with you?"

"Certainly. What sort of paper do you use in your
copier?"

"Just the usual white multipurpose kind that everybody
uses."

Peter didn't say much until they'd locked themselves into
the Buggins Room; then he took out the autopsy report yet

again and spread it out on the glass top of the copier. "Could I have a clean piece of paper, please?"

Helen handed him one. He laid it over the text of the report, leaving only the name and address of the county medical examiner, and pushed the start button. "Drat! It's got a black line where the edges overlap. What do I do now?"

"Slide this little widget a tad to the right before you push the button again. The printing will be a tiny bit lighter but the line will be gone and the change in depth of tone will be indiscernible to the untrained eye."

"By George, you're right." Peter ran off another copy just for the practice. "So that's how it's done. I'm going to call Chief Ottermole and then let's go get an ice cream."

25

HELEN SUCKED UP THE LAST DROPS OF HER CHOCOLATE-RASP-berry ice-cream soda through her straw with a defiant gurgle, regardless of some newly elevated seniors who were holding a solemn colloquy on the subject of ladybugs; partly because they really cared about ladybugs and partly for the edification of a few green freshmen who'd come looking to buy what they called double-deckers whereas any knowing Balaclavian would have asked for a bullhorn.

Having kindly set the freshmen right on how to order an ice-cream cone Balaclava style, the upperclassmen, three of whom were women, went back to their ladybugs and their college ices, though none of them quite realized what he or she was doing here. "College Ice" had been a name coined back in the Roaring Twenties when in fact it had been mainly the bulls who roared. In those decorous times, male students would have taken off their straw boaters before inviting a female student to join them for a stroll around the pigpens by the light of the silvery moon.

The College Ice was by now nothing more than the name of the shop. Anybody who wanted a scoop of ice cream covered with strawberries, chocolate sauce, chopped nutmeats, whipped cream, and/or whatever other embellishments might strike his or her fancy just asked for a sundae, little wotting that a sundae had become a sundae long ago for purely humanitarian reasons. By 1926 or thereabouts, a young student who'd worked hard all week, attended divine service on Sunday morning, and wanted to take his girl out for some fresh air and a little wholesome refreshment later in the day would, the then college president had conceded, not be breaking any of the Ten Commandments by ordering ices on Sunday, provided she or he made sure to ask for them with a lowercase *s* and a final *e* in place of a more orthodox *y*.

Anything in the category of local color was grist to Helen's mill. Peter, on the other hand, had been in and out of the never modernized ice-cream parlor with its marble counter and its twisted-wire tables and chairs too many times to stay on imbibing the atmosphere once he'd eaten his sundae and licked the spoon.

"What do you say, madam? Are you up for another soda or shall we put the show back on the road?"

He looked around for a waitperson, sorted out the exact amount of the check, and added a modest tip. Large tips were frowned upon in Balaclava Junction as being citified and sometimes embarrassing to students and townsfolk who were none too flush with their spending money. This included just about all of them, according to their own estimates, even though half the town thought the other half were lying and the other half knew damned well they were.

Having made sure that Helen didn't want a second helping of superfluous calories, Peter tucked her blue mohair stole around her in a protective and husbandly way while the three female seniors looked on, trying their best to sneer at such outdated gallantries.

Naturally the Shandys couldn't leave without pausing every other step or two to exchange pleasantries with some of their acquaintances and scatter a few encouraging nods among the incoming first-year students. They ran into colleagues they hadn't seen since the semester began, and hearing new gossip kept Peter and Helen chatting far longer than they'd meant to. By the time they got back to the Crescent, Jane was more than ready for a catnap and telling them about it. Having missed their usual bedtime though, her two humans were wide awake again.

"Feeling sleepy, Helen?"

"Oddly enough, not a bit," she replied. "I hadn't realized a raspberry-chocolate float could be so reviving. What do you say we sneak out back and see if we can get a sight of that lonesome screech owl who's been serenading us ever since he—or maybe she—moved in among the spruces?"

"Why not? You'd better not wear that light blue outfit, though; it shows up too much in the dark. How about wearing the black raincoat you bought last year in Toronto? I'll put on my old brown cardigan and we can go as a pair of misinformed leaf peepers. No, Jane, you'd better not come with us. A great horned owl might mistake you for an overweight mouse. No offense intended."

"And none taken, I'm sure," said Helen. "Sweet dreams, Jane." Now suitably attired for owl-watching, she and Peter slipped out their back door into the autumn-smelling night.

Most of the houses around the Crescent showed nightlights of some sort: a quasi-colonial lantern on a hook outside the front door, a lamp left burning in the foyer, nothing special except at Christmastime when the Grand Illumination was in full swing, and then only for good and sufficient reason. Ms. Tripp didn't appear to be wasting electricity, at any rate, unless she had all the blinds down. If she didn't, she must have the gall of an ox. Not many people would choose to sleep alone in a dark place where someone had so recently died in so gruesome a way. Helen shivered inside her black raincoat, wondering whether this had been such a great idea after all but not wanting to back out so soon when she herself had been the one to suggest the midnight owl walk.

"See any owls?" Peter's voice was hardly a breath. He was taking their impromptu outing seriously, practicing for this year's annual owl count. Last year's had been a complete bust from his point of view, though nobody could have called it a dull one.

Helen knew better than to answer. She moved her head slowly from right to left and back again, remembering that owls could see in the dark far better than most humans and not wanting to miss getting a glimpse of the little owl that had entertained her and Peter on many a summer night with its dying-away call but never waited around for their applause.

There had been a time when many acres of college land had grown nothing but trees. Selective timbering had kept the students warm in the fall when they'd cut and stacked cords of firewood and again the next winter when they lugged it inside to feed the wood-burning stoves and open fireplaces. As time went on and the college flourished, more trees had been cut and more space made for farmland, barns, stables, classrooms, greenhouses, dormitories and other amenities; but common sense had prevailed. The trees and shrubs, though less rife, were better cared for and duly cherished. Arboriculture was high in the curriculum. The Crescent was proud of its plantings: the Shandys' blue spruces were among its chief treasures.

Overhead, the screech owl pulled out the tremolo stop to its utmost quaver and let its voice travel sadly down the scale. Its wings, muted by the soft down under the feathers, spread their stubby width as it glided back to where the trees grew thicker while Peter and Helen watched in delight at having finally seen their shy tenant.

As the bird disappeared, a tiny dot of light showed itself for a fraction of a second. Peter held out his hand; Helen took it. All of a sudden it dawned on them both that they'd seen a shooting star.

Or had they? There was the dot again, coming this time from behind a windbreak of hemlock and fir; the merest blink, then gone. A flashlight, of course, held in a human hand. Feet that knew just where to go but didn't want to step on anything that would make a noise. Relieved that they'd put on dark clothing, Peter pulled Helen down behind a hemlock that had grown out low and bushy, held her tight, and wondered what was up.

Whoever the visitor might be, he or she was heading for the cellar door of the house that was still technically Jim Feldster's. The person in the dark was tall and bulky and did not knock at the door. Instead, he—surely this must be a he—simply lifted the door off its hinges and set it to one side. With his egress assured, he flicked on his light just long enough to make out where the stairs to the first floor were, and went up. Helen turned her head carefully toward Peter.

"Who's that?" she mouthed.

Peter's only reply was, a "damned if I know" kind of shrug. He eased her away from the greenery and headed her toward home. "I'd better stay here," he whispered. "Can you slip back home, lock the door, and call Security? For God's sake, be careful."

"You too." Helen wrapped the black raincoat more snugly around her, sneaked back as bidden, and locked herself inside her own house, thankful that she and Peter had left a few lights on.

Purvis Mink took Helen's call; she explained what she and Peter had seen, trying to keep her voice from shaking. "We don't know whether there's anything going on over there, but considering what's happened lately—"

"Sure, Helen. I'm on my way."

Purvis wasn't just saying that to calm Helen's nerves. He showed up on a bicycle almost before she'd got her raincoat off. "Where's the professor?"

"Over behind that stand of hemlock that Jim Feldster used to keep clipped down. Want me to go with you and show you where he is?"

"Sounds to me as if you'd better stay here by the telephone. Got a police whistle in the house?"

"I think there's one around here someplace. Probably in the culch drawer. If it doesn't turn up, I can always scream."

"Just so we'll know where you are."

Not one to hang around and ask foolish questions, Purvis biked off to where the hemlock grew thick to the ground. "What's up, Professor?" he muttered.

"Don't ask me," Peter muttered back. "Might be anything. Want to go?"

A shrug was answer enough. Purvis shoved his bicycle out of sight and followed the leader. When they came to where the cellar door had been taken off and left leaning against the house, he whispered "Who done it?"

"Somebody big." As big as Elver Butz? Peter thought he'd better wait and be sure.

They heard voices from upstairs. Ms. Tripp was trying on what she seemed to think was a high-class accent. It was more squeak than chic but Peter thought she deserved at least a C-minus for trying. The second voice was deep and masculine and sounded a cajoling note.

Having Purvis Mink with him gave Peter a stronger feeling of confidence than he'd anticipated. He was further relieved to know that Helen was back home with the door locked and the telephone close to her hand. Peter did wish, however, that President Svenson could be among those present. It wasn't that he and Purvis couldn't handle this odd late-night meeting by themselves; it was just that watching the Nordic Nemesis in action was always such an uplifting spectacle. Too bad they wouldn't have time to sell tickets.

Since the night of the president's reception, when Peter, Helen, and the Porbles had first set foot in this house, Peter had been in and out enough times to know the layout. He deduced from the odor of fresh-brewed coffee and from the direction that the voices overhead were coming from, that Ms. Tripp was entertaining Elver Butz against her will in the breakfast nook. It would be safe enough for Peter and Purvis to creep up the basement stairs and hide in the little mudroom between the deck and the kitchen, ready to spring either forward or back as the circumstances might require.

From here, they could hear every word that was uttered. The conversation must have been going on for a while by now; the participants were parking their gentility and getting down to business. Ms. Tripp was, of course, taking the initiative.

"So what it boils down to is that you two got me here under false pretenses."

"I love you,' said Elver. "You said you loved me."

From the tone of his voice, Peter suspected he had been saying that same thing over and over. He had heard that love was blind, but this?

"And you said you were Florian Feldstermeier." Perlinda Tripp sounded angry and disappointed. "Mirelle's been telling me about him for years—how big and handsome he was, how classy, how rich. And then when you showed up in Claverton and said how I could have this house and you and all I had to do was find those damn letters for—"

"You look so much like Mirelle," Elver said softly.

"Yeah, yeah."

"She was so beautiful, so elegant."

"I don't suppose it ever occurred to you that your elegant little angel-pie was getting it on with every good-looking salesman or repairman that came along. You think you were special?"

"I was! What we had was wonderful! I did everything for her—stole that Lincoln to snatch Jim in, trussed him up like a Thanksgiving turkey and sent that beautiful car crashing over the rocks. All I had to do was get rid of Jim for her and she'd be free. We were going to get married."

"In your dreams! She set you up for a fall guy. You kill Jim, she gets a nice widow's settlement, you get the bird."

"That was wrong and I was wrong to believe her. But you and I— We'll go away together. I'll cherish you. I'll give you everything I have. I'll—"

"Which is what? A broken-down van and some coils of electric wire? I thought you had millions. You're a loser, Elver, just like all of Mirelle's men. And I'm tired of taking her leavings. You and that mastermind friend of yours can just forget it. I'm selling this house, I'm selling her things and if I ever find those letters, I'm selling them, too. So you can just go tell him—"

"NO!"

His roar was so loud that Peter and Purvis almost tumbled down the basement stairs.

"What are you doing? Ow! Stop, you're hurting me!"

"I won't let you laugh at me again, Mirelle. I won't! I won't!"

"Elver, honey, don't. I'm not Mirelle. I'm Perlinda. Honey, I was kidding. I do love you, I do!"

"All I ever wanted was a lady like you to love, Mirelle. Someone beautiful and—but you laughed at me, so I came back when you were drunk and asleep and I painted you in red. Red is the color of my true love's hair."

"Please, Elver, no."

"And when you were all wet with the sacrificial blood, I touched your lovely breasts with those bare wires and—"

Perlinda screamed in terror as Elver grasped her with one huge hand and dragged her from the kitchen into the porcelain-crowded parlor.

Peter moved in. He grabbed a Staffordshire dog and flung it straight at Butz's head. Peter's throw was a work of art; but that crash of pottery dog against human head served only to whet the electrician's fury. He was totally out of control now, a maddened animal glaring around for something to kill.

There wasn't much choice of victims. If somebody had to go, Peter wouldn't shed many tears over Perlinda Tripp, who was, Peter supposed, more to be pitied than censured. Purvis Monk was pure gold; Elver Butz a raging maniac. Peter was Peter and he hoped to God as he snatched the biggest Staffordshire dog that this one would do the job, at least for long enough to get Butz stunned, sedated and packed off to a high-security zoo.

The barrage of porcelain that Peter was laying down was beginning to bother Butz. He started backing away toward the staircase, reached under his black pullover and took out a pint-sized bottle. As he yanked out the cork, the smell of gasoline came sharp and vicious. He simultaneously flicked a lighter and took a swig from the bottle, sprayed it between his teeth as he climbed the stairs backwards, spitting flame down on those below, setting fire to the curtains, howling with glee as he watched the flames driving those below out of the parlor that was now a shambles.

"You're dead," he kept screaming. "You're all dead!"

When he wasn't yelling, Elver was still spraying gasoline. He was up to the second floor now. His clothes were smoldering around the edges now; he didn't seem to notice, and the others had neither time nor inclination to wait and watch. The fire was spreading through the downstairs rooms faster than Peter would have thought possible; the flames were roaring almost but not yet quite loudly enough to drown out the madman's howls of "You're dead! You're all dead."

But they weren't. Perlinda might have been, if Peter hadn't shoved her out the side door onto the deck. He made sure Purvis Monk was out safely and leaped for his own life as a huge puff of flame exploded behind him.

Peter didn't know what was happening with Elver Butz and he didn't give a damn. Even as he raced across the yard to make sure Helen was all right and his own house hadn't caught fire yet, he was thinking that the Feldster house would be no great loss.

To avoid huge boulders that would have had to be blasted out of the inconveniently situated lot, the by now long-dead builder had scamped on length and breadth. He'd compensated by raising the ceilings and tacking on a full attic, which he'd then rendered all but useless by carving the space into quaint gables, turrets, a stained-glass cupola, and other architectural extravagances that had been in vogue back during the heyday of Belter and Eastlake. Now voracious tongues of flame were licking at those fantastical excrescences that had never been worth the cost of building and would, within another few minutes have ceased to exist.

Peter was halfway across the yard before he realized that he was being pelted by fire hoses. They were keeping a screen of water between the burning house and his own precious blue spruces. Once he'd got the water out of his eyes, he could see why the firemen had sensibly given up any hope of saving the Feldster house. He'd seen one of the college security guards shepherding Perlinda Tripp. Assuming there was nobody left inside, they'd concentrated on saving the Porble house as well as the Shandys', the Jackman's with their four young children, and a few others that were less vulnerable but still within possible range of flying embers.

News of the fire had spread faster than its sparks. Already the Crescent was full of fire trucks. Volunteer firemen and firewomen, most of them Balaclava students, were pumping water up from the Wash Pond and down from the Skunk Works Reservoir, more properly named Oozak's Pond. Locals were running over to see what was happening, tourists from Lumpkinton and Hoddersville were arriving in carloads and on bicycles, getting in the way of the fire engines and being given strict orders to stay behind the lines or go back where they'd come from.

Chief Ottermole was out there on his bike like Napoleon on his horse, cutting a fine figure in his flawlessly pressed uniform, attracting more respectful attention than he'd ever got before the old wreck he'd been stuck with by an overzealous budget committee had done him the favor to fall apart in the middle of a busy intersection.

All this Peter gathered more or less by osmosis as he dodged the writhing hoses, ducked under the curtain of water, and burst soaking wet into the kitchen that, thank God, he and his wife still hadn't got around to remodeling. Helen was where he'd last seen her, clinging to the telephone like the boy on the burning deck. Just now she was trying to convince a representative from the Scarlet Runners of Lumpkinton that his contingent hadn't better jog over to Balaclava Junction with their hose cart and the firehouse Dalmatian because there was literally no room for them on the road; but it was kind of the Runners to offer. When she spied Peter come dripping through the door, she hung up quickly.

"Are you all right?"

"Are you all right?"

They spoke in unintended unison, then burst out laughing. Peter was all revved up to pull out the old chestnut about two hearts that throb as one, but Helen beat him to it. She herself was in good repair, having had sense enough to close all the windows and batten down the hatches as soon as smoke began to roll out of the Feldster basement. Peter was a mess. He hadn't noticed at the time how much in the way of smoke and gasoline fumes he'd inhaled while he'd been having his go-round with Elver Butz, or how many cuts and scratches he'd collected from all that broken china.

The prolonged bombardment by hose and the frenzied leaping of the partially contained flames were turning the whole Crescent into a community steam bath. Everybody was coughing and sweating, nobody was even thinking about leaving. Fire engines kept coming, their sirens screaming like creatures from another planet. There was no place to park, their help was not needed; there was little they could do except add to the uproar. That part, it should be said to their credit, they performed without a flaw.

As Peter had been expecting, the Feldster house had by now become little more than an oversized chimney. Those inside rooms on which Ms. Tripp, like her sister before her, had lavished so much care must be totally gutted by now; all

Mirelle's expensive fripperies destroyed, nothing left of her overflowing collection except that one paper bag half-filled with shards of porcelain, sitting down cellar in the Shandys' jam cupboard.

"For a cap and bells our lives we pay,

"Bubbles we buy with a whole soul's tasking . . ."

Peter knew the New England poets; they'd been friends of his ever since he could remember his father reading to him from *Tales of a Wayside Inn.* There'd been a lot of Whittier and Longfellow quoted around the Shandy house. When they were kids, "You look like the wreck of the Hesperus" had been a favorite insult. How many today would know anything about the schooner *Hesperus,* or even about Longfellow? Of those few who might still know, how many would there be who'd give a damn? Why should he think of that now, when a house that he'd lived beside for more than half his life by now was about to fall in on itself?

"Oh! Peter, look!"

Helen was clutching his arm, scooping up Jane and adding her to the family armload. Peter didn't need to be told; every eye in the crowd was staring at what he was seeing now. Guards were shoving spectators back out of harm's way. The racket was truly infernal; but there was one horrendous noise that out-roared all the rest.

The electrical currents in the Feldster house had blown. What light there had been afterward must have come from the fire that by now was raging its way up the stairs and into that crazy attic. Totally maddened, Elver Butz had forged his way, sometimes inside the smoke-filled dark, sometimes clinging to the outer shell, to the topmost peak of the highest turret. There, a century or so ago, the builder had affixed an elaborately conceived wrought iron lightning rod, twisted and curlicued into a creditable semblance of a sunflower.

To this rod Elver Butz was holding; howling, laughing like the mindless thing he had become. This couldn't be real; it was a replay of some early horror movie; it was Dr.

Frankenstein's loathsome but pathetic monster, mouthing its last hurrah. The pointed roof was beginning to cave in. Elver ripped the iron sunflower loose from its smoldering mooring, flourished it over his head like a trophy, emitted one more drawn out, death-defying howl, and flung himself, still howling, into the heart of the inferno.

26

"YEEPERS CREEPERS, SHANDY!"

By this time Peter was sick of the Feldstermeier saga, but this was Dr. Svenson's chance to be filled in on some of the background. "So, Shandy. While Jim Feldster was yammering for a divorce, Mirelle was egging on Elver Butz to kill him, right?"

"Putting it in a nutshell, yes. Jim must have been giving the matter serious thought for quite a while. Mirelle got hold of a pocket diary in which he'd jotted down names and addresses of some divorce lawyers and figured she'd better get cracking. Their marriage had been a fiasco from the start but there wasn't much they could do about it. Jim's father, the patriarch of the clan, wasn't a cruel man but he was dead set against divorce. Forster kept to the old man's beliefs and had warned Jim long ago that any breach of vows would not be taken kindly by the family. Jim didn't care; he wouldn't take a penny from them anyway, but Mirelle was ready every month to cash old Forster's allowance checks.

"This went on far too long. Jim had his cow barns and his lodge brothers. Mirelle had her bridge club, her hair appointments, her shopping with Forster's money, and her occasional flings. She must have really panicked when she ran across that pocket diary of Jim's. Mirelle wouldn't mind dumping Jim if she could be assured of skipping off with a chunk of the Feldstermeier money, but how could she get it? Whether it was herself or Jim who got the divorce, the checks would stop the minute the decree was signed. There was only one way for Mirelle to have her cake and eat it; and that was to find a way to murder her husband in a discreet and ladylike manner. Then she could sit back and enjoy the fruits of her labors as the merriest and richest widow in town.

"After promising herself to Elver if he'd dispose of Jim, she tried to back out of the bargain. He didn't take it very well, as you saw."

President Svenson summed it up. "Why hog blood?"

"He had access to it while wiring the farrowing barn and the abattoir," Peter said. "He needed something wet to ground Mirelle when he electrocuted her and I guess the blood seemed symbolic. Who knows why a madman does anything?"

It was early afternoon now and though Peter had grabbed a few hours' sleep, he still felt tired. He'd ruined a perfectly good pair of pants climbing out of the Feldsters' kitchen window with his socks on fire. Thanks to whatever guardian angel might have been clerking in the celestial menswear department, those pants had been tailored from genuine, old-fashioned, fire-retardant sheep's wool. Peter would have hated having to disappoint Helen of her conjugal prerogatives.

He had taken time for a shower, which had been pretty much an exercise in futility. By the time he'd got undressed, the water pressure had been down to a few dribbles short of zero. Peter didn't feel particularly bereft; he'd already been subjected to a thorough drenching from the fire hoses while trying to escape the still-burning remains of the house that Ms. Tripp had thought she wanted. At least he'd had clean clothes to put on, even if they did make him smell like a pound of finnan haddie.

Being next door to the aftermath of a horror show was not

conducive to gracious living. The yard was a quagmire, the stink of wood smoke was all-pervasive. Peter and Helen thought at first of moving to Ellie June Freedom's inn for a week or so, but Ellie didn't allow even the best mannered cats, so they would make the best of it.

For every drawback there was a compensation. Neighbors who'd been feuding for years had found themselves manning the same fire hose and gone home after a few hours' hard spraying, each now convinced that old So-and-So was only about half as big a bastard as they'd thought he was. Mrs. Mouzouka, head of restaurant management, lived two miles off-campus and needed her sleep; but as soon as the sound of many sirens penetrated her slumbers, she'd flung on a uniform over her nightie and a bathrobe over the uniform, had driven hell-for-leather to the faculty dining room, and opened its kitchen for the benefit of those weary, sooty, hungry firefighters who'd saved most of the Crescent and were now bewailing the fact that there were no new fires to conquer.

Iduna and Daniel Stott had been the hit of the night. It had been worth getting up for, watching the august head of the animal husbandry department tending the grill while his buxom helpmate flipped towers of flapjacks, made toast enough to feed a regiment, dealt out the loaves and fishes to all comers.

Sometime around daybreak a brisk wind had sprung up. This helped a little, but it would be a long time until winter gales carried away the rank odor of wet ashes. Despite the smell, Peter and Helen and Jane had slept soundly for four or five hours before he was summoned to the president's presence.

"Autopsy?" he queried.

"Um—yes. I asked Chief Ottermole to call the county coroner and see if he could send us another copy. He faxed it to the library last night."

"Urgh?"

"Oh yes, no question. Mirelle Feldster was electrocuted. Once all the blood was washed off, the marks were clear to see. And not a trace of Coumadin in her own blood."

"Ungh."

"And well you may say so. Poor Mirelle. And poor Jim, too."

Svenson nodded, not being one to waste words. "Coming back?"

"I don't know. Jim's always taken his work here very seriously, but I shouldn't be too surprised if he felt it his duty to take on the family responsibilities. He'd need lots of help, of course, but help would be available. His nephew Florian Feldstermeier the something or other, I suppose, is next in line as head of the family and seems quite amenable to seeing that Jim gets all the coaching he needs."

"Yumping Yaybirds! What's that racket?"

"Oh, that must be Jim." Knowing what to expect, Peter sauntered nonchalantly out toward the helicopter that was just settling itself on the lawn outside President Svenson's office window.

"Couldn't wait till the cows came home."

For some reason, Dr. Svenson found it amusing to watch the newly rechristened President James Feldstermeier descend from the helicopter dressed much like Prince Charles but taller, grayer, and not carrying his little tin pail. His escort, an equally impeccable cutout from *Gentlemen's Quarterly* was, of course, the real Florian Feldstermeier, heir apparent and aide-de-camp par excellence. Jim introduced his nephew to President Svenson as casually as though they were all three mere human beings, which also, of course, was ridiculous.

It immediately became obvious without being said that this was more a visit of state, an act of closure, rather than Jim's return to the cow barn. Ever so tactfully, Florian made it clear that during the next month or so, the new head of International Dairies would be flying in one of the company planes to France, the Netherlands, Germany, Switzerland, Great Britain, Wisconsin, Duluth, and a few more places, just to get the feel of the business end and also to lecture on the fundamentals of dairy management to demonstrate that here was a genuine, hands-on dairyman as well as a highly honored name in the annals of lactescence.

Suave diplomat that he was, Florian suggested that perhaps President Svenson might invite President Feldstermeier, CEO, to begin his new life on the milk circuit by delivering his by now almost historic lecture right here and now at Balaclava Agricultural College, where he had served so flawlessly for so many years. The suggestion was accepted on the instant: Even though it was Sunday, President Svenson collared Professor Stott. Stott collared some of his brighter students. The bright students rounded up classmates of more bovine temperament. All this was done in about ten minutes. Professor Feldstermeier, as they now knew him to be, stepped to his old familiar podium at the front of the room.

While the usual flurry of getting the class seated went on, Florian drew Peter and Thorkjeld Svenson outside. "Not to interfere with the program, but since I expect to be hearing this same lecture a number of times during our tour, I wonder whether perhaps we might slip off for a few moments."

"Oh, I think that could be arranged, Florian. Did you have anything special in mind?"

"Several things. First, I should tell you that we have made arrangements with your excellent and discreet Harry Goulson to transport Aunt Mirelle's body to our ancestral burying ground for a private interment."

"Urgh," said Svenson.

"Second, the Feldstermeier Foundation wishes to make a significant donation to endow a James Feldstermeier Chair in Dairy Management here at Balaclava."

"Urf."

"Third, would you happen to know an acquaintance of

mine? While I was cruising in the Caribbean a few years ago, I happened to meet a doctor and his wife who mentioned that they lived not far from the college where Uncle James taught, in a house that had been in a doctor's family for several generations. I'd hoped to get a look at the place when I stopped to see Aunt Mirelle last week, after Uncle James disappeared; but I was running so late that it just wasn't possible. Their name was Melchett. Does that ring a bell?"

"Loud and clear," said Peter. "As a matter of fact, we were just about to drop in on Melchett when your helicopter dropped in on us. What do you say, President; shall we ask him to join the party? It er—may not turn out quite the way you're expecting, Florian."

"Excellent. I enjoy surprises. This wouldn't happen to have something to do with Uncle James's little problem, would it?"

"Probably quite a lot. The Melchett house is just up beyond that stand of hemlock; we can walk it in five minutes if you're game."

"Then we're going in the opposite direction from Uncle James's house?"

"Sorry, Florian. As of last night, your uncle doesn't have a house, at least not in Balaclava Junction. It burned down, didn't anybody tell you?"

"No. But was it really Uncle James's? Don't those houses belong to the college?"

"They do indeed. Jim's was the only house that couldn't be saved because that was where the fire started. The rest were protected by a wall of water from all the fire hoses in the county, just about. Including my own house, I'm relieved to say."

"As am I relieved to hear." Florian did have a human side to him when he chose to let it loose.

"That's the Melchett house we're coming to," Peter said.

"It is a handsome place." Florian slowed down and took

his time studying the layout of the fine old structure. "I hope there are children to carry on the tradition."

"I don't know of any," said Peter. "Do you, President?"

"Dog. Size of a squirrel."

"Foo-Foo."

Peter recalled the too-cute name from the diatribe Mirelle had unleashed when he'd refused to go hunting for Jim Feldster. He still felt a twinge of guilt every time he thought about what he should have done and had failed to do on that fateful night when Elver Butz was busy turning a stolen gray Lincoln into a torture chamber.

"A Peke? How perfect." Florian was enjoying his brief sight-seeing tour.

Peter was not. As they approached the wide veranda that had been added to the Melchett house sometime around 1880, he was less than overjoyed to see Mrs. Melchett. She was holding not a Peke but a Pomeranian and not looking much happier than Peter felt, despite her clearly displayed pleasure at seeing both the president and the resplendent Mr. Feldstermeier coming up to her very front door. Or rather the Melchett door; the brass plate beside it that bore the family name had been almost obliterated by time and many polishings over the generations but was still doing what it had been put there for.

"Why, President Svenson, Mr. Feldstermeier, what a surprise! I do wish I'd known you were coming, I'd have had something ready. Perhaps you'd like to see the staircase, it's said to be rather a special one."

She was floundering, not knowing what to say, clinging to the tiny dog as if it were her protector. The atmosphere inside this precious antique was thick enough to cut with a bucksaw. The reason for it became obvious when Dr. Melchett poked his head out of his office door, took one quick look, and decided to pull it in again.

But not fast enough to escape the mighty foot of Thorkjeld Svenson that was jamming the entrance. "Come out here, you yackal!" He flung wide the door and dragged the terrified doctor out into the hallway.

"Talk!"

"Buh—buh—what did—I didn't do it! I only picked him up and gave him the hypo. It was Elver who—I only meant—"

"To kill Jim Feldster, right?" Peter hadn't realized until now just how deeply he despised the self-important doctor. "Why?"

"Because I couldn't stand it any longer. She was bleeding me white, I needed the money. She said if I'd help get rid of Jim— All those years, holding that damned pack of letters over my head—"

"Whose letters, Howland?"

Coralee Melchett was hanging an icicle on every syllable she uttered. "Whose late-night emergency calls? How many of your lady patients did you entertain on your examining table? Do you think you ever fooled me for one second? I'm through covering up for you, Howland. I'm going home to father and you can take what's coming to you."

She turned to her distinguished guests. "I do apologize for washing our dirty linen in front of you, but it had to come out sometime. I fully intend to strip this whited sepulcher of everything he's got. I shall splash his name all over the county as an example of a disgusting old buck rabbit trying to pass himself off as a wolf. What letters, Howland? Why did you think Professor Feldster had to be killed? And how did Elver Butz get into the scene? Because you were too much a coward to kill the professor yourself?"

"I gave Elver strict instructions. I told him straight out that I didn't want Jim to be left hanging there alive, starving and dehydrating until he— Elver was supposed to—"

"To what, Howland? No, don't tell me, I don't want to know. Just as soon as Mr. Feldstermeier leaves, I'm going to get in my car that Daddy gave me, take FooFoo with me to the best divorce lawyer in Claverton, and start proceedings against you. And I want those letters for evidence. Where are they?"

"All right, all right! Anything to shut you up. It was Mirelle. She—I—she used to be a knockout when she was young, I fell for her in a big way. You were such a god-damned prude, always gassing on about what Daddy would—"

"Oh, shut up, Howland! Mirelle blackmailed you, is that what happened? And then you killed her?"

"I had nothing to do with *her* death."

"Maybe not, but you sure tried to put it on Jim when you realized he wasn't dead," said Peter. "You sneaked the real autopsy report out of the station while Chief Ottermole was out on patrol, then substituted a phony one that said she'd died from an overdose of blood thinner. No wonder Edmund was so grumpy. He'd already clawed you for shoving him around."

"Urrgh!"

This was no time for a chat. Melchett dashed back inside the office. They heard him locking the door after him. It took President Svenson only a few mighty yanks to rip the heavy door from its hinges but by then the plunger had already been filled and emptied. The eyes were half open but not seeing, the mouth an ugly hole in the cyanosed face. The point of the hypodermic syringe stuck quivering in the intricately laid oak parquet floor, where it had fallen from the dying doctor's hand.

"So that is that."

Having delivered the eulogy, Florian Feldstermeier unfolded the pristine white linen handkerchief that must have been tucked into his breast pocket by the incomparable Curtis and spread it over the head of the last Melchett. Coralee thanked him politely, went to the telephone, and dialed the number of the Goulson Funeral Parlor.

Harry Goulson would know exactly how to manage the whole affair without any hint of unpleasantness. The

Claverton Crier would get a brief but not too brief obituary, the *Balaclava County Fane and Pennon* would accentuate the positive and eliminate the negative. Coralee Melchett would be spared the costs and embarrassment of a divorce. She and Foo-Foo would deed the old Melchett house to the college, as had been promised in her so recently late husband's will, and go home to help her father in the store.

"And all is for the best in the best of all possible worlds."

Florian did have a way with words. "Let's go see whether Uncle James is still enlightening the multitudes. And I shall need your recommendations on a good restaurant, if there is one around these parts. Uncle James will want a little something before we go on to our next stop, don't you think?"

"I'm sure your uncle will want something." Peter could not envision a Feldstermeier who wouldn't. "And the best place to get it is right here in the faculty dining room. We can put in a reservation with Mrs. Mouzouka and go pry Jim loose from the cow barns if you're intending to make another stop today."

Peter was right. They practically had to get the fire hoses out again to disperse the clamoring students. Professor Feldstermeier was promising more talks on dairy management as soon as his schedule permitted. Professor Stott was agreeing to join his longtime colleague at the luncheon table. Peter was hoping the food would hold out. A Svenson, a Stott, and two Feldstermeiers all at once were a test even for Mrs. Mouzouka; but she marshalled a squad of student cooks and waiters and met the emergency like the trouper she was, notwithstanding the run on her kitchen during last night's fire.

It was not until Stott and Svenson had left for their afternoon duties and Peter was walking the honored guests back to the helicopter that Florian broached a tender subject. "Uncle James, not to leave a dark aftertaste from a most interesting visit, but one good thing has come out of last night's fire. Everything was burned, including those letters

Dr. Melchett wrote to Aunt Mirelle. We don't have to worry about the Feldstermeier name being dragged through the tabloids."

Jim Feldster had never been much of a laugher, but he laughed now. "We wouldn't have, anyway. I burned those letters myself about twenty years ago. There was nothing in the envelopes but a bunch of circulars advertising a bean supper and beanbag toss for the benefit of the Beantown Buglers' annual Bean-hole Bash. We were all going to wear propeller beanies but our shipment got hijacked so we decided the hell with it, we'd just buy a pound or so of Mexican jumping beans and think of innovative ways of employing them to the general good. But then we got to beaning each other with the beanbags and things sort of fell apart. We never did get around to sending those circulars, so I figured I might as well get some use out of them. It tickled me to think of Mirelle mooning over bean-supper circulars. This has been great, Pete. See you in a month or so, if the cows come home and the milk don't go sour."

Peter did not wait to see the helicopter safely out of sight; he'd had a beautiful thought. He and Thorkjeld Svenson could swipe a couple of bulldozers, drive them over to what was left of the Feldster place, spend a cathartic day or two burying the ruins, and turn a hideous memory into a park where horticulture students could practice what Professor Shandy preached. Exit the milkman, on with the mulch.

PLEASING, PERPLEXING MYSTERIES FROM ACCLAIMED AUTHOR CHARLOTTE MACLEOD!

- ☐ CHRISTMAS STALKINGS
  (0-446-40302-2) ($5.50 US, $6.99 Can.)
- ☐ THE CORPSE IN OOZAK'S POND
  (0-445-40683-6) ($5.99 US, $$6.99 Can.)
- ☐ EXIT THE MILKMAN
  (0-446-40398-9) ($5.99 US, $6.99 Can.)
- ☐ MISTLETOE MYSTERIES
  (0-445-40920-7) ($5.50 US, $6.99 Can.)
- ☐ THE ODD JOB
  (0-446-40397-0) ($5.99 US, $$6.99 Can.)
- ☐ THE RESURRECTION MAN
  (0-446-40332-6 ($5.99 US, $6.99 Can.)
- ☐ SOMETHING IN THE WATER
  (0-446-40446-2) ($5.50 US, $6.99 Can.)

579-D

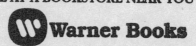